MW00936354

The Traitor's Chair

a novel by Jon Carter

illustrations by Joanna Carter
cover illustration by Emma Carter

SKOOB
PRESS

to Joanna and Emma,
who climbed in their own hemlock

.

I am indebted to the Greats—
George MacDonald, G. K. Chesterton,
C. S. Lewis, and Walter Wangerin Jr.

Prologue

Ben woke with terror coursing through his veins, not because his window was open and a strange man was standing near him in the darkness, but because the claws of his dream still scratched at his skull. He told himself to breathe slowly. He had dreamed of a world without sheep. No, it was worse than that. It was a world with sheep, but they were as stupid as any other animal, mucking around in fields for grass, and humans treated them with contempt. It was as though half the world had gone mad, and the other half—as though men's eyes had grown dim.

Ben could hear the man breathing, each lungful every bit a gasp as his own. He was nervous, but trying to keep quiet, fiddling with something under his vest. A knife? Ben leapt up, threw his blanket over the man's head, and wrapped his arms around him. "Why are you here?"

He thought the man would wriggle, fight in some way, but he just went limp. They stood for a moment in silence, Ben wondering what to do next. Slowly the man tried to raise his right arm, shaking the blanket loose.

Ben tightened his grip on his arms. "Drop it."

He felt the man unclench his fist and heard a rustling on the floor. It had not been a knife. Ben unclasped his hands and pulled the blanket from the man's head. "Who are you?"

The man bent down and picked up the piece of parchment. Moonlight caught the patch on his shoulder, a beam of light shining through a window onto an ornate chair, the insignia of the Senate Guard. He put the paper in Ben's hand. "A message from the Chairman of the Senate," he whispered. Then, without the least bit of noise, he slipped out the window and disappeared into the forest.

Ben knelt beside the window and unfolded the paper in the moonlight. The writing was in the rotating hoof marks that made up the forty-seven syllables of sheep-scrawl.

Benjamin Edmundson, we have reason to believe that Royalists are hiding fugitives from beyond our borders in your valley. Senator Clovenhoof has been given authority to investigate. I beg you to avoid any discussion of this issue in your upcoming debate, even if it may be politically beneficial to you.

Ribald Barkloin,
Chairman of the Senate

Ben folded the message back up and stuffed it in his pocket to examine later. He rested his arms on the windowsill and let the cool breeze fill his lungs. It tasted of pine and hemlock. Was he serious about wanting to be a senator? He had never imagined it would involve covert messages delivered in the middle of the night. Royalists?

People of his father's generation saw one lurking around every corner, but he had always thought of them as a thing of the past. The republic had been rooted for nearly fifty years. Religious folks talked about the return of the king, but merely as a matter of myth.

Chapter 1
Conviction

Benjamin Edmundson sat apprehensively on the stage, watching the old hall fill with the people and sheep of Blackwater Valley. The room throbbed with the rhythm of convivial chatter. Sconces lit the high wooden walls of the great hall where latecomers filed down the aisles. Few of the benches were now empty, and ushers were asking folks to move toward the center to make more room.

Ben hoped they had come sincerely to hear a debate. In three months of campaigning, he had yet to feel that anyone was taking him seriously. He saw his former history tutor, a scrawny old ewe who had made him memorize every king from the Slave Revolt to the Constitution, nudge her way past two scruffy looking forest yeomen and crawl up in an empty seat, lowering the back to the flat position that accommodated a sheep's hindquarters. She squinted her eyes at Ben in the same disapproving manner that she had used when drilling him as a child. How could this boy make history if he could not even learn it? Ben slowly pulled himself out of his slouched position and adjusted his collar. She emitted a snort, then stuck her head in her purse and emerged with a hank of straw, which she began to munch on contentedly.

Eli Simeonson, the spokesman for the miner's union was talking loudly to someone near the front, his long moustache flaring out with each syllable: "I'm voting for the boy. It's a mistake to keep biting into the same rotten onion."

Ben winced. He would have to show them that he was more than a boy. He looked across the stage, and his eyes inadvertently locked with his opponent's. Professor Helfroth Clovenhoof was an ancient politician, one of the writers of the constitution who had served since the conception of the republic. How many terms had he served—twelve? No one had ever seriously challenged him before, but he was getting old. He sprawled on his flattened chair, old and fat like a bloated carcass, staring with a condescending smile at Ben. A variety of grasses lay littered around the sheaf of parchment  before him. He chewed steadily on a clump of coriander as he eyed Ben. Every now and then, he nodded as though he was reassuring himself that this debate was already settled.

Conscious that he did it too casually to seem natural, Ben forced his eyes to stray beyond his opponent's. Clovenhoof had a new page, a pretty girl about Ben's own age—late teens or early twenties—with a shy, mischievous smile. She was gazing around the room like a child who had just crawled under a circus tent. Yet she seemed afraid of Clovenhoof. Once, he motioned her to fill his inkwell, and she scurried away from him as soon as she had accomplished the task. Ben had never seen the girl before, which meant that she wasn't from Blackwater or Chirbury. She must have come back with him from Eddisford. Ben shook his head at the thought: his own experience was so limited. She could probably talk circles around him about political life in the capital city.

Ben's page, Dunstan Proudsnout clopped onto the stage and thrust a parchment into his hands. "Look, I've scrawled out your notes."

Ben pushed it back into Dunstan's mouth. "They'll make me look like I don't know what I'm talking about."

Dunstan blinked behind his glasses.

Ben pointed at his own head. "I've got it in here. Trust me."

Dunstan shrugged and put the parchment on the small table beside Ben's chair. "Just remember that when you don't know what you're talking about, the less said the better. This whole idea of a debate has scared me from the beginning. You've been gaining people's confidence recently. You could so easily lose it."

6

"Very encouraging." Ben took a handkerchief and wiped a string of Dunstan's slobber off the parchment.

"I'm sorry. I'm just very nervous about this. You've been gaining people's confidence lately. You could so easily—"

"Dunstan!"

"I'll just sit down and watch."

As Dunstan retreated sheepishly down the stage ramp, a hush came over the crowd. Edric Williamson, the mayor of Blackwater, clad in a bright orange vest and black knickers, had entered the room, and was striding in his businesslike manner toward the stage. He stopped only to let Dunstan clear the ramp and sit on one of the front row seats. Once on stage, the mayor bowed to each candidate and turned briskly around to the crowd. "Welcome to our first ever Blackwater Senatorial Debate. On my left, representing the Socialist Party is the incumbent, Senator Helfroth Clovenhoof. On my right, representing the Republican Party is his challenger, Benjamin Edmundson. I will be your moderator tonight. I wish both candidates well, and let's begin with the first question." He pulled a rolled up scroll out of a deep pocket inside his vest and examined it dramatically. All eyes in the audience fixed on the scroll. Ben could see why Williamson had survived three elections.

"We'll start with the incumbent," the mayor said. "Professor Clovenhoof—or should I call you Senator Clovenhoof?"

"Is that the first question?" Clovenhoof asked.

Laughter spilled through the audience.

"I haven't taught in a few years now," Clovenhoof continued, "having retired from the university, but people still call me Professor."

The mayor nodded and examined the top of the scroll again as though he hadn't looked at it yet. "Professor, the senate has raised taxes every term for as long as I can remember, and each time you have voted for the raise. Do you expect that the government will need even more of our money this term?"

Clovenhoof furrowed his brow as though he thoroughly sympathized. "I'm a taxpayer myself, Mayor. We would all rather keep our money, wouldn't we? Yet when I see what the government is doing with my taxes—providing food and medicine for needy children, building much needed roads so that disadvantaged farmers can get their goods to the market, building a solid army that could crush the Ilgoths if they were ever to cross our borders again—when I see the necessity of these things, I'm willing to sacrifice."

The mayor turned to Ben. "Mr. Edmundson?"

"The Republican Party has always spoken for a lighter load on tax payers," Ben said. "I believe the burdens on our people are great enough as it is."

A man in the back stood up and clapped. A few sheep bleated enthusiastically near him, and heads turned his way, but the mayor interceded. "Folks, we are not in this hall to hear your opinions, but to hear the opinions of the candidates. No interruptions, please."

Ben caught himself glancing at Dunstan for reassurance, but his page was pointing a hoof toward one

8

of the entrances and raising his eyebrows over the top of his glasses. Ben squinted. The lanterns had been dimmed near the back, so it was hard to see his face, but his father's form was unmistakable. Ben felt his remaining sense of ease drain from him. Though it was his father, with his vehement views on politics and religion, that had first stirred Ben's interest in matters of state, he never felt free in his father's presence. He always found himself shying away from topics his father was most passionate about; his own views seemed weak merely because they were milder.

It surprised Ben that his father had come to the debate. Why was he here? A prominent lawyer, he had been called away to a murder case in Chirbury. Two sheep—a husband and a wife—had been found dead in their basement, and their lamb had gone missing. The sheriff had arrested a vagrant thief for involvement in the murder, and his father had been embroiled in the case for several days, sleeping over at the inn in Chirbury.

Williamson unrolled the scroll a little further and challenged the crowd with a sweep of his eye. "And now," he began, but something stopped him. "What is it, Mr. Haroldson?"

Edmund Haroldson was walking quickly down the aisle with purpose, his hand thrust out toward the mayor as though he had some authority to stop the proceedings. "Could I have a word with my son? I'm sorry to interrupt."

Williamson might have objected, but Ben's father gave him no time. He was at the edge of the stage in a moment,

9

beckoning his son with short, impatient motions of one hand while he still held the other outstretched toward the mayor. Ben stooped down to hear him.

His father spoke in low tones. "I know you don't take the idea of a Royalist revolution seriously, but don't downplay it in this debate. Those sheep that were killed in Chirbury—we think they were Royalists with connections outside Redland."

Ben was stunned for a moment. Royalists again. But Barkloin had told him to avoid the issue—what had his words been—even if it may be politically beneficial to you. "You came back from Chirbury to tell me this?"

"And to ask the senator some questions after the debate." He pursed his lips shut as though he could say more but shouldn't.

Ben nodded slowly. He couldn't go against the Chairman's instructions, but as they were delivered in secret, he couldn't tell his father about them. Could he really believe that Royalists were still a threat to Redland? He wondered what his father wanted to ask Clovenhoof. His instinct was to just ignore it all. People seemed to think they were giving him information he needed to act on, but he had no idea how to use it.

Behind him, the mayor was shuffling around impatiently. Ben settled back into his seat on the stage and watched his father pick his way to an empty seat at the back of the great hall.

"And now to the second question," Williamson began again, "Mr. Edmundson, do you think the government should play a role in bringing more jobs to our valley?"

Eli Simeonson sat up in his seat. Ben hadn't made him any promises, but he had certainly been courting his vote. The two had eaten lunch only the day before, talking breezily over the rights of miners.

"As I remember it," Ben said, "the last time the government interfered to bring in more jobs, an upholsterer in Eddisford opened a textile mill in our valley. Since wages were good, we had an influx of workmen from Warburton, and unemployment remained relatively the same." Ben felt himself easing into his speech like one might put on a pair of well-worn gloves. This was familiar territory. "Promises were made," he said, "promises to improve the trail over the Runcorn Mountains so the textiles could be transported easily, but none of them were fulfilled. Having negotiated deals to bring the mill into our valley, Senator Clovenhoof had nothing left to trade, and the trail was left the wreck it is today. The mill closed within three years. Here's the great irony: now we had more workmen in our valley, so jobs were scarcer. Men were willing to take work for lower pay. Senator Clovenhoof can ask Mr. Simeonson how he felt about that." He paused long enough to see the audience gage the reaction of the miner and the senator. Simeonson folded his arms with a dignified air; Clovenhoof glanced at him with a detached sympathy, as though he were a drowning man too far away to save. Ben continued, "The concept of bringing jobs, or any kind of outside help for that matter, in from the outside is wrong-headed. Whatever we do economically, we must do locally. We want a self-sustaining economy. If the government can

11

encourage local expansion, I'm all for it."

His eyes raised in mock surprise, the mayor turned toward the senator. "Well, Professor, you've heard some fighting words. A rebuttal?"

Clovenhoof cleared his throat and wiped his eyes. During Ben's speech, he had fished some more grass off his chair and eaten it. "Yes, yes, the textile mill was a disappointment. Bad business that. I would have liked to bludgeon the manager of that mill a few times, and the sad thing is that he ran back to Eddisford when the mill closed, so we couldn't string him up. What year was that, Mr. Edmundson?" He cast a mischievous look at Ben. "I think it was twelve years ago. What were you, eight years old then? Amazing how close attention you paid to the economy at such an early age!" He smiled and looked toward the back of the audience where Ben's father now sat. "Or maybe your father gave you the details. I know he's a man of strong political convictions. Next question, Mr. Mayor?" Clovenhoof dipped his hoof in the ink well that his page had provided him, and scrawled a note on the parchment before him as though he had closed the issue.

Williamson unrolled the scroll further, peered at it intently for a moment, then unrolled it even further. "Ah, here it is. Since you've brought up the Runcorn Trail, professor, we'll go to that question. Can we count on you to introduce a bill that will improve the trail, and maybe more importantly, do you have the leverage in the Senate to make it happen?"

Clovenhoof nodded his head thoughtfully. "Of course to a person who believes we should have a totally self-sustaining economy in our valley, improving the Runcorn Trail wouldn't be much of a priority." He glanced toward Ben playfully. "But if he did want to improve it, a new senator from our valley would have no political leverage to push for its improvement. I say that with no disrespect for Mr. Edmundson; it's the simple truth. The trail is unfortunately an issue that only benefits our valley. Assuming I am elected again, this will be my last term of office; you might have noticed some signs that I am aging—wrinkles, dry wool, a shameful weakness for parsley." He chuckled and foraged some sprouts out of a pocket. The audience laughed. "I have had a long and happy career in the Senate and have made a great number of political friends, even among those of the Republican party. I believe the Senate will offer me a last request, so to speak. I'll see the Runcorn Trail improved, Mr. Mayor."

Clovenhoof said the last bit with such feeling that Ben could almost touch the audience's sympathy. The words "last request" had certainly resonated with them. Who could deny an old ram his dying wish? Williamson, furrowing his brows at Clovenhoof, seemed to be as caught in the sentimentality of the moment as the crowd. Ben couldn't afford to wait for his question.

"If you give a person twelve terms to get something done, and he hasn't done it, do you give him a thirteenth, thinking, 'This time will be the trick'?" Ben looked slowly around the auditorium, meeting the eyes of various folks in the audience. "Vote for change. Vote for a person who will truly speak for you. No, I am not an insider in Eddisford. This will be my first trip to the capital." He paused thoughtfully. "To be honest with you, I've never even been over the trail. But I have lived the last twenty years in this valley and know your hearts. I believe that in his years in the capital, Senator Clovenhoof has—"

"You say you know our hearts!" The words flew at him like an arrow from the back of the auditorium.

Williamson heaved out his chest. "I'll ask the questions here!" He strained his eyes into the shadows to see who had spoken. "I'll ask the questions here," he said again, this time looking at Ben.

"You won't ask the ones I want to hear!" Again the voice came from the back, a bit playfully as though the man were slightly drunk. To Ben's surprise, a few murmurs of assent tripped through the crowd.

The mayor rose to his feet. "Ushers," he said, snapping his fingers toward the entrances. Heads turned as two burly rams in red vests appeared at the entrance closest to the troublemaker. "Escort that man out."

The ushers started bumping their way through the row of people and sheep to get to the man, but they came to a heavyset elderly ewe who blocked their way.

"Let the man ask his question," she said.

The ushers looked imploringly toward the mayor.

"Madam," the mayor began, but again he was interrupted.

"How do you feel about the Sacrifice, Senator Clovenhoof?" The playfulness had disappeared. The man stood up and raised a fist in the air. Ben didn't recognize

14

him, but he wore the heavy flannel of a farmer, and his voice betrayed the lolling vowels of the Blackwater Valley. "Do you mean to outlaw our holiest of sacraments, the means by which a sheep can assure the salvation of his dearest friend?"

Indistinct murmurs rippled through the auditorium.

Williamson opened his mouth to object again, but Clovenhoof waved a hoof at him. "I think everyone here knows the firm stand I have always taken against the Sacrifice, that a sheep giving his life for a man is tantamount to—"

"Murder!" It flew from another end of the auditorium.

Ben recognized his father's voice and cringed. He had half been expecting it, knowing his father's inflammatory feelings on the subject.

"No more outbursts!" Williamson cried. "Ushers, take the man away."

The ushers looked at each other, confused as to which man the mayor was referring. One of them made up his mind and tried to squeeze past the elderly ewe. She rose to her hooves and pinned him to the seat in front of her. The other usher tried to cajole her, apologizing for his partner's behavior, but insisting that they had to do their duty.

"Recently—" Clovenhoof tried to continue. "Recently, I have wondered—"

"Senator Clovenhoof," Williamson snapped, "Professor, I ask you not to respond directly to outcries in the audience. This is a formal debate."

Clovenhoof rolled his eyes, but the mayor either didn't see it or ignored it. No one was paying attention anyway;

15

all eyes were on the ruckus at the back. The ushers had reached the rebel and were now wrestling him out of his chair.

"It's because of what I asked, not because I asked it. Mark that, all of you!" the man shouted. "You won't see my question anywhere on that scroll in his hand. The Senate is killing our faith right under our noses! And calling it religious freedom! You heard him say it was murder—our most cherished sacrament!"

"He didn't say it was murder! I did!" Ben's father jumped out of his seat into the aisle. "How does plunging a knife into the heart of his friend atone for the evil in a man's life? What sort of god would demand such a barbaric practice? It's because of backwards thinking, pious, arrogant religious fanatics like you that—"

"Mr. Haroldson!" The mayor's voice thundered. He glanced at Ben. "If for nothing else, for your son's sake, let this go."

If anyone in the room hadn't known that this was Ben's father standing in the aisle with his chest heaving, now they did. Ben looked down at Dunstan, who had buried his head between his forelegs. By now the ushers had clamped their jaws onto the shirtsleeves of the other man and were dragging him down the row. Folks were vacating the row quickly to make way for them. Ben saw that his father was trying to push past the people in the aisle to get at the offender. Ben bounded off the stage, ran down the aisle, and grabbed his father from behind.

"Don't," he said. "Please, don't."

His father turned furiously toward him, his eyes bulging.

"This isn't the way," Ben said. "If you really cared about this, you wouldn't make a f—" His eyes suddenly fell from his father's.

His father tried to shake himself loose, but Ben hung on.

"I wouldn't make a fool of myself, right?" his father raged. "It's all just words to you, isn't it—something to get you elected. Very likely, there's a sheep somewhere out there in Redland this very night who is offering a knife to a man, and that man is going to stab him through the heart in the name of love and self-sacrifice. And you want to deal with this calmly? It's murder!"

"There isn't anything you're telling me that I don't know," Ben said. He looked imploringly at his father. "Please."

His father shook himself loose. "I won't disturb your political discussion anymore," he said, and turned on his heels.

Ben reached for him, but only half-heartedly. He felt the crowd's eyes on him and didn't want to extend the scene. Further up the aisle, the ushers butted the other man toward the door. He made a final lunge to get loose, and would have gotten free, but tripped. As the ushers pulled him off the floor, his face twisted in passion, he spat, "May the Lord of Grace trample you! Long live the king, the anointed one!" Before he could yell anything else, a third usher reached him and gagged him. They dragged the man kicking through the doors, and all became quiet.

17

Folks filed back into the empty row. Beyond them, Ben's father slipped out a different door.

"Mr. Edmundson?"

Ben turned to see Professor Clovenhoof in the aisle with him, extending a hoof. "You handled that most nobly."

Ben took his hoof in his hand. "Thank you."

"If you'd rather not continue—" An odd look of sympathy fell over the sheep's face, as though it were an unfamiliar feeling to him, as though he had looked up to find rain falling from a clear sky. Ben had seen the look before, usually when Clovenhoof was speaking of hard working folk or hungry children, but he had never seen him uncomfortable with it as he was now.

Ben gathered himself. "No, we've come to debate. Let's give them something to vote for." He suddenly felt a strange camaraderie with Clovenhoof.

"Good then," Clovenhoof said, again somehow blinking at his own friendliness. He turned quickly and headed back to the stage ahead of Ben.

Dunstan intercepted Ben on the way to the front. "Don't think for a moment he's being sincere," he whispered. "Can't you see what he's doing? He's patronizing you in front of everyone. Look around at the audience when you get up there. They're all thinking what an embarrassment you've endured and what a good sport Clovenhoof is for coming down and offering to call it quits."

"Do you think there really is a Royalist threat?" Ben asked. "He was going on about the Sacrifice, but did you hear what he said about the king?"

"You can worry about that after you defeat Clovenhoof," Dunstan said. "If you don't win this debate, it won't be your business, will it? Take one enemy at a time. I'll be honest with you. It's a good thing we've dispensed with your father, whatever the cost has been. You're never yourself when he's in the room. Now go up there and fight."

Ben nodded slowly. "All right." He took a deep breath and stepped on the ramp to the stage.

Chapter 2
Sacrifice

Ben had a hard time believing it himself when the mayor announced the results of the election. Members of both campaigns, prominent folks and reporters from Eddisford and Warburton, as well as Blackwater, had gathered in the great hall at the appointed time.

Williamson cleared his throat in his usual dramatic fashion. "By the narrowest of margins, Benjamin Edmundson has upset the long-time incumbent, Professor Helfroth Clovenhoof. Tallies for the whole of Blackwater Valley, including the towns of Chirbury and Blackwater and outlying areas, are as follows: 12,872 for Mr. Emondson and 12,359 for Professor Clovenhoof."

The town hall erupted in exclamations and animated conversation. Ben's friends and volunteers immediately surrounded him, throwing hats in the air and whooping. Dunstan knocked him over in his exuberance. When he stood back up, smiling and shaking hands and hooves, he could see the old professor intently answering questions quietly on the other side of the room.

When things had calmed down, Clovenhoof clopped over and gave him a strained congratulation. He looked even older than he had at the debate, and he could not bring himself to meet Ben's eye. Clovenhoof's page hung behind him, biting a strand of her long black hair and looking as though she wanted to apologize for something but couldn't think what.

"I have a favor to ask you," Clovenhoof said. "There's a matter we need to discuss now that you are replacing me."

"We could talk this afternoon," Ben said.

Clovenhoof went stiff for a moment, as though the idea had frightened him. "No," he said. "I must get my things in order first. Perhaps tonight. . . ." His voice trailed off, and he stared at Ben's feet unable to continue.

Ben had never seen him like this, but after all, Clovenhoof had never suffered a political defeat before.

His page rescued him. "I'm sure you'll be celebrating tonight, Senator, but could you spare a few minutes, perhaps afterwards?" ·

She had an odd accent that Ben couldn't place. Her voice was pleasant though, and confident. "Yes, certainly," he said.

"Your party will be at the Blackwater Inn? I'll find you there." She nodded a goodbye and led the old professor toward the door, her hand gently settled on the back of his waistcoat.

Dunstan spent the afternoon turning what had been projected to be a small consolation party into a great victory celebration. He made a list of folks he needed to see—the inn keeper, caterers, security officials, a belloret band from Chirbury, folks he hadn't originally invited—and paced back and forth with his slate, sure that he would forget something before leaving on his rounds. Ben saw the last of his supporters out the door and then strolled over to his parents' home. He planned to leave early the next morning and wanted to spend some time with them.

He was just closing the latch on the gate when they were already upon him, beaming with such crystal pride that it made him uncomfortable.

"Mr. Simeonson told us," his mother cried, "but he didn't have to. He was walking by the house, and I could see it on his face." She kissed both father and son. "Everything has turned out well."

An unspoken truce had followed the night of the debate. Neither Ben nor his father had brought up the incident or the issue of the Sacrifice. Ben had been sure that if he had lost the election, his father would have blamed himself. Now his father seemed downright giddy to be out from under the effects of his outburst.

"Think of the opportunities you have to reform society," his father said. "Progress is in your hands."

"I'll be the youngest and newest member of the Senate. I doubt I'll be able to do much."

"Don't talk that way, Son. Think of your ideals."

"Are you coming to the celebration tonight?"

His father's face clouded over. "I don't think so. I need to walk back over to Chirbury for a hearing early tomorrow."

"I thought I'd pack you something for your trip," his mother said. "Maybe I could just drop it by tonight before you go home."

His father's face brightened again. "My own son, off to Eddisford. I still can't believe it." He opened a cabinet and fetched a piece of paper. "I've written down some issues you'll want to bring up when you meet with the Chairman of the Senate."

After a long lunch in which his father laid out wild plans for the reform of the whole country while his mother shoved one thing and another in front of him to eat, Ben finally shut himself in his old room to lie on his bed and at least let his mind wander if he couldn't catch some sleep. He was a senator. He would give his acceptance speech tonight and leave for Eddisford in the morning. He had convinced a majority of the valley that he could do this, but now it filled him with wonder as much as it did his father. What were all those voters thinking? He was twenty-one years old and barely out of the university. He had no experience in the world. All he had were his convictions and a nagging sense that most of those were simply grafted branches on a weak sapling.

His thoughts could not keep the evening from arriving. By the time Ben donned his finest black coat and ambled self-consciously into the inn, half of the valley seemed to fill the feast-hall. Looking around, he wondered how many of these folks had actually voted for him. For a moment he was just one of the crowd; then Roland Simeonson, a short statured bald man who had hovered around him at every political event since the past summer, called out his name, and every head turned toward him with anticipation.

"Speech!" someone cried.

People applauded while sheep drummed their hooves on the floor.

Ben blinked at them for a moment, then finding his legs, he grabbed a goblet of wine from a nearby table. "Not until everyone has drunk a few of these. I really didn't expect to win, you know, so I'm not as prepared as I ought to be. The less you remember of what I have to say the better. Please, eat, drink, dance. I'll give a short, forgettable speech at eight o'clock." He motioned for the band to start a song, turned from the crowd, and drained his goblet.

The victory celebration built energy as the evening drew into night. Ben glided around the room cheerfully accepting congratulations. He had lost his inhibition and was now swimming in the affection of all these faithful friends. He was looking for Dunstan. He wanted to show everyone how much he appreciated him—maybe tear off his own tie and hang it around Dunstan's thick neck, or maybe douse him with wine. He couldn't think of anything wild enough to fit his mood. Six months ago Dunstan had told Ben that he would make him a winner, and now here he was.

"Ben!"

He turned around to find his father smiling awkwardly at him, one of Dunstan's victory cigars dangling awkwardly from the crook of his mouth. "You came!"

"Your mother made me come after all. She'll be here in a while. She hasn't finished packing the food for your trip." His eyes roved around the room until they rested on some of Ben's old classmates raising their glasses and singing a slightly off-color song. Ben noticed Dunstan in the middle of the pack. "Too much cheerfulness," his father muttered. "Politics is serious business."

"I'm glad you came," Ben said. He grabbed a goblet of champagne from a passing waiter's tray and offered it to his father.

"No thanks," he said. He took his cigar out of his mouth and exhaled a slow stream of smoke through his frown. "Someone needs to keep his head to make sure you don't make a fool of yourself." A corner of his mouth twitched a little as though he were holding back a smile. "That sort of thing runs in the family at political events."

Ben took a sip of the champagne. "You will always have my deep respect, Father." He patted him on the shoulder and raised his goblet toward the singers.

Dunstan caught his eye and pointed a hoof at him. "The man of the hour!"

The singers finished their song in a flourish, lifting their glasses toward Ben.

"And," Ben shouted, leaving his father and rushing over to Dunstan, "the ram of the hour!"

He and another friend picked up Dunstan and carried him around on their shoulders, nearly colliding with a chandelier lit with candles in their exuberance. The room filled with cheers, and the band struck up a boisterous polka. The two men broke into dance, the sheep swaying

25

precariously back and forth. Soon a crowd formed a circle around them, clapping wildly.

"Let me down!" Dunstan cried. "I'm getting dizzy!"

"The crowd's loving it!" Ben said, "One more time around!" and the two men careened around the floor yet another time. Ben motioned others to join in the dance as he lowered Dunstan to the floor. All around people joined hands and sheep stomped hooves to enter in.

Ben pushed his way through to a window at the edge of the room, assuming that Dunstan was right behind him, but the sheep had staggered off in a different direction. He was probably angry, but he'd be fine after stewing a bit. Ben felt a headache coming on. The band, the singing, the shouting, and the clapping—it all suddenly felt stifling. If he could get out of it for a bit—he checked his watch; he had a full hour until he would give his speech. He edged behind the curtain, slipped over the ledge, and found himself alone on a small verandah. It was the work of a moment, and he was quite sure nobody had seen him. He laughed at his luck; he laughed at his sense of guilt. Now that the election was over, he didn't have to be so perfect, always smiling in the spotlight. Dunstan might miss him and panic, but Dunstan needed to relax more. His new job as page was going to be a lot easier than his job as campaign manager. The night air bit his neck and sent a shiver down his back. He turned up his collar, folded his arms, and braced himself.

The dark trees creaked against the wind. The nearest of the hemlocks stretched a thick branch over the edge of the verandah. Ben studied the tree. He could climb nearly to

26

the top and look out over the night fires of Blackwater. He hoisted himself up and crawled along the limb. Reaching the trunk, he climbed up to another branch, and then another, his hands and knees sticky with sap. The effort brought warmth and joy. He finally reached the perch he had identified from below. The tree was taller than most and rooted on the sloping edge of the valley. It gave Ben a marvelous command of his hometown. Lanterns near and far twinkled and flashed as the wind blew through the grove. He could even see a small stretch of coast to the north where ribbons of waves tumbled onto the rocks. All was snug and familiar. Behind him the eastern range leaped to the sky. He would have to cross over these mountains for the first time tomorrow to another world where he sensed he would be someone peculiarly different.

A gust of wind brushed through the tree, and he found himself swaying precariously. He was feeling for footing on a sturdier branch when his eye caught a movement below him. He shimmied himself around into the shadows of the tree and looked down. Someone had emerged onto the verandah, a young woman in a gown. He could only see the top of her head and shoulders, so he couldn't see who she was, but something about her seemed familiar. She leaned over the railing, looking around below her

as if she had dropped something. She paused for a moment, then threw the shawl back and looked up at Ben. A shiver passed through her as if she felt his eyes on her, but she couldn't have seen him.

"Hello?" she called.

It was Clovenhoof's page. Had she seen him? Would it seem foolish to her that he had climbed the tree? Then again, did it really matter?

She leaned over the railing again and called below her, "Mr. Edmundson?"

Ben shifted his weight. "I'm up here," he called. "Wait just a moment." He dropped down a few branches, edged around the tree and dangled to the next, working his way down to her.

She waited patiently, smiling up at him. When he finally landed beside her on the verandah, she said, "You're an excellent climber."

"I wanted to see the lights of the valley one last time," he said. "I don't suppose it was very senatorial." He felt his chest heaving from the exertion. She was still smiling at him. What a child he must seem to her.

"I don't think there's another senator in Redland who could climb as high as you just did. It's an achievement," she said, laughing.

He looked back up through the branches and shrugged his shoulders.

"The professor is wondering if you could meet him now," she said, her dark eyes suddenly serious.

"Now?"

She stepped over to the edge of the verandah, and placed her forearms on the railing. She gazed out into the dense forest. "You still have an hour until you have to give your speech, right?"

"Folks will wonder where I am."

A breeze caught her hair and lifted it out of her hood. She brushed it out of her eyes and rested her chin on her arms. "I can see his fire from here." She rolled her head to one side as if trying to get a better look into the woods. "He's worried it will rain soon, and then it would be too late."

Ben leaned over the railing himself. "Are you saying he's out there in the forest?"

"Mr. Edmundson, I had been thinking how crazy I was going to sound asking you to come outside to meet the Professor. When you slipped behind the curtain, I thought to myself, 'This is supposed to happen,'" she said. "I don't believe in coincidences. This is the work of the Lord of Grace."

"You still sound crazy," he said, but he could see the campfire she was looking at. He could understand why Clovenhoof wouldn't want to show up at the party, so maybe there was some sense to it.

"If anyone starts to worry where you are, I'll tell them," she said. She placed her hand on his arm for a moment. The gesture seemed to carry more weight than a simple reassurance. Before he could ask her what she meant by it, she had unlatched the window and lifted her legs inside. In another moment he could hear her greeting someone on the other side of the curtain.

Ben turned back toward the woods, and it dawned on him that she expected him, so long as he was already out here, to climb down the tree he had climbed up a moment ago. All was dark. The wind brushed through the branches. He crouched down. There. Up the slope, barely discernible through the tangle of trees, the light flickered. Ben climbed out on the branch, slung his leg to a lower one, and dangled down to the next, working his way to the ground. The clamor of the party thumped against the walls. He hesitated for a moment at the base of the tree, then crept into the forest.

Soon he was close enough to see the flames licking at the night. In front of it, his back toward Ben, sat the huge old ram, the edges of his striped vest shining in the firelight. Ben skirted the edge of the campsite until he came around in front of him. "Senator Clovenhoof?"

The sheep started. "Oh, you scared me. You wait and wait for something, and it still startles you. I believe you're the senator now, Mr. Edmundson—Ben." The old ram rolled over and scratched his back against a log.

Ben stepped out into the opening. The heat from the fire slapped his face and arms. "You were confident I would come?"

"Hoping, at least. Of course there was a big part of me that was hoping you wouldn't come, but you'll understand why soon, I guess . . . ." His voice trailed off, then came back suddenly. "She's a pretty girl, don't you think?" The sheep chuckled. He shoved his nose to the ground and rooted out a clump of grass. He chewed on it for a moment and then stood up on shaky hooves. "It feels good to win, doesn't it? I remember the feeling. Everyone's clamoring for your attention, congratulating you."

"What can I do for you?"

"I was hoping for maybe a little small talk, but I see what you mean. You're concerned about your party guests, and then here I am out here in the woods." He paused again, chewing intently. "It's hard to tell you." A bit of the grass dangled from the edge of his mouth. "What can you do for me?" He hobbled over to the fire and kicked a log into it. He looked at Ben quizzically. "Your father might have figured it out by now."

Ben flinched at the mention of his father. His words on the night of the debate came back to him. "There's a sheep somewhere out there in Redland this very night—"The thought was preposterous though. Clovenhoof had always opposed the Sacrifice. But what had he started to say at the debate when the mayor had interrupted him?

Clovenhoof saw the effect of his words. "I'm sorry to mention your father. That was wrong. You are your own man, Ben. I think everyone can see that but you."

Ben shuffled his feet, afraid to speak further. Clovenhoof's words suddenly came back to him: "Recently, I have wondered . . ."

"I know it doesn't make any sense," Clovenhoof said.

"Haven't you always opposed the Sacrifice?"

Clovenhoof nodded slowly. "I have, but . . . ." He squinted his eyes as if trying to spit out something stuck in the back of his throat.

"It's murder," Ben's voice came out in a cracked whisper.

Clovenhoof lowered his head to the ground and remained that way for an interminable moment. Then he fumbled beneath a pile of sticks and came up with a dagger in his mouth. He slowly walked over to Ben and dropped it before him. "I'm asking you to sacrifice me, to trust that my soul will open the way for yours into the life to come."

Ben backed away. "Neither one of us believes in this."

"Things have happened recently to change my mind." He flopped his hind end down and wagged his head seriously. "It isn't right to throw it on you like this. I realize that. The night of the debate, the thought of offering myself to someone was still just a small seed in my mind. When your father stood up . . . just because his intensity gets the best of him at times doesn't mean that he can't see things clearly. Ben, the sacrifice is either a holy sacrament or a murder. Your father and that lunatic at the

32

debate were the sane ones. People like us—we've taught ourselves to look at things dispassionately, and everything has become academic or political. We've lost the sense of things." A weak smile worked its way across Clovenhoof's trembling face. "I chose you that night. As you clung to your father in that aisle, trying to recover any remnant of dignity left you, I knew I must offer my life to you."

"I can't help feeling this is some kind of trap," Ben said.

"I'm sorry," Clovenhoof said. "I'm as surprised at myself as you are, but I really have changed my position on the Sacrifice. Circumstances that I am not at liberty to share with you have led me to it. If I could only share them with you, but I'm bound by an oath . . . ." His words seemed to wind into a hole deep within himself before they reappeared with more vigor. "Please trust me in spite of your very good instinct. There's nothing political here."

"Then why me, of all people? You're my political enemy."

Clovenhoof looked fully into Ben's eyes for the first time since Ben had stepped into the light of the fire. "That's the very reason. I want it to be a real sacrifice— with no sense of personal gain whatsoever. I want to throw away the part of me that has been my greatest treasure. I don't know how to say this without offending you—of course you know it already—but I have looked down on you with such disdain!" He suddenly groaned. "Please forgive me. I suppose I've chosen you because you seemed the unlikeliest person to choose. Yet the moment I chose you, the disdain, the personal loathing, fell away like a snake's skin. Ben, I want to do this for you."

The old sheep's steady, earnest gaze, filled with an almost childlike expectation, sent a chill down Ben's spine. Clovenhoof was dead serious. Ben had half a mind to run. The old sheep, the fire, the woods—it was all so ancient and ugly. The knife lay on the ground before him, the fire flickering in the shiny blade. In his mind's eye, he watched his hand take hold of the dagger and lift it into the air. No, it was inhumane, barbaric. They had both always said this; it had hardly been an issue in the campaign. Now here they were eye to eye with the thing before them. Could he even go through with it if he were to accept?

"I'm scared," Ben said, taking a step backward.

"You think I'm not, boy?" Clovenhoof looked up at the sky. The hemlocks swayed gently beneath the night sky. Tufts of low sailing clouds dragged the tips of the trees as they passed. All around, the hemlocks creaked and groaned. A tremor crossed Clovenhoof's lips. "I need you to say yes, Ben."

Something akin to longing stirred within Ben, a faint, dark joy he had felt once standing on the edge of a cliff. He fought against it. "I don't believe in the Sacrifice. You know that." Even as he said it, Ben felt the certitude fall away like a ledge slipping from under his feet. If something did lie beyond the edges of this life—"I'm an educated person."

"And I'm a university professor."

Clovenhoof walked over and touched Ben's arm with his ear. "Believe," he said. "We are all supernatural. I want to give you my life."

Later, when Ben tried to explain the shift that came over him, he found that he couldn't put it into words. It was not just a feeling. It was as though one moment he was standing with his nose against a wall and the next moment the wall was a rough pane of glass he could see through, though only dimly. The texture of each stone and the mortar between them was still there, but what had been opaque was now faintly translucent. He could never think of his new faith as anything but a gift (or a curse), something from outside himself.

Ben spoke slowly, listening to his own words as if someone else were speaking them. "I don't think I can do it."

The tacit agreement hung between them in the air like a vapor. The sheep heaved a huge sigh, letting his breath out slowly. "The courage will come. It's a holy thing I'm asking of you. If we see it properly, not one of us can face a holy thing with our own courage. It must be given to us." He stood up and shook the dust from his trousers. "Throw the rest of that wood in the fire," he said. "I'm a fat sheep. It'll take a big fire to reduce me to ashes."

Ben tossed a log on, and then another. The fire crackled, and a volume of sparks flew up into the sky. He picked up the dagger and tested it on his fingernail. It sliced the tip off easily.

"It's sharp enough," Clovenhoof said. "I made sure of that. I need a good clean thrust, Ben, straight into the heart. I'm not about dying slowly."

Ben dropped the knife. It stuck in the ground upright by his foot. "This is barbarous. It's murder. Even if there is a life to come and a Lord of Grace—why blood sacrifice? How could he require such a thing?"

Clovenhoof nodded his head vigorously. "That's the crux of it, isn't it? I asked another sheep that once." A log in the fire snapped loudly, and Clovenhoof bristled. "Ramsportion—that was his name. He was my father before he offered himself to King Egeland."

"Your father offered himself to the king?"

Clovenhoof nodded. "Reinard's father—only a few months before he died and handed the kingdom to his son."

"I never knew that."

"You really are young, aren't you? I should have played that up more in the election." Clovenhoof chuckled and shook his head as if to shake loose the memory. "I was furious. In giving his life to the king, he took it from me. He was still young. He could have waited many more years. There were older sheep—why didn't they offer themselves to the king? I argued all this, but it seemed only to increase his resolve. 'The Sacrifice,' he said, 'is the greatest gift I have ever been given. Since I first breathed air, I knew I would come to this. It fixed my nose to the only principle that can bring happiness, that can bring true love, that can bring change to our world—self-sacrifice.' Those were his words. For years as a senator, I tried to deny it. I glued myself to the rights of man and sheep as if life were something we each deserved in our own right." Clovenhoof's voice broke and trailed off into angry tears. "I thought my father had committed—"

"Suicide," Ben muttered.

The sheep nodded. He sniffed loudly, stepped over to a thistle that sagged near the heat of the fire, and grubbed it up. "Suicide is an escape. The Sacrifice is an offering. Suicide is hoarding your life, throwing it away rather than letting anyone have it. The Sacrifice is giving away your life, offering it freely for another's good."

The old ram lay down and turned over on his back. His hooves dangled in the air awkwardly. He turned his head to the side, and it rested on Ben's foot. There was something sad and weary in the gesture. "The Lord of Grace has never appeared to me like a shining light or a trumpet sound," he said, "but I know he's real."

"What if neither of us has enough faith?" Ben asked. "Will it still—work?"

Clovenhoof closed his eyes. "Give us faith, Lord of Grace."

Hearing Clovenhoof's trembling voice, Ben wondered if he had ever heard a sincere prayer before. "But if it's not enough?"

"It's only a picture of what's to come," Clovenhoof said. "Ultimately it doesn't depend on us. The faith to do it is enough faith. They say that someday the Lord of Grace will offer himself to the king, and that is where the power will—"

"King?" Ben backed away, his mind whirling. Clovenhoof's head thudded to the ground. "But you're a senator, a founder of the republic." Even as he said it, he wondered at his own naivety. Those who worshipped the Lord of Grace waited for the return of the king. Everyone knew this. All sacrifices were merely a picture of what was to come.

"It all goes hand in hand, doesn't it? It's like jumping stones across a river. You can't skip one, or you fall in. Take your time, and jump each one, Ben."

"But I'm a senator."

"And you'll be a fine one."

"I'm not a Royalist."

"You don't have to be."

"I don't see how that can work."

"Ben, if you know that something will one day happen, you don't have to try to make it happen. The king established the Republic before he left. You don't have to undermine his wishes."

Ben stood in silence for a long time, holding the knife, working it over in his mind. He kept arriving at dead ends.

"I haven't worked it all out myself," Clovenhoof finally said, "but I've come to believe in the Lord of Grace and his sacrifice. It's my starting point. Everything else will have to fall into place, but I have this sense that it will."

Ben could see this. It actually helped that they were pretty much in the same place. Had Clovenhoof talked with the arrogance of certainty, he might not have agreed. They were both new believers taking a risk, and Clovenhoof more than he. He nodded his head.

Clovenhoof picked the knife up in his mouth and placed it in Ben's hand. "I believe I am supposed to give you a blessing first. Benjamin Edmundson, may your knife be sure. I take your sorrows and your faults and carry them with me to the next world. Take what little wisdom I

38

have to give with you as you travel the rest of your journey on this earth." He swallowed a lump in his throat and gazed around at the edges of the forest. "I want to say this right so you understand. I've only learned this recently. Nothing of value in this world is gained from achieving, earning, or taking by force. Give and receive, Ben. Love freely, and live in expectation. I spent most of my life talking about rights—what the law requires—and I suppose as senators it is right and noble to defend the rights of people, but I brought it home with me, into my meals, my library, my classroom. Don't do that, Ben. Live with open hands; give and receive. Remember this, and meet me on the other side." He closed his eyes and waited. "I'm ready," he said softly.

Ben stood up, shaking. He straddled the old sheep and lifted the blade with both hands above his head. Sweat dripped down his face and neck. He hesitated for only a second, then plunged it into the old ram's heart. Clovenhoof shrieked a deafening squeal. His whole body constricted, convulsed, while Ben gaped in horror, his hand steady on the knife. The squeal faded into a final gasp, and Clovenhoof fell limp. Blood flooded from the wound into the thick wool and pooled into the jacket. Ben rolled over onto the ground, short of breath, heaving. He lay on his back, staring up at the night sky and the sparks wandering upward into it until the terror passed.

At last he felt chilled and crawled over close to the fire. It wasn't over. He had to roll Clovenhoof into it. He yanked the knife out of the sheep's heart, and wiped it off on his handkerchief. He tried to drag the body to the fire, but he got in his own way. He hadn't counted on him weighing so much. Finally he sat down with his bottom in the dirt and pushed the body into the fire with his feet. It seemed so inhumane to do it this way that tears came to his eyes. The fire collapsed as the sheep's body pushed the logs out of the way. He had to go around to the other side of the fire and shove the logs back up against the body. As he worked, he resisted looking into Clovenhoof's face, but some devil inside him kept making him look at it.

By the time the fire was at last roaring around the body, Ben was drenched with sweat, and his clothes were soiled with blood and grime. He collapsed a little ways from the fire and hugged his knees. It came into his mind like a dream that the others at the party would be looking for him. He needed to get back. He had forgotten about his acceptance speech. What could he possibly say that would explain this? Some sort of bellow escaped his lungs—part laugh, part anguished cry—what it was he couldn't say. "I have to come to my senses."

He was contemplating what to do when he detected a motion in the woods, a shadow behind a holly bush. A twig snapped; some leaves rustled.

"Who are you?" Ben called.

A slight silence followed. Then "Is it finished?" Clovenhoof's page stepped out into the clearing. She had donned a wool fleece over her dinner dress and a fox-fur hat, but still shivered with the cold, or maybe with fear. She walked cautiously toward him, her eyes wide. She tripped over a root, and one of her feet lost its fine evening slipper. She had not dared to look at the fire yet.

40

"It's finished," he said, stepping to her and reaching out a hand to steady her.

She closed her eyes and took a deep breath. "I'm all right," she said. "Thank you." She smiled up at him, then set her face and looked down at the fire. She gave a yelp. The fire was slowly pealing Clovenhoof's body away from his bones. His clothes had long burned up. Some of the snaps from his jacket had fallen into the ashes and glittered beneath the gleaming logs.

The girl moved past Ben, stumbling with trembling limbs, around the fire to where she could see Clovenhoof's face, now a mere skull. She knelt down and reached her hand out as if to touch his cheek.

"I'm sorry," Ben said.

Her hand wavered tenderly a few feet from his face. "I didn't think he could go through with it," she said. "He was so scared."

"He was braver than I." Ben thrust another log onto the fire and stoked it with a stick. The flame flickered for a moment, but then surged up, refreshed.

"You need to get back," the girl said. "You need to give your speech."

"I can't go back there."

"You have to. You can't disappear on the night you've been elected a senator of Redland."

"I can't just give my speech as though nothing's happened." Clovenhoof's writhing body in his last moment suddenly burst before Ben's eyes. He flung himself down on his knees. "What have I done?"

The girl took a handkerchief out of a pocket in her fleece. "Here." She took his hands and wiped them.

He stared at the blood staining the handkerchief. His body suddenly convulsed, and he choked on tears.

"Just believe," she said. "Believe in what Clovenhoof has done for you." She put the palm of her hand softly against his cheek.

Something in the gesture stirred his courage even more than her words. He nodded his head. "Will you tend the fire? I'll be back as quickly as I can. Maybe you could help me bury him then."

There was nothing to do but start off into the woods.

"Hey," she called. "I need to tell you—there's a basement window on the East side of the inn. If you can slip past the people in the courtyard and climb in the window, someone will be waiting for you."

He walked back to her. "Who?"

"Her name is Thistle. She's Clovenhoof's granddaughter. I didn't want to bring her out here yet." A look of understanding passed between them. "And someone needed to make sure you could get back in the inn without any trouble. She has a change of clothes for you."

It dawned on him that he hadn't asked her name. "What's your name? How did you and Thistle get into the party? Did Dunstan invite you?"

"There are all sorts of people at your party," she said. "You'd be surprised."

"Just tell me your name, and I'll go."

42

"Miriam." She smiled and gave him a push toward the woods.

Ben turned and picked his way through the trees. What could he possibly say? He would just have to tell them what happened with as few words as he could manage. His mind reeled at the response this news would bring. Better not to think about that. He felt as though he had awoken to a new world as someone else. Had he, Benjamin Edmundson, really lifted a blade and plunged it into a sheep? The Sacrifice. He could talk about sacrifice. That would put a good face on it. What had Clovenhoof said about it? He would have to write it down when he got the chance. It wasn't coming to him now. The trees loomed large overhead. His own small size in comparison suddenly filled him with a sense of foreboding. They would not understand.

Chapter 3
Speechless

Ben came around the back of the inn and stopped in the cover of the trees. Some of the party had spilled into the courtyard. A few sheep—two council members and the sheriff's deputy from Chirbury—were lounging on the cool stones, smoking the Barcanian cigars that Dunstan had bought with leftover campaign cash. A woman with her arm wrapped around a post giggled at their talk. Ben wondered who she was. An inn boy in a silk shirt served from a punch bowl near the sliding glass doors that opened out onto the porch.

Ben skirted the building, keeping out of sight, until he saw the propped basement window.

One of the sheep on the stones, the sheriff's deputy, heard Ben's feet rustling the underbrush. He propped himself up on a hoof and looked Ben's way. "Did you hear something?" he asked the others.

"Yeah, a party with music and laughing," the lady joked.

One of the other sheep looked out into the forest. "What are you looking at? It's probably just an animal.

Hunting season starts next week. Not a time to be in the forest, if you know what I mean, what with jittery humans and their spears. There've been too many mistakes. I foraged out all the remaining clover, vetch, and filaree I could find on my land this afternoon. I have 'No Hunting' signs up, but you know how it is?"

"I fenced my land this year," the sheriff's deputy said.

Ben waited as the conversation rolled onto the management of prime forbs on one's land and whether it was better to sell them at the market early or hold off till winter. At last the sheep were in an animated argument. Ben slipped out of his cover and padded across the side lawn to the window.

"What was that?" the woman suddenly cried.

Ben grabbed the ledge and slung his legs through the opening. He landed on some boxes piled under the window and pulled it shut behind him, crouching in the darkness of the basement room. He could hear the footsteps of the sheep and the woman outside.

"I could have sworn I saw somebody run across the lawn," the woman said.

"There's nothing here," one of the sheep answered.

"I better let Dunstan know, all the same," the sheriff's deputy said, and then the voices and footsteps trailed away.

Ben breathed a sigh of relief, but he had to act quickly. If he was lucky, Dunstan would come down to check the basement himself. More likely, he would send someone else.

"Did you sacrifice my grandfather?" a small voice came from the darkness.

"Thistle?"

He could hear something dragged across the floor, and a little lamb stepped into the dim light from the window, holding a sack in her mouth.

"Yes," he said, "I sacrificed your grandfather." The words sounded foreign to him.

She lowered her head and released the sack. "These are your clothes."

"I'm sorry," he said.

She peered up at him as though she were trying to recognize him, and said nothing. He had expected her to break into tears, but her face remained blank. There was no time to work it out. He lowered himself onto the floor and fumbled with the drawstring of the sack. Inside it, he found a set of dress clothes, neatly folded over a polished pair of shoes.

"There's a lantern here," she said, "and some water." She stepped back into the darkness and reappeared with the lantern hanging from her mouth.

Ben took it and lit it. In the corner of the room sat a bucket of water, a towel, and a mirror. He squatted down in front of the mirror. His own appearance in the glass shocked him. Blood speckled his face. Dirt and blood caked his hands and sleeves. Sweat had run the muck together in gruesome dried streams.

"I'll wait in the hall," Thistle said, as he pulled his shirt off. The door opened, and the brighter light from the lanterns in the hall blinded him for a moment. As he pulled off his trousers, he felt the notes for his speech in his pocket. Dunstan had written them out neatly for him as usual. It would be pointless to use them now. He took out the contents of his pockets—the note from the Chairman of the Senate, some change, his house key—but left the notes for his speech. His old clothes off, he squatted again in front of the mirror and washed his face and hands thoroughly. Blood had clotted in his hair behind his left ear. He was working at it with wet fingers—there just wasn't enough water—when the door opened again.

"I'm not ready yet, Thistle," he said.

"What are you doing?" Dunstan's voice erupted in a mix of panic and frustration. He pushed the door shut behind him and clopped into the dim room. "Where have you been? We've been looking all over for you."

Caught off guard, Ben stared at his friend in the mirror. A trickle of blood crawled down his neck.

Dunstan caught a glimpse of it. "Did someone hurt you? Someone just ran across the yard from the woods. Did he hurt you?"

Until that moment, Ben had not considered lying to Dunstan. The thought of concealing what he had done in the woods stole into his mind like a quiet intruder. Ben turned from the mirror, hesitating.

"Where have you been?" Dunstan repeated. His eyes, now adjusted to the dim room, wandered over Ben, the mirror, the bucket of water, the neatly folded fresh clothes, and landed on Ben's soiled clothes. Dunstan stared.

"I'm not sure what I've done," Ben said. "It happened so quickly. I have to tell you—"

Dunstan slowly picked up the soiled shirt in his mouth and dragged it over to the lantern. He examined the sleeves. Even in the dim light, a dark red shown clearly. Dunstan grabbed the lantern and held it up over the bucket. The liquid inside gleamed the same brownish red. He looked up at Ben, his eyes now confused with accusation.

Ben shook his head, his lips trembling. "I sacrificed Professor Clovenhoof."

Dunstan staggered back. "Sacrificed—"

Ben searched for words, but so little of what he'd done made any sense. The clarity that had come to him in the forest seemed like a dream in the presence of his friend. "Clovenhoof was waiting for me tonight, out in the woods behind the inn."

"Waiting? How long have you been planning this?"

"We—"

"Clovenhoof!" The name had taken a moment to fully land in Dunstan's mind. "When have you even talked to him?" A nervous agitation seemed to take over him, and he started turning circles, his brow furled. "How did I not know about this? But I thought you both opposed the Sacrifice! Ben, this is murder!" He stopped abruptly. "Do you—Ben, you know this is murder."

"We didn't plan it," Ben said. "He was just out there. I wouldn't have planned this without telling you."

"Well, someone planned it if he was out there. How did he get you to go out there in the first place?" A sort of wild recognition came into Dunstan's eyes. "Ben, what has he gotten you to do? This is the eve of your election! You can't go out into that feast-hall and tell them about this. You can't—Ben, I—" He fell silent, his eyes roving around the room in desperation.

Ben waited for him, increasingly frustrated with himself. What had seemed a personal decision in the woods now shaped itself clearly as a betrayal of his friend. They had given the last six months of their lives to reach this point, and he had thrown it all away.

"I cannot believe you have done this to us," Dunstan finally said.

"If I had time to explain—"

"Well, there isn't any time is there? People are waiting out there for you to—Ben you can't tell them you've sacrificed Clovenhoof. Listen to me. Now I'm using the word 'sacrificed'. Tell me you haven't called this murder at least once or twice a week over the last six months."

In the pause that followed, Ben heard voices outside the door—someone wanting to come in and Thistle asking him to wait. Ben pulled on the clean trousers and stuck his arms through the sleeves of the shirt. His hands trembled as he tried to button it up. "There's no time right now for me to explain to you what has happened to me," he said.

"What has happened to you? Listen to yourself," Dunstan said. "This isn't something that has happened to you. This is something you've done." He took a couple of steps back and heaved a sigh. "Ben, I can't be your page." He shook his head. "You're going to have to find someone else."

Ben gaped at him. "You're resigning over this?"

Dunstan set his jaw.

"Are your feelings about it that strong then?"

"It's either a sacrifice or a murder, isn't it?" Dunstan said.

"But you've never—"

"We both agreed. Everyone agreed. Even Clovenhoof agreed. There was no reason to talk about it. It was a peripheral issue, wasn't it?"

"But now it isn't," Ben said. He meant it as a question, but it came out as a statement.

The two friends stared at each other.

"I'm sorry," Ben said.

"I'll just slip out the door at the end of the hall," Dunstan said. He turned, walked to the door, nudged it open, and disappeared through it.

Ben sat down and put on his socks and shoes. Thistle came in as he was combing his hair.

"Do you see any blood on me?" he asked.

She checked him over. "I'm sorry about your friend."

He shrugged, trying to make little of it. He had to focus on his speech.

"I believe in you," she said.

He turned from the mirror and looked down at her. "I don't know what I'm going to say."

"I'm sure the right thing will come," she said.

"Who were the folks at the door?" he asked.

"I told them to round everybody up and that you'd be out in a few moments."

He smiled. "That was rather presumptuous. A born leader, I see—like your grandfather."

Her warmth had encouraged him to mention Clovenhoof again, but now here was the same vacant expression she had given him under the window.

"I'm sorry," he said. "Let's get going."

Thistle walked out of the room ahead of him. Ben took a few steps toward the door and stopped. Feeling like a coward, he went back to his old trousers and retrieved his original speech. Of course, he would tell them what had happened in the woods, but he might use some of his old material. Just feeling the crisp parchment in his pocket was a comfort at the very least. He followed Thistle up the ramp to the first floor, his heart beating faster with each step. The hallway had been emptied except for the host of the inn and one of the waiters, who motioned Ben toward the door where he would make his entrance. Ben had rehearsed this with Dunstan earlier in the evening. Facing the door, he paused on the pretext of looking himself over. He took a deep breath. Should he tell the crowd right off, or work his way around to it?

The host and the waiter smiled up at him, their shoulders ready to swing the doors open. He would work his way around to it. He had other things to say first, people to thank—all of which he knew would be lost if he started with the Sacrifice.

"All right," he said, and smiled widely.

The doors swung open before him. The feast-hall erupted in cheers. Smiling faces greeted him on all sides. Sheep pounded their fore-hooves on the floor as people clapped. He started moving toward the platform slowly, shaking hands and bowing to each person he recognized. Eli Simeonson appeared on his left, clapping him on the back. Egbert Bullshanks, the wealthy tree farmer who managed the western slope of the valley, was nudging his way between some miners from Chirbury. Behind them stood his friends from the university, Dunstan conspicuously missing from their presence. Every one of these folks had played a part in the election. Their numbers were astounding.

Yet each drop of their gratitude and support added to the pool of apprehension gathering in his heart. He found himself silently measuring each smiling face even as he enthusiastically proclaimed his thanks. Would this person turn his back on him? Would he continue to support him? Would he care at all? A small voice in the back of his head said, "What does it matter? The election is over." Another said, "You have betrayed every person you see." Still another said, "You are the politician. You can make them think what you want them to think." Even so, he smiled, shook hands, and bowed, moving ever closer to the platform.

And then he came face to face with his father.

In the moment he looked into his father's shining eyes, Ben realized that he could not tell this crowd what had taken place in the forest. Had he truly not considered his father until now, or had he been pushing his father's image out of the forefront of his mind all evening? The Sacrifice was a chasm that could never be crossed. He stood on one side, and his father stood on the other.

"I am so proud of you," his father said.

Ben hugged him, more to avert his eyes than anything, and then stepped up onto the platform. The cheers faded to an eager silence as he turned to the lectern. Ben took Dunstan's notes out of his pocket and unfolded them.

"I have so many of you to thank," he said. "I want to start with—" Dunstan had written numerous names, including his own with a smile next to it. What was meant to be a joke now pierced him with guilt. "I want to thank my campaign manager, Dunstan Proudsnout, whose efforts brought us here more than anyone else's."

The crowd cheered and hollered. Heads turned in all directions looking for him.

Ben continued before anyone could ask where he was. "I also want to thank Eli Simeonson for his leadership in breaking the miner's union from the cloying grip of the socialist party, his cool-headed ability to choose reason over emotion, and his unparalleled dedication to the working man." The other miners pushed him forward. He raised a fist in the air, and everyone applauded.

Ben moved down the list with apparent ease, thanking those who had helped his campaign the most and throwing in an odd person here and there who had done some specific task. He knew what gratitude meant to folks; he wanted every person in the room to feel that, though it wasn't likely to happen, Ben might just call his name and thank him. The crowd loved it. They became more exuberant with each person he honored.

His heart relaxed. It was all a matter of timing. There was no betrayal in waiting. His father would surely think there was, but it was his father who made it impossible to be honest. He did not want a repeat of the scene at the debate. And whatever Dunstan's views were, the Sacrifice was a peripheral issue, a personal issue that would hardly affect the way he voted on anything that was likely to come up in the Senate this term. "And so I go to Eddisford as your representative," Ben said, "as the small but clear voice of Blackwater Valley, ready to speak for the ideals that we hold dear." Dunstan had listed them neatly for him. Of course, there was nothing about the Sacrifice. It was an important personal issue, but not a political one. He marched confidently down the list, waiting for applause between each issue he mentioned.

"Lower taxes and less wasteful spending!"

Applause.

"A strong military with a sense of purpose!"

Applause.

"Repair and enhancement of the Runcorn Pass!"

Explosive applause.

As he neared the end of the list, a wild whim overtook him. He could not say where it came from, perhaps his guilt. The moment it came into his head, he knew with certainty that he would do it. He also knew with certainty that he should not do it.

"Finally," he said, "I would like to say something about Senator Clovenhoof."

Someone shouted, "Professor Clovenhoof, not Senator Clovenhoof!" Laughter spilled through the crowd.

"I guess you're right," Ben said with mock surprise. When the laughter died down, he continued. "I want to speak well of him even as I celebrate our victory. He has served this valley for forty-eight years, and has been a model of self—" His voice suddenly broke. He could not bring himself to say the word. Had he actually broken from the prepared speech to bring himself here? This was the pivotal moment. If he were going to tell them about the sacrifice, it would have to be now. The crowd waited for him, moved by his respect for his opponent.

Ben looked into his father's face—a face filled with admiration.

"I'd like to drink a toast to Professor Clovenhoof," Ben said. He signaled to one of the waiters to bring him the traditional goblet of wine.

Within a few moments, waiters emerged from the kitchen with fresh goblets, and everyone who wanted to drink to the old professor was given a full goblet. The waiter whom he had signaled brought Ben a goblet and filled it for him.

When all was ready, Ben said, "To Professor Clovenhoof, may his goblet run over," and slammed it down on the podium so that the wine swirled over the rim.

"To Professor Clovenhoof," the crowd responded. The sheep slammed their goblets on the floor, while the humans slammed theirs on the palm of their hands. Wine sloshed over the rim of every goblet, and everyone drank.

As he lifted his own goblet to his mouth, Ben caught a glimpse of Thistle through a gap in the crowd. He had put her out of his mind as easily as he had put his father out of his mind earlier in the evening. She stood on a low serving table at the back, her eyes wet with bewildered pain. The gap in the crowd closed as quickly as it had opened.

Ben stepped back from the lectern to signify that he was finished. His heart grappled with shame. He knew that he had failed the first real test of his new convictions.

What hurt most was that a mere child had seen through him. The feast-hall filled with one last burst of applause and hoof stomping, and the evening was over. Folks drank the last of their wine, said their good-byes, and filtered slowly out of the hall. Ben stayed on the dais, smiling and waving to folks as they left. He was in no mood to mingle. Waiters circled the room, gathering goblets, mopping up spilled wine, and rolling out tables for the next event. Ben's father hovered near the front of the stage thanking people for coming. If only he would leave too, but Ben knew he would have to speak to him.

As the feast-hall emptied, Thistle became visible again. A waiter asked her to get off the table she had been standing on, and she complied quietly. Ben watched her as she curled up in a corner. She did not look up at him once.

She laid her head down, closed her eyes, and waited for him.

At last, Ben could avoid his father no longer. As he descended the ramp, his mother walked in one of the back doors. He could not have been more grateful. Her needs could take precedence; he could sweep his confession to another time. He reached his father first.

"Is something troubling you?" his father asked. "I noticed—"

"I'm exhausted," he said. "Look, here's Mother."

She came up to them in a flurry of feeling. "I have everything you could want," she said, "a loaf of bread, hunks of cheese, carrot strips, boiled eggs, even some smoked salmon." She smiled up at him through tears. "I just can't believe you're going. I'm so proud of you, but we'll miss you so."

Ben took the knapsack from her. "You're the best mother in the world." He gave her a warm hug.

His father stepped forward, started to shake his hand, thought better of it, and slung his arm around his shoulder. "Follow your convictions, Son. We may be a long way away, but we're behind you."

"You sure you don't want to come over to the house for a little while?" his mother asked.

Ben looked across the hall toward Thistle. "I'm sorry. I promised to deliver that little lamb to—" He wasn't sure what to call Miriam. He couldn't call her family. Now that he thought of it, where was her family? Why was she in her grandfather's care?

"Poor darling," his mother said. "Children so often get dragged to these things, don't they?"

"Looks like it's long past her bedtime," Ben said. "I better go."

His father relinquished his squeeze, and he kissed his mother on the cheek. His parents continued to look at him as though more were expected.

"Well, I'm off," he said, smiling weakly.

It took another few minutes to extricate himself, but finally they let him go. He wondered how long Miriam had been waiting in the woods now. He suddenly felt an urgency to get back to her. He approached Thistle warily.

"Are you awake?" he asked.

She dozed on. He nudged her. She was either in a deep sleep or pretending very well. He had no choice but to pick her up as she was. As he took her up, she struggled against him for a moment, but weariness took over, and she nestled into the cradle of his arm. He wrapped his coat tightly against her and carried her out the door onto the verandah. Ben stopped and turned around at the edge of the patio. But for a few waiters closing up shutters, the place was empty. He fought back a strange emptiness he had never felt before and plunged into the woods.

The wind had picked up, and low clouds brushed in among the tops of the trees. It felt like rain. He hastened his pace, bounding over roots and sidestepping bushes. The jolting awakened his bundle when he was nearly at the fire.

"Where are we?" she asked, peering up his collar. "Is someone chasing us?"

"No one's chasing us. We're going to see Miriam." He nearly said Clovenhoof, but caught himself. What would he do when he got to the opening? Should she see the remains of her grandfather in the ashes? He stopped beneath the canopy of a particularly large hemlock. Its branches brushed the ground in front of them, obscuring the fire. He hesitated to mention Clovenhoof directly.

"Thistle, why are you with Miriam? Where are your parents?"

At the mention of her parents, she tensed up like a cramped muscle and dug her hooves into his side.

"I'm sorry," he said. "I'm sorry." He backed through the branches, hunching over as the bristles scraped his neck, and pointed to the firelight. "Miriam's over there. I want to take you to her, but I'm afraid to." He drew a long breath and let it out. It was cold enough that he could see the vapor rise and dissipate in front of him.

Thistle lifted herself up and turned her head toward the firelight. "I hardly knew my grandfather," she said, a firmness hardening her voice. "It's cold here, and I want to see Miriam."

Ben looked into her eyes. She stared back at him. What did he see there? Fear, anger, resolve—a tangle of feelings that must surely have been alien to her child's nature.

"All right," he said, and carried her into the clearing.

They found Miriam curled up, asleep, her chin tucked warmly into her fleece and her evening gown splayed on the dirty ground like a fan.

Ben opened his jacket, knelt down, and laid Thistle beside her, facing the forest. Thistle snuggled close to

Miriam, and Miriam put her arm around her.

"Hey, little buddy," she whispered. "So, we made it this far."

Ben sat down on the ground beside them, too tired to think.

Chapter 4
Assassins

Ben lay quietly beside the fire, listening. He felt watched. A dense fog had settled in so that he couldn't see beyond the first trees. Clovenhoof's bones now protruded from the fire at various angles; the hollowed ribs framed what was left of the flames. Miriam stirred and turned toward him, her gown glittering in the firelight.

"I want to go with you," she said softly.

"Where?"

"To Eddisford."

"I can take you there."

"No, I mean I want to go with you as your page." She sat up, took off her fleece, and placed it over Thistle. Her shoulders shook from the cold. She crawled closer to the fire for warmth. "Senator Clovenhoof was going to take me with him to Eddisford, but now—" She took a deep breath and looked off into the forest. "He was so good to me."

Ben smiled wryly. "I supposed you've guessed that Dunstan resigned."

"I expected that he'd come back out here with you, but since he didn't—"

He took his jacket off and gave it to her. "I suppose I could use somebody who knows her way around Eddisford."

"I've never been to Eddisford actually. I helped the professor here in Blackwater. I ran errands for him. I feel like I can get around anywhere though. You wouldn't regret it if you took me on."

"I don't remember seeing you before the debate."

"I suppose you and the professor had very different constituencies."

"Not as different as you might think. Really, our views weren't that different, or at least I didn't think they were until tonight."

"But you agreed to accept his sacrifice, so they weren't that different after all."

Ben frowned. "Did he ever say anything about King Reinard to you?"

Miriam stood up and cupped her hands in front of her mouth. "He never shared his personal beliefs with me," she said. "It's cold. This fog is getting us all wet. Shouldn't we be digging a hole? He's all ashes now."

Ben pointed at a squat fir behind her. "He left the shovel leaning against that tree. Bring it here, and I'll dig." He dragged his foot across the ground to clear a spot.

She retrieved the shovel. "So, what will you do if the king returns?" she asked.

He took the shovel and jabbed it in the ground. "It's been nearly fifty years since he established the congress

62

and left. He was what, twenty then? Do you think there's any chance he would return now? How old would he be? I mean, they say that sometime in the future according to prophecy—"

"But let's say he did," She said, pressing it on him.

"We're a republic now. I don't see how a country can go back to a monarchy. Once people have certain freedoms, they won't willingly give them up."

"A lot of people talk like they hate the king." Miriam rubbed her thighs with her hands. "I can't seem to get warm. The fog's got my gown damp."

Ben jumped on the shovel, bent it over, and scooped out a mound of dirt. "If the king came up to my father's door announcing his return, my father would shoot an arrow through his heart."

"Open the door and whiz, just like that?" Miriam laughed.

"I'm serious," Ben said, "no questions asked. He's a real patriot."

Miriam kicked at the fire, spreading it out to help it die. Several times she stopped and looked at him as if she would say something, but didn't. Ben went back to digging. The fog was turning to drizzle. The rain-soaked ground began to fill the bottom of the hole with water. He slipped in it and got his shoes soggy. Then his feet stung with cold.

"You must be very disappointed that Dunstan isn't going with you to Eddisford," Miriam finally said.

"When we first started talking about running for office a year ago, we wanted to do it together," Ben said. "We weren't sure which one of us should be the candidate. We could have done it the other way round just as easily. I've always thought he might have been the better candidate. He certainly knew the issues better than I did."

"How did you decide?"

"We threw dice."

"You threw dice?"

He shrugged. "It was a partnership. Then I started acting cockier like the big senator I thought I was certain to become, and he seemed perfectly satisfied to be my page, the hidden mastermind behind the campaign. Finally tonight I betrayed him. He created my image, and I destroyed it. I'm the one headed for Eddisford, and I can only imagine what he's doing or thinking right now."

"I know I could never fill his shoes," Miriam said. "It just seems like I could help you right now, and you could help me, at least for the time being."

"You'd be switching parties," he said. "Aren't you a Socialist?"

"It doesn't seem to matter much, does it," she said, "when it comes to things that really matter?"

He had reached a tree root that wouldn't give. He jabbed at it violently with the shovel. "All right," he said, "I'll take you on. I want to leave for Eddisford early tomorrow morning though."

She was already nodding, smiling at him as if he had offered her a diamond necklace. "You will not regret this, Sir," she said.

"Don't start calling me 'Sir'," he said. "You're probably older than I am."

"I'm nineteen, and you're twenty-one."

She smiled on at him, her dark eyes sparkling in the glow of the dying embers. It made him uncomfortable. He leaned on the shovel and wiped his brow.

"I think that's deep enough," he said. He climbed out of the hole and scooped the shovel into the ashes. Something in the coals snapped loudly, and a volley of sparks rose into the air.

Thistle stirred, rolling deeper into Miriam's fleece. Miriam knelt down and patted her. The fleece rose and fell steadily. "I have one more favor to ask you," Miriam said. "Thistle goes wherever I go now. She's no trouble. I promise—"

"What happened to her parents?"

Miriam stood up and came close to Ben. "They were killed."

"When I asked about them, she tensed up like a fist. Why were they killed?"

"At first I thought it might have been the professor himself."

"The professor?" Ben dropped the shovel. "I can't believe that." But he remembered the strange looks Thistle had given him in the basement when he mentioned her grandfather.

Miriam looked nervously around, fidgeting with her hair.

"I'm still trying to believe he offered his life in the sacrifice tonight," Ben said. "I can't believe he would kill his own kin. Was it his son or his daughter that was Thistle's parent?"

"It was his son. They haven't had anything to do with him for years. Thistle didn't know he was her grandfather until I told her, and that was after they died. I think he disowned his son at some point."

"I've heard of people disowning their children, but I can't see anyone killing them."

"I told you. He didn't kill them. I'm fairly certain of that now. I—I was there when the news came, and he seemed genuinely surprised. Is your hole ready?"

Ben picked up the shovel and passed it to her. She scooped up a pile of ashes and unloaded it in the hole. It sizzled as it dipped into the water, and a puff of steamy smoke rose from the spot. Ben leaned over to relieve a knot in his back. Sweat and drizzle dripped from his hair.

"It was a few days after the debate, about two weeks ago. I was still new with the professor," Miriam said, continuing to work the shovel. "A messenger appeared outside Professor Clovenhoof's gate. He was breathless, and he had a wild, almost crazy fear in his eyes. He wouldn't come in, said he had somewhere else he needed to get to quick. Where, I don't know. I haven't seen him since, and I keep wondering about that. Anyhow, he said that Professor Clovenhoof's son wanted to see him; he needed to drop everything and go right then.

"Clovenhoof wouldn't have any of it. 'Impossible,' he said. 'I have no son.' Then he looked with a suspicious eye at the messenger. 'Who sent you?'

"But the messenger didn't answer. He just turned and ran away.

"The professor cursed the messenger until he was out of sight. Then he turned to me. 'You go and find out what they want from me. You're my page, aren't you?' He seemed furious.

"What could I do but go? When I arrived at their gate, it was locked. That made no sense because they were supposed to be waiting for the professor. I circled to the back gate, but it was locked too. I climbed a tree." She smiled at Ben. "I can climb too. I climbed a tree and jumped into the back yard. I knocked on the back door, but no one answered. I knocked on the front door, but no one answered. Now I was stuck in the yard. The limb I had jumped from to get into the yard was too high to reach. I sat down on the front step to wait.

"After a few minutes just sitting there picking at the weeds growing in the cracks of the steps, I noticed a scraping noise behind me at the window, just a small, timid sort of noise. Someone was home. Who would be home but not answer my knock? Why would everything be locked up so tight if someone were home?" Miriam stopped and handed Ben the shovel as if she expected him to answer.

"Thistle?" he ventured.

"She was shaking all over, peering out of the crack between the shutters when I turned around. At first she seemed unsure whether to let me in or not. I smiled at her, and it was like something clicked within her and she trusted me. She bolted out of the house like lightning, squealing at the top of her lungs. She plunged into my arms and clung to me.

"I didn't know what to think, whether to go in the house or run and pound on the fence and scream for help myself. Well, I wasn't stupid enough to go in the house, and I'm just not a screamer. I took her around the side of the house and sat us down on a bench. The sun shone on everything brightly there. I thought it might calm her spirits.

"'I'm going to ask you some questions,' I said. 'Is that all right?'

"She nodded and wiped her little nose on my shirt.

"'Do you think we're safe here in the yard?'

"She looked toward the fence as if the danger were outside now. That set my mind more at ease.

"'Is there still danger in the house?' She didn't seem to know how to answer, so I rephrased it. 'Is there a threat to our lives if we go back in?'

"She shook her head.

"'Can we go back in?'

"She wouldn't do it. We sat out there in the sunlight for it must have been an hour before the laundry woman arrived and unlocked the gate. I gave Thistle to her, took her keys, and explored the house. It was a mess—chairs knocked over, the contents of drawers scattered everywhere, cupboards overturned. They must have been looking for something. It was scary. I expected to see dead bodies around every corner I came to. The door to the cellar was ajar when I checked the kitchen. I was hoping beyond hope that I might find someone still breathing." Miriam stepped closer to Ben. "Her parents had both been stabbed. They were splayed out on the ramp to the cellar.

68

They must have hidden Thistle down there."

Miriam took a long shuddering breath.

Ben mused, "She probably heard her parents die. She might have even seen them die."

"And she had to climb over them to get up the ramp to the window where she could see me. She's a brave little one."

Ben shoveled the last of the ashes and bones in the hole. "So why did you think it was Clovenhoof?"

"I told you it wasn't him. He had already—changed by then, started to believe."

"But you thought it was at first. I'm trying to get a picture of the sheep who gave his life for me." He handed her the shovel and pointed at the pile of dirt, and she shoveled a few scoops of it over the ashes.

"Do you have any idea why Thistle's parents were killed?" he asked.

She looked up at him, her brow furrowed. "I haven't put it all together. I think Thistle knows more than she's told us."

Ben reached over and pulled the hood of the jacket over her head. "The rain's ruining your hair," he said. "If you're too tired, I can start filling the hole in. I'm eager to get—" He paused mid-sentence. He had heard something in the forest.

"What is it?" she asked.

"Well then," he said, ignoring her question, "if you're going to be my page, tell me what you do know about Clovenhoof." His eyes shifted back and forth, scanning what contours the mist provided. The coals in the hole offered precious little light now, and the moon had long ceased to brighten the mist. That might actually be to their advantage, he thought. He kicked a heap of dirt on the coals and they went black. "Shovel some more in," he said.

Miriam slowly turned to look around. "No," he said as casually as he could. "Let's just keep talking. You were going to tell me more—" Again he broke off.

"If you're going to pretend to be casual, you'll have to stop breaking off your sentences," she said.

"I'm not any more prepared for this kind of thing than you are," he said. "It's pitch black now. I can't see a thing beyond the nearest trees. Maybe he can't see us any better than we can see him."

"You think there's someone out there?"

"I'll look around. We're a larger target together than apart."

"Very reassuring," she said.

He started to take the shovel from her—"I might need this"—but something flashed on the edge of his vision, and he shoved the shovel at her with all his force instead. An arrow flashed between them an inch from his nose. Miriam fell backwards into the hole, the shovel on top of her.

"What was that for?" she gasped.

Ben crouched down. "Didn't you see the arrow?" he whispered. "Stay there and hold the metal part over your head." He had not seen the arrow himself, only heard and felt the puff of wind between his face and hers.

She obeyed. He crept to the nearest tree on all fours and slipped behind it. He felt his heart pound in his ears. Which direction had the arrow come from? He had no weapon. Miriam might use the shovel if they stumbled on her. They—how many were there, or was it just one? If he could find a tree limb the right size, he might have a weapon. And poor Thistle slept there somewhere in the opening—he couldn't see where—oblivious to it all. Lord of Grace, may she sleep on, he prayed.

What should he do? It was no use skirting around the campsite. He would head right toward the archer, and in this kind of dark, movement was death. He took hold of a branch and lifted himself up slowly and noiselessly. It took twice the strength, but he dared not scrape his feet on the bark. Once on the first branch, he felt more secure in the shadow of the tree's canopy. He ascended to the second branch, which was still thick enough to make no movement as he heaved himself onto it. Holding a third branch above him to steady himself, he sidestepped out as far as he dared.

From there, Ben could look down on the whole opening. Thistle lay inside Miriam's fleece, a heap that could be mistaken for a rock or bush in the darkness. He was glad for that. Miriam's shovel, on the other hand, wet as it was, glittered above her. If it had been still, it might not have drawn his attention, but Miriam was all movement in the hole. She twisted one way and then another like an insomniac.

A shadow approached, a lone figure, a bow stretched taut before him. It crept from tree to tree around the  opening, the arrow pointed toward the squirming shovel, away toward the forest, back toward the shovel. It couldn't seem to get a fix on Miriam though. A patient hunter. Ben waited, patient himself. How often had he waited like this in a tree for a deer to approach? Yet this was a man with a weapon. Miriam's life depended on him. The archer moved faster now, eager as he closed in, and probably frightened. Hadn't he seen two figures? Could there be more than one in the darkness down there on the ground? He stopped about five yards from Ben's position, put the arrow to his cheek, and took aim.

The angle wasn't what Ben had hoped for, but he had no choice. He dove. His hands swiped the archer's arm as it let the string go. Ben heard the ping of the arrow on the shovel as his face crashed into the man's belt, his arms clasped around his waist. The man crumpled.

The bow, tangled with them, found its way over the archer's head as they fell. When they stopped rolling, the man's arms were incapacitated. It was a fortunate thing, for he was burly and strong. As he struggled, Ben wormed behind him, wrapped his arms around his neck, and squeezed with all his might. The bottom end of the bow stuck in Ben's ribs, and as the man writhed around, Ben felt it grind against him, tearing his flesh. He gasped in pain. He was certain his rib cage would collapse at any moment, but he hung on.

The man flailed his lower arms wildly to no avail. He managed to rise to his feet, Ben on his back, and the two spun around and collapsed again. A searing pain split Ben's chest. He loosened his hold and fell limp on the ground. He could hardly breathe. The man rolled over and turned toward him, panting and furious. He threw the bow off his shoulders and grabbed Ben by the shirt.

He was reaching back to pound Ben with his other fist, a menacing shadow above Ben's helpless eyes, when the shovel broke his skull. His stunned body dropped onto Ben's chest. Ben lay under the inert man, unable to move or speak, staring up at the shadow that must have been Miriam.

Soon a smaller shadow crept up, the face close to the ground near Ben's. Her warm breath made him smile.

"Is he alive?" she asked.

"I might have killed them both," Miriam said.

"He's smiling," Thistle said. "Dead people don't smile, do they?" She backed away, and Miriam stooped close.

Ben managed to turn his head a bit.

Miriam yelped with joy and pulled the archer off of him. The release of pressure brought fresh pain. Ben gritted his teeth, moaned, and curled onto his side.

"What hurts?" Miriam asked.

"My ribs," Ben gasped.

"We need to get you to a doctor."

"Home."

"It may not be safe. Can you stand?"

Hugging his ribs and pivoting on his head, Ben rolled onto his knees. He gripped his chest tightly and straightened himself up. He rested in this position for a moment, breathing light, quick breaths. "Check the body," he said. "Anything to tell us who he is."

Thistle nosed into the archer's pockets as Miriam steadied Ben and brought him to his feet. She walked him to the tree from which he had jumped and leaned him against it.

"Here's something," Thistle said, "but I can't read it. It's too dark." She brought it to the tree and tucked it into the pocket of Ben's trousers.

"We'll take it with us," Miriam said. "The main thing is for us to leave quickly."

"Home," Ben repeated.

"That's where they'll look for you next," Miriam said.

"Me? He was shooting at you."

Miriam took him under her arm again and led him into the woods. Thistle trailed behind.

"You're the senator," Miriam said. "Why would he shoot at me?"

"You tell me," Ben said, but the pain was too much for this sort of arguing. He was shivering from the cold, and each convulsion jarred his ribs. He had to concentrate on walking, on breathing lightly, on holding his arm just so under his ribs. He would let her lead him. But where was she taking him with such deliberate steps? They were moving up hill and farther into the darkness.

Chapter 5
Convergence

How long they had hiked, Ben couldn't say. He had asked Miriam several times if she was sure where she was leading them, and now she was clearly angry. She kept beating at the ground with a stick she had picked up. The blackness had turned to a charcoal, and the off-key warbling of a curlew hung from some branches nearby.

"I'm tired," Thistle said for the fourth time.

Miriam stopped abruptly and threw her stick against a tree. She sobbed and thrust her face into her hands. "Maybe we walked right by it. I don't know."

"You've been saying, 'Trust me, just trust me,' all night. Maybe it's time to tell us where we're going."

"It's this impossible mist," Miriam said. "How could I hope to find our way in this?"

"I'm tired," Thistle said again.

Ben reached down to pick her up, but she eluded his grasp with an angry scowl. He couldn't have picked her up anyway. Simply bending over had jarred his injured rib. He gasped in pain.

"Here. Let me." Miriam squatted and welcomed the little lamb into her arms. "You're shivering all over, poor thing."

"It'll be light soon," Ben said. "If we're close by, we'll find it." He scratched his head. "Maybe we can help you if you tell us what we're looking for."

"It's an old hermitage. A friend of my father lives there." She wiped her nose on her sleeve and sighed deeply. "I should have gone to him in the first place," she muttered.

"What do you mean by 'in the first place'?" Ben asked. "Who is he?"

"He's an old hermit named Roderick. He's supposed to be good with medicine, and he lives all alone—good person to go to when you may have a broken rib and people are trying to kill you." She hesitated and then looked at him questioningly. "I was hoping you might have heard of him."

"Should I have?" Ben said.

"I might have known!" Miriam broke into fresh tears.

Thistle buried her head in Miriam's arm pit.

"You might have known what?" Ben asked.

"I'm not even certain Roderick is still alive." Convulsing, she squeezed Thistle until she bleated.

Exhausted and near tears himself, Ben leaned his head against a tree. His mother's knapsack full of food appeared in his mind. He had forgotten it in the hall when he had picked up Thistle. He kicked at the tree. A long silence followed, broken only by Miriam's sniffles and the dripping of morning dew off of branches. They had been steadily climbing the eastern slope of the valley, veering south away from the sea. The early morning air, though damp with the mist, was fresh and crisp. A breeze brushed Ben's face and he started. "Miriam?"

"What now?"

"Smoke!" He drew in a deep breath. "From a stove pipe."

She lifted her head.

"Come on," he said, stumbling upwind. "If it isn't your old hermit, at least it's someone with a warm kitchen."

Miriam put Thistle on the ground. "Just a bit farther now, little one."

Thistle broke into a trot with revived energy. A few hundred yards through the mist, the smoke thickened in puffs of a warm, delicious smell. They climbed over a log, pushed through some brambles, and there in front of them stood a small cottage, smoke pouring from a stovepipe in the roof.

They could see a vegetable garden, a patio with a table and chair, and a small red door, but no path or road leading to it. "This must be the back," Miriam said. The company circled the cottage, but found no other entrance, path, or road.

"It's a hermitage all right," Ben said.

Thistle trotted up to the door and knocked. No one answered. She looked around longingly. "I'm tired."

"Try the door," Ben said.

Miriam turned the knob, and it opened. Warm air curled out the door, inviting them in. The cottage was one room, and in the dim light, Ben could see that it was empty. Miriam breathed relief. "I half expected to find the old man dead after all we've been through."

In the corner to their right sat the pot-bellied stove. A full flame crackled within it, tossing warm shadows across the room. Thistle clopped over and lay down with her tail to it. Ben limped over to a large bed at the far end of the room and lowered himself gently onto it. Miriam sat down at the kitchen table, which was covered with a cheerful red tablecloth.

"He can't be far with a fire going like this," she said.

The warmth of the room soothed them and hushed further speech. No one came. Before long, Ben had given up on listening for footsteps. He studied the rafters, content to let all his questions slip behind the forefront of his mind. Various nets of onions, cloves, ginger, potatoes, and the like hung from hooks in the roof. He could live in a quiet place like this. He could dirty his hands in the soil and see what he could grow. What business did he have going into politics? He vaguely remembered Miriam laying Thistle on a corner of the bed before he drifted to sleep.

He might have slept all day had the sun not woken him—not the light streaming through the window above the headboard, but the intense heat it produced on his cheek. He was dreaming of flames, of Clovenhoof's cheek as Miriam might have touched it the night before if the flesh had not been burned away. He felt an intense ambivalence—a wild joy at her touch and a depthless despair at having lost his life. He opened his eyes and looked into hers. Then he slowly turned away from her toward the flame, and as he did so, it seemed the feelings reversed. The memory of her touch seemed a yawning chasm of despair, the loss of his life a pool of joy. It stirred his heart awake. He sat up with a jolt and yelped in pain.

"What's that!" a quaking voice cried. An old man with beady eyes and a mop of gray hair stared at him from the table where Miriam had been. His leathery cheeks sagged into a goatee of bristles that he kept scratching. Though the room was warm, he was wrapped tightly in a dark green cape as though he were shielding himself from a cold wind. Thistle lay on her corner of the bed sleeping soundly. Her little chest rose and fell in deep, sonorous heaves.

"Are you Roderick?" Ben asked, squinting and rubbing his eyes.

The old man nodded quickly and waved the question away. "Were you dreaming just now? There was such anguish in your face, but something else too."

"I was Senator Clovenhoof. I've never felt that way before. It wasn't like a dream. It was like I was truly him. I guess I should tell you first, last night I sacrificed—" The words came so easily that it startled him.

"Yes, I've been told."

Ben shuddered. "I was in the flames, as though I were Clovenhoof—no, I mean, I was Clovenhoof—and Miriam touched my cheek." He touched his own cheek as if to feel it all over again. "I turned from her into the fire. It was this thing I suddenly had to do even though I knew it would burn me."

The old man scratched his chin thoughtfully. "You are right that it was no dream. It was a convergence."

"What?"

"The two merged, you see. It's written on your face." His eyes widened into large ovals. "It was a convergence, a vision. Let it speak to you."

"It was just a dream," Ben said. He prodded his chest with his fingers until he found the sore spot. If it were broken, could he feel a crack?

"You said yourself a moment ago that it was more than a dream. You must give her up, Ben. You must die to her."

"Her? Who?"

"Miriam, of course."

"What do you mean 'give her up'?"

"I don't have the slightest idea what I mean. It's your life, not mine. I only know that you must give her up. You were Clovenhoof. She touched your cheek, and you turned from her into the flames. What did you feel when you did this?"

"Despair," he said, "and joy."

"See, it's what I saw in your face."

"I only met her last night. How can I give her up when I have no attachment to her?"

"No attachment?"

"Well, she did ask to be my page."

The old hermit shook his head. "No, no, too insignificant. It can't mean that. Are you sure you aren't in love with her?"

"I met her last night."

"Irrelevant. I was young once. I know how these things happen." The old man raised an eyebrow and smiled. "You cannot ignore the vision. She has a deep hold on you, and you must let her go."

"Everyone suddenly talks in riddles," Ben said, growing frustrated. "Everything was so simple until last night."

"It wasn't any simpler than it is today. You just didn't know it." Roderick pushed his chair back and ambled over to the stove. He ladled some batter into a skillet and poised a spatula over it. "Care for some corn-cakes?"

"I'm starved," Ben answered. "That would be great." He bent down to wake up Thistle, but the old man motioned frantically with his finger to his mouth.

"One thing at a time," Roderick said. "You must acknowledge your convergence."

"I give up," Ben said. "Tell me what a convergence is." He gently lowered his feet to the floor, and rolling slowly to his right, stood up. He moved to the table and sat down, annoyed with Roderick's excitement that he didn't understand, and annoyed with himself for not understanding it and being annoyed.

Roderick flipped the corn-cake on the skillet. "I see you have a knack for sarcasm. Nothing will kill your spirit more completely if you let it grow."

Ben flinched at the accusation. His father had often accused him of sarcasm. It had won him countless votes in the election. He and Clovenhoof had both excelled at it. "Forgive me," he said. "I am cynical. I'm only just learning how to believe in things."

"You accepted Clovenhoof's sacrifice," Roderick mused. "That could not have been done without conviction."

"It seemed like the right thing to do at the moment. I wish I could call it conviction."

"You didn't want to hurt his feelings?"

"I've said things to hurt his feelings plenty of times, with hundreds of people watching."

Roderick scooped up the corncake, dropped it on a plate, and set it on the table in front of Ben. "You will have dreams, Ben, sleeping dreams and waking dreams, in which the eternal will press itself upon the temporal, in which the world of being will fuse with the world of becoming.  Each convergence will tell you, in some different way, how you must die to this world to live for the next. Senator Clovenhoof's sacrifice has opened the door of eternity for you. The Lord of Grace will give you glimpses through that door. You must never turn your back on those glimpses."

"So I need to give up Miriam, whatever that means."

Roderick nodded gravely, sitting down on a stool beside the stove. "I'm afraid so."

"Does that mean she's going to die?"

"Of course eventually she will, but no. It's you who must die."

"You mean physically?"

"You mustn't fragment your life like that. It makes a coward of a man. How can you die spiritually if you are unwilling to die physically?"

Ben poked at his corncake with his fork and took a bite. He chewed slowly, then took another bite. He had too much to work through in his head. Miriam had told the old hermit about the sacrifice. What else had she told him? What else did she know to tell him? Things had been happening so fast that he had no time to think.

Roderick poured more batter into the skillet and seemed content to flip corncakes and let him think.

"So how do I die to her?" Ben finally said.

"I don't know. It would look different to me than it would to you. Some people have to let go of things they clutch; others have to clutch things they're afraid to grasp. Whichever way means self-sacrifice, it will be your greatest challenge and your greatest joy."

"You sound like Clovenhoof."

"Hmm, Clovenhoof? Not as I knew him. He didn't know the meaning of self-sacrifice."

"Apparently he did at the end."

"That's what baffles me. When Miriam told me he had given his life for you—" The old man shook his head and lapsed into silence.

"How did you know him?"

Roderick stacked two more corncakes on Ben's plate and sat down at the table with him. "I was once bishop of the valley, likely before you were born. Clovenhoof has always been wary of the faith, ever since the conception of the republic. Any thinking man knows that the faith is wrapped up in the monarchy, though it's actually the other way around. Meaning, truth, reality—all flow out from the center. Democracy is a kind of decentering isn't it? We don't trust the Lord of Grace or the king always to give good gifts, so we erase the center. Now instead of hoping to receive good gifts from them, we strive for our own rights and barter with each other. We give up an unknown for a known, though we know the known is evil. We all know our own selfish desires, but we think if there are enough of us together, we'll do good. Safety in numbers." Roderick laughed, then seemed to realize that Ben wasn't following him. "I'm sorry. Remember I'm not used to talking to people, and I go off on tangents. A senator has a lot of power, I think more than King Reinard ever intended. I don't know. That's his business. Senator Clovenhoof set spies on me right from the start of the republic. They were always around. I guess I got lazy after a while. They intercepted one of my messengers one night, and next thing I knew, he and I were in a private meeting discussing my dismissal."

"A messenger to whom?"

Roderick smiled and winked. "To the king, of course."

"The king? Suddenly everyone I meet loves the king. So you're a Royalist too. "

"Nonsense, I was the king's friend. I didn't want to lose track of him. Do you know what the message they intercepted was telling me? He and his new wife had—" The old man stopped mid-sentence, his mouth still open in the shape of his last syllable. He scratched his head. He swiped a piece of parchment folded neatly under a candle on the table and held it close to his eyes. "Hmm, not a hint in here, but it's undoubtedly true. That girl's a crafty one." He handed the paper across to Ben, smiling a gummy smile in a knowing way.

Bewildered, Ben took it and read.

"Dear Senator Edmundson,

I know you'll think me a coward, but my traveling with you has just become too dangerous. Please don't hold it against me. Maybe it was a silly girl's dream to go to the capital as your page.

Roderick has agreed to allow Thistle to stay with him. It breaks my heart to leave her. Please assure her that I'll be back when I've gained some responsibility, and it won't be long.

Affectionately yours,
Miriam"

Ben stared at the words. He felt strangely abandoned. He shook his head. He had only met her last night. Assassins were after him now, and she was frightened. Who could blame her for going home? Ben folded the letter and put it in his pocket.

"You won't need that anymore," Roderick said, holding his hand out. "Why don't you let me throw it in the fire."

Ben furrowed his brow. "What does it matter?"

"You see how hard it is for you to give her up."

"You're making too much of it. It doesn't surprise me that she left," he said. "She was breaking apart before we found your cottage this morning. I suppose she went home."

"Not likely."

"She said you know her father. Do you know where she lives?"

"You only met her last night, right? She can go as she pleases."

Ben put his fork down. "I'm just curious. That's all."

Roderick leaned forward onto the table. "Are you going to let her go?"

"Does what I do really make a difference?"

"It makes all the difference in the world, Ben. Now that you are a believer, you will have to think and act on universal principles." He smiled gently. "The first of those, if you accepted Clovenhoof's sacrifice, is that as the beneficiary of grace through him, you will in turn throw away your own life as the Lord of Grace shows you how. As strange as it sounds, the most important thing for you to do right now is to decide that you do not have any claim on Miriam in any sense. You must give her up. It is your present calling, never mind what else transpires in your life or in the nation as we speak."

A curious elation sprung into Roderick's tone as he spoke these last words. Ben leaned back in his chair and studied him. Roderick was hiding something that he wanted to tell. The old man scraped his chair on the floor, rose, and turned back to his skillet. "We should be waking little Thistle up," he said. He reached into a bag, drew out a handful of sprouts, and spread them on the skillet. "I'll just brown these a little. She'll like that."

"All right," Ben said, "I'm willing to give up Miriam." He looked at Roderick expectantly.

Roderick smiled. "You think I'm going to reward you? You think I'll clap for you or sing you a song?" The contents of the skillet sizzled. Roderick set the spatula on the edge of the stove and turned around. He spoke in a slow, steady voice. "Now I am going to surprise you. The young lady you saved from the arrow of an assassin last night—and yes, it was meant for her—is Miriam Elaine, the only daughter of King Reinard of Redland, your true king."

Ben rose to his feet, his hands on the table, his eyes fixed on the old man in shock. His mind tumbled backward over all that had taken place since he had first seen Miriam at the debate. How many times had she mentioned her father? She had been Clovenhoof's page! Had he known? Was this the source of Clovenhoof's conversion?

Thistle's voice suddenly burst from behind him. "You're not supposed to tell! Why did you tell him!"

Roderick raised his hands in a gesture of defense, but the incensed little lamb wouldn't stop.

"Why did you tell him?" She stood on the bed waving her head wildly back and forth. You can't trust him! He's a senator of Redland! He's the enemy!"

"He is no longer the enemy," Roderick said firmly, "not after last night. If your grandfather could trust him with his life—"

"Miriam!" she yelled, ignoring him. "Where's Miriam?" She scrambled off the bed and careened around the room, looking out windows, under the tablecloth, into a closet. Finally, she ran to the door, flung it open, and hollered at a pitch that Ben would never have guessed she could reach, "Run, Miriam! Run! You've been betrayed!"

Ben's mind reeled between the news and Thistle's reaction to Roderick's telling him. If she hadn't run around so wildly, he might not have believed it. "The princess?" he said.

Roderick nodded.

Thistle finally lost steam. She stood, a shadow in the bright sunlight of the doorway, glaring back and forth between them.

Events were linking together in Ben's mind. "She must have told the old professor," he said.

"Yes, I've been thinking the same thing," Roderick said. "I've been wondering what could change an old man's mind about something like the Sacrifice? But the arrival of a princess—"

"What's she doing here?" Ben asked.

Both men turned to Thistle.

"How long have you known that Miriam is the princess?" Ben asked.

Thistle pursed her lips shut. She blew air out of her muzzle and studied the floor. Ben was about to let it go when she looked up at him. "When the bad men came into my house—" She furrowed her brow into a deeper canyon and took a threatening step toward Ben. "When I hid in the basement, I overheard them. They kept shouting, 'Where's the princess?' They kept shouting that. They kept saying, 'We know you know where she is,' things like that. When Miriam came, she was so—well—"

"You guessed who she was?"

"Yes."

"Did you tell her you knew?"

Thistle shook her head. "I was afraid. And at my grandfather's, it was too dangerous—" She broke off and stuck her head back out in the yard. "Miriam?" she called again, but more faintly as though she had lost hope of being heard. After a few moments, she came back inside and nudged the door shut behind her. She blinked up at them. "Is she gone?"

"She wants you to stay here with Roderick," Ben said. "You'll be safe here."

A long silence followed as Thistle swallowed the news. Roderick scraped the contents of the skillet into a bowl and placed it on the table. Thistle glanced at it, but seemed hesitant to leave her vigil by the door. Ben studied the little face in the doorway. The one person in the world whom she felt she could trust had abandoned her. She had no reason to trust Ben. She had witnessed his cowardice in the face of political pressure the night before. If he could betray Clovenhoof so easily on the very night that

Clovenhoof had given his life for him, how could she expect him to keep Miriam's secret?

Ben stood up and went to her. "I was weak last night," he said. "You have every right to mistrust me." He knelt down slowly, a hand on his rib to steady himself, and looked into her eyes. "Please, forgive me, Thistle."

She heaved a sigh. "The bad men. I saw them in the basement where—they came one day—"

Ben nodded. "Miriam told me. You don't have to explain."

"The light was shining from the door at the top of the ramp. One of the men had a patch on his shoulder. The patch had a beam of light shining through a window onto a throne. Where the light hit the throne—"

"It fanned out into the colors of the rainbow."

She nodded.

"The insignia of the Senate Guard!" Ben sat back in wonder. Miriam had at first thought that Clovenhoof might have been behind the murders. Somebody in the Senate was.

Thistle now eyed him carefully, as though she were testing his response. "You seem surprised," she said.

"Did you know what the patch was at the time?"

"My mother had showed it to me before. She said not to talk to anyone who wore it, but I didn't know what it was."

"She knew they were coming then."

Thistle nodded again. Her ears twitched nervously. The wrinkles under her eyes deepened.

"Did she tell you why?"

91

Thistle shook her head.

"But they were looking for Miriam?"

"Yes."

"Do you remember your parents ever mentioning a princess, saying anything about her?"

"No. I don't think they knew her, but I don't know." She glanced toward Roderick. "I'm scared."

She didn't trust him. What could make her trust him? He had nothing to offer her. Then he remembered the piece of parchment Thistle had foraged out of the dead man's pocket the night before. If the men who killed Thistle's parents were looking for Miriam—

He pulled it out of the pocket of his trousers and unfolded it.

"We believe the princess is now in Clovenhoof's service. Seek Warwick for assistance. He will have further instructions. Find her and take her."

Ben took the paper to the bed and spread it out on top of the covers. He grabbed his jacket from the bedpost, slipped another piece of parchment from an inner pocket, and spread it out next to the other one on the bed. The hoof marks matched. "Barkloin," he muttered.

Roderick left his skillet, hobbled over, and perused the two notes. "Hmm," he said at last, "it looks as though the Chairman of the Senate's out to catch our princess."

"Not if I can help it," Ben said, putting an arm through a sleeve of his jacket. "I'm going after her."

"You'll do no such thing." Roderick turned him around and shoved him onto the bed with surprising strength.

Ben hugged his chest and bent over with pain. "What—" he gasped.

"Be quiet and listen," he said. "You are meant to give Miriam up. That is your present calling, however you feel about it. You have agreed to this. No, don't shake your head at me. From what you said to Thistle, it sounds like you've already had a poor beginning at following your new convictions. Now you're threatening to go off and do the very thing your vision has warned you not to do."

"They'll kill her!"

"You don't know that. What you do know is that you cannot be her savior."

"Will you take me with you?" Thistle had come up behind Roderick. She bounded onto a low chest and then onto the bed and looked intently from the note to the letter. "These people have to be stopped," she said.

Roderick rolled his eyes. He suddenly noticed smoke billowing from his skillet and rushed back to it, banging his head on one of the onion sacks. He poured some oil into the skillet. "Made me about ruin my best pan," he muttered. The oil sizzled loudly.

Ben folded the two pieces of parchment back up and stuck them in his pocket. "Do you trust me then?" he asked Thistle.

"I have no choice," she said.

"That is nearly always a lie," Roderick said. "Neither one of you have any business chasing after murderers."

Thistle winced at the word.

93

"Miriam wanted you to stay with me," Roderick said. "She knew who those men were after and wanted you out of harm's way."

"She doesn't know the Chairman of the Senate sent them," Thistle said. "Someone needs to warn her."

Ben sat back down at the table, suddenly hungry. He took a bite of his corncake. In his mind, another archer crept toward Miriam. "Why was there only one man last night?" He asked. "The note said to seek—who was it— Warwick for assistance."

Thistle scrambled down from the bed as Roderick picked out some of the unburned sprouts from the skillet for her. "Maybe he was there?" she said. "The one you killed didn't see you or me until it was too late. Maybe we didn't see a second man."

Ben and Thistle stared at each other.

"He might have followed us here," Ben said.

"He might have been waiting out there for her," Thistle said.

"This is all conjecture," Roderick asked.

Ben took another bite of corncake, avoiding Roderick's eye.

"Assuming nothing happens to her on the way, what are you going to do with Thistle when you get to Eddisford?" Roderick asked.

Thistle jumped in. "Can I be your page, Sir? Both Dunstan and Miriam have abandoned you, but I promise I won't."

Ben set his fork down. "You're a child!"

She leaned toward him eagerly, inadvertently poking one of her forehooves into her food.

"All right," Ben said, "at least until we can arrange something else, you can call yourself my page."

"In that case, Miss Thistle," Roderick interjected, "before you eat your meal—and I will insist that you eat it—I want you to go outside and around the house. You'll find the door to the cellar there, under that window." He pointed to the window above the bed. "There's an old knapsack from my fighting days, and fetch some more comfortable clothes for yourself, and something you think will fit the senator here too." He pointed his spatula at Ben. "You can't go over these mountains dressed in a silk shirt and vest. Thistle, you'll see some bundles of herbs on the far wall. Just stuff some of what you like in the knapsack. Go now. You have no time to waste."

At the word "cellar," something knotted up inside Thistle's face. She raised her head slowly from the sprouts on the floor and walked with determination to the door. There in the sunshine, she stopped. Twice she put her hoof over the threshold to go out, but retreated again. Finally, she braced herself and disappeared into the yard.

"Why are you making her go down there?" Ben said.

"Isn't it obvious?" Roderick replied. "If she's going to follow you into this folly, she better be prepared to face her fears."

Chapter 6
Intimidation

Snow had been falling since early afternoon. Ben pressed on, Thistle tripping along in his tracks, but it was getting too deep for her to continue much longer. The wool sweaters and fleece jackets Roderick had given them were growing inadequate for the flurries at this high altitude. The shivering made Ben's sore rib ache. He stopped and scanned the mountainside for shelter. The trees were thin this high up. They should have stopped at the shelter at six thousand feet, but he had given in to a sense of urgency that kept him going. He had been certain that they could reach the next shelter by the time darkness fell. The clouds and the snow had thickened and slowed them down.

Thistle bumped into the back of his boots. "Sorry," she said. "I wasn't watching."

"I'm looking for the next shelter," he said. His nervousness would edge on panic soon, but he must hide it from her. He could feel the knapsack digging into his shoulders. He was carrying more than he had wanted to carry, especially with the pack pulling against a sore rib.

Roderick had forced most of it on him in that impractical generosity of the elderly that wouldn't be denied. He would have dumped a lot of it long ago if he had known how to explain it to Thistle, who had treated every piece of it as treasure. He was grateful for the fold-up sled. It was a round, lightweight tin thing made of eight pie-piece shapes that folded into each other for portage. It would shorten the distance down the eastern slope.

Thistle cast her head around, but she could barely see above the snow. "Do you know how to build a house made of snow?"

He laughed. "You sure know how to cheer me up, kid."

"We could go back," she said.

"No." It flew out of his mouth.

Thistle cocked her head. Bits of snow landed softly on the roof of her muzzle as she gazed up at him. A blue and green knit tube-cap covered her head and wrapped itself around her chin and neck down to the collar of her jacket.

"I think we've gone over half way to the next shelter," he said more calmly. "It would be farther to go back. I'm sure it isn't too far ahead. We can make it while there's light." He turned and continued walking, case closed.

She came quietly panting behind him. A hundred more feet and they would reach the crest of the slope they had been ascending. Beyond that, he wasn't sure what he would see. It could descend hundreds of feet before rising again on another slope. The ceiling of clouds dragged snowy strands across the upper slope. If the mountain merely plateaued and then rose again as he hoped, even

97

then they would climb into snowy fog. Wouldn't that be treacherous?

Thistle nudged his leg. "Only," she said, "only we could slide back down a lot more easily than climbing up."

"It's going back," he said. "We do not go back."

"Never?" she said.

He kept climbing for an answer.

She straggled behind. "You've never been over this pass, right?"

He stopped, turned again, and glared at her.

"Sir," she said, pathetically trying to affect politeness to please him, "Sir, do you think we'll be able to see anything when we enter the clouds up ahead?"

"Thistle, we're in a hurry."

"I don't want to die."

He closed his eyes. Her worries were reasonable; they were in fact the voice of common sense that he had been battling in his own head, this last statement the most poignant. Why was he in such a rush? Here he was charging madly to save a girl he had only met the night before. She was the daughter of the man the Chairman of the Senate considered the greatest enemy of the republic. Was he turning himself into a traitor by helping her? Even if she did deserve his sympathy, his dream—what the old man called a convergence—had warned him to turn his back on her. Was that even real? He could hardly remember it now. The flames—not the image of the dream, but the real body of Clovenhoof burning—suddenly came back to him. It had only been the previous night, and yet it seemed a long time ago. Perhaps life was better measured in changes of conviction than minutes or hours. It felt as though his whole life before the sacrifice had been compressed into a few moments and each wavering of his convictions since had consumed decades of time. And now he was wavering again.

"We'll decide what to do when we get to the top of this slope," he said. "See it up there?"

"The snow gets in my eyes."

"Trust me then."

The wind picked up as they approached the top, hurling sheets of white in a blinding fury. The snow grew deeper around Ben's boots. He plowed through it up to his knees. With snow above her head on her left and right and Ben in front, Thistle was shielded from the wind. She found it easier and regained some of her breath. Above the din, Ben heard her singing wildly in a pathetic bleating voice that made him shake his head:

If I die here on this mountain

And my nose becomes a crystal
And my blood a frozen fountain
May this song my last epistle
Join the winds . . .

But there it did join the wind, and Ben lost the rest of it. They had reached the top, and the wind poured over it in blizzard force. He stopped and stared ahead. Beyond a few yards, it was all a blank, a swirling turmoil of white. It was futile to go forward. Even returning seemed hazardous now, and he kicked himself for demanding this last stretch of hiking.

He motioned for her to go back down a bit. There he stooped over to her level. "You think we can make it back to the last shelter?"

"Yes, I do," she said.

"You think we can find it again in all this snow? I've been considering your idea of a snow house."

"I remember how we came," she said. "I thought we might have to go back, so I memorized it." She drew in the snow between them with her hoof. "We went up a steep slope for a long time. Then the trail turned to the left by a clump of five trees with white bark. Then we went flat for a ways through an open field and then up some more. Then we went down, so far down I thought we were starting over going up." Here she broke off, looking up at him with her mouth dropped open.

"I can remember the rest," Ben said, sitting down cautiously and easing his pack from his shoulders.

"Sir, what's that? Look," Thistle said. "There's something there. Look." She pointed past his shoulder at a lone fir clinging to the mountainside only a few yards away over the ledge. They had not been able to see it before, but the wind had dragged the blanket of fog back for a moment.

Some sort of orange material flapped against a lower branch. Ben struggled over the ledge and tugged at it, but it wouldn't come loose. "It's probably nothing," he shouted. "Wait, there are strings. It's just caught a bit." He pried the tangled strings loose and brought it back to Thistle. It was a winter parka, a wide sheet of canvas with a wool lining at the neck and a drawstring where it could be tied  around the waist against the wind. "It's ripped in a few places, probably from the tree," he said.

"Why would it be flying around up here?" Thistle asked.

"Maybe someone took a rest, and then forgot it. It's not always this cold up here. I could see someone getting hot from hiking, taking it off, and then forgetting it."

"Maybe that someone needs it now and is freezing to death out there somewhere. Maybe we should go on."

Ben shook his head and looked around him. "Thistle, you said it yourself a few minutes ago. If we stay out here much longer, we're going to freeze to death ourselves. There's nothing we can do."

"Do you know what Miriam was wearing?" Thistle asked.

The question had been hovering in the back of his mind. He shook his head. "We should have asked Roderick. I don't know why we didn't. Come on, it's not likely to be hers. All sorts of people come over this pass." He slung his knapsack onto the snow and stuffed the parka into it as best he could. "We can look at it more closely when we get back to the shelter." He unclasped the sled from the pack, fanned it out, and locked it open. Then he climbed onto it, sitting cross-legged with his knees bracing the sides. "Sit on my lap," he said.

Thistle wriggled onto his legs and leaned her side against his stomach. It made a snug seat for her.

"Here we go," he said, and pushed off.

The sled picked up speed quickly. Ben dragged a hand on either side to slow down or steer. They sped down straight slopes and slowed for turns, the snow blinding them. Shivering, Thistle put her nose to the air to see the way. They swooped like a rock from a slingshot up the slope that Thistle remembered ascending until they gradually slowed and then had to walk the rest of the way back up. Then boarding, they flew down again, Thistle pointing the way with her little hoof. Each landmark seemed to laugh at Ben for his wasted effort.

Light dimmed quickly as they descended, till dusk swallowed the mountains down its gray throat. As they slid around the final turn, Ben dragged his gloved hands on the snow until they were barely moving. "I don't see it," he said. "Where was it?"

"Somewhere down there," Thistle said, pointing indefinitely at a grove of pines.

"It's all gray. I don't see anything," he said.

"Just go over there."

He steered the sled toward the trees and a bank of snow. As they approached, the mass of gray took individual shapes, emerging as trees and bushes. Above the bank of snow, Ben saw a row of cut logs. "That's it," he said. "That's the roof. We'll have to dig through for the door. Curse me for plowing on. We could have been snug inside with a fire going."

"Where was the door?" Thistle asked.

"Your guess is as good as mine," Ben said, pacing back and forth in front of the piled up snow. "Let's try the middle."

They had no shovel, so they went at it with hoof and boot, kicking the snow aside until they found the top of the door and could from there work outward. As the pain in Ben's chest increased with the jarring, he had to allow Thistle to do more and more of the work. The heavy clumps seemed to groan as they fell away. The further down they worked, the more packed the snow seemed and the more laborious their work became. Several times they thought they had finished, but had to claw out more hollow space to get the door open.

When they finally edged into the dusty darkness of the shelter, they collapsed with exhaustion. Ben fastened the door behind them, and they leaned against it, panting in the semi-warmth, safe from the cold and wet. Their breathing gradually slowed. Ben fumbled in his jacket pockets for his matches. He couldn't identify them with his fingers. He sat still, thinking what he'd done with them. In the stillness, a strange sensation came over him. Thistle had stiffened next to him. She must have sensed it too. The cadence of their breathing whispered that three people inhabited the blackened shelter.

What should he do?

Every moment of silence revealed his awareness of the alien person. Act calm. Get his knife ready. It was probably an ordinary traveler. Still, why hadn't the person identified himself? He reached for the pocket of his trousers. He felt his knife and pulled it midway out of the pocket and let it hang there, poised. He felt around deeper in. Nothing there. He groped in his other pocket and found the matches.

The person moved. A faint rustling of clothing. Still the measured breath continued.

Ben struck a match, held it up for a moment, then waved it out. What had he seen in that moment? Beside him, unprepared and surprised, Thistle had jumped to her hooves. What else? Log walls, empty cots, no face anywhere, a bundle of something on one cot. A person turned the other way? Asleep! He was nothing to be afraid of, just a traveler. An assassin wouldn't have slept through the scraping and banging of their entrance. A sword leaned against the wall in the far corner, but out of reach. Ben rolled to his knees and crept forward.

"What are you going to do?" Thistle whispered.

"Wake him up."

"What if he's dangerous?"

"Then we're in trouble, but better to surprise him than have him surprise us, and I want to get some sleep tonight." Ben felt around and found the right cot and the sleeping mass on it. It rose and fell with each of the stranger's breaths—breaths that reeked of alcohol. That explained some things. "Wake up," he whispered, jolting the body. "Wake up."

The stranger moaned. "What?"

"Wake up," Ben said more firmly, shaking him.

"What? The Chisel!" The man suddenly squirmed away, kicking at Ben and writhing in fear. "Get away! No!"

"What's the matter? Get back here." Ben crawled after him.

"I couldn't do it! Forgive me! Mercy!" He wiggled off across the cots to one of the near corners.

Ben could hear him breathing heavily now in the darkness. "We're not going to hurt you, but we're going to be here together all night," Ben said. He crawled back to the other corner and retrieved the sword. Why hadn't the man thought to lunge for it if he was so afraid? "There are some things we need to know."

The man sniffled. "I know what you mean by that." His voice came out slurred, as though his tongue were coiled up in his mouth and had to be unwound.

"I don't mean anything by it," Ben said. "Who is it you think I am?"

A long pause followed. "I know the Chisel sent you."

"I'm Benjamin Emundson, Senator of Redland."

"I knew it! I knew it! Please, don't play games with me. If you're going to kill me, do it quickly." He scrambled

105

forward, feeling blindly across the cots until he found Ben's shirt. Clutching it, his breath a thick vapor in Ben's face, he cried out, "Why does she have to be killed? Why couldn't we just take her captive, banish her somewhere where no one will know who she is? I'm not a murderer."

Ben took hold of the man's hands and pried them from his shirt. His mind jumped to the note in his pocket. Warwick—was that the name? The note had said, "Seek Warwick for assistance." Ben took a chance. "Where is she, Warwick?" he asked, threat deepening his voice.

The man gasped in the dark. "Don't hurt me! I'll tell you what you want to know."

"Then answer my question!"

"She's at the next shelter, maybe the one after, but not likely. She would have been much further, but she doubled back on me. I wasn't fooled; I'm a good tracker. Still, for a princess—Sir, you people hired me to track, not to murder. That was the other fellow's job."

"If you lead us to her, we'll handle it," said a small voice from across the room, "I'm sure the Chisel will understand when you report to him."

The name, whoever it was, maybe Barkloin's henchman, seemed to inject terror into the man's veins in spite of the small voice that invoked it. "Report to him! I can't go back without—"

Ben took hold of Warwick's shoulders. "Listen, if you know what's good for you, just lead us to the princess, and everything will turn out fine for you."

Warwick wilted onto one of the cots, his relief palpable. "I'll take you to her then. She won't escape me, however clever she is."

"Now that that's settled, let's have some light," Ben said.

"There's a lantern hanging from the rafter behind you," Warwick said.

Ben felt around and found it. He lit a match and held it to the wick. The room filled with an orange glow. He examined the tracker for the first time. He was a small, balding man with a curious scar on his neck below his left ear.

"How'd you do that?" Thistle asked.

"What, this?" he fingered it. "It was Senator Clovenhoof gave this to me. Funny what power does to a person." Seeing their faces at the mention of Clovenhoof, he laughed loudly. "The respectable old professor, yes! Now there's something you could have used against him in your election. Only, you start digging in the other fellow's pile of manure, he starts digging in yours, right? And none of you senators want that."

Thistle lowered her little head menacingly, but Warwick didn't notice. He fished under his cot for his bottle, suddenly cheerful.

"This is what you get when you don't obey a senator's commands, little miss. You'll learn soon enough if you stick with him." He glanced at Ben. "Years ago, Senator Clovenhoof hired me to track for him. He sent me after traitors, said they were in league with the tribe of Miliuc. For a while there, you remember, every shadow in the

107

forest was a traitor from Miliuc. So we caught the traitors with a bag of letters, only it wasn't what we thought. You wouldn't believe who they were from."

"Was it the king, or the Bishop of Blackwater Valley?" Ben asked. He was beginning to think that everything in the world really was tied together in a string of inextricable knots.

Warwick swallowed hard, clearly taken aback. "You know everything, you do. I'll walk down a dark road for you. I might even kill a man for you if I know he's wicked. But I won't go against the Lord of Grace or his anointed. I'm a praying man."

"What did you do?" Thistle asked weakly.

"I hid them in a hole in the ground and said we never found them, but I was betrayed. You can figure out the rest. A Rangellian sword can be very convincing, especially hooked into your neck a few inches from where you draw the breath of life."

Thistle turned slowly away from the light, clopped over to a cot in the far corner, and climbed in it. She buried her head in a pile of wool blankets and lay quietly, her chest heaving. Ben could only imagine what was going through her head. She might have only just convinced herself in the last few days that her grandfather had had nothing to do with the slaughter of her parents, and now she had this to open the question again.

"What's the matter with her?" Warwick asked.

Ben took one of the blankets and spread it over her. "Rest a bit, Thistle. I'll fix us something to eat." He leaned over, nuzzled her head with his forehead, and whispered, "May the Lord of Grace give you rest." He wondered at himself. The words came out naturally, as though he had believed all his life.

When she sighed and nodded, he went back over to his pack and foraged in it for some food. He was about to empty the pack when a thought struck him. "What happened to your partner?"

"Last night in the woods outside Blackwater—we were told the princess would be there, at someone's sacrifice. When we got to the spot, a sheep had died all right, poor fellow. They were burying him when we arrived. I wonder what he did to make Clovenhoof want to kill him?"

"You don't think it was a real sacrifice?"

"Not for a moment."

"It was Clovenhoof that arranged his death," Ben muttered. "You're right about that." He turned the pack upside down, but it was so full that nothing fell out.

"Go ahead and mock. That was someone's life. There was another fellow with the princess, the one who must have done the killing. When he caught onto us, I slipped away. When a plan goes wrong, you abandon it. That's a good rule to live by. My partner would still be alive if he'd followed it." He lifted the bottle to his mouth and took a swig.

"How do you know he's dead?" Ben shook the pack, and the contents fell out in a heap.

"I don't know for sure, but he never turned up at the rendezvous spot. He was a brute with no sense—probably went blundering in and got himself killed."

"You didn't go back to the spot?"

"Are you kidding? Resisting urges like that is what's kept me alive all these years. The princess was bound to come west. I knew that. I came up to the pass and waited. When I caught onto her, she was alone and traveling fast—which proves my point about not going back. That other fellow's no doubt still waiting there to ambush me when my curiosity gets the best of me. Only it won't." Warwick leaned back in his cot, satisfied with himself, but then suddenly sat up straight. "What's this?" He grabbed the parka from the pile in front of Ben. "What are you doing with this?"

"Why do you want to know?" Ben asked slowly.

"She was wearing this. The princess was wearing this up on the pass."

"We found it a ways up."

The tracker looked at Ben suspiciously. "Found it? What do you mean?"

"It was stuck on a branch up on the pass."

Still the tracker studied his face as though Ben were hiding something. Finally he lowered his eyes to the parka and examined it, turning it around in his hands. "It would be a cold night on the mountain without this," he said.

110

Chapter 7
Final Authority

"Fly away my spirit of sorrows
Ride the wind beyond these windows
Eyes no more will see your mother
Eyes no more will see your father
Skip away on mountain snows."

Thistle sang softly to herself, and the tune came flitting back to Ben, who was trudging behind her. Warwick was a few hundred yards ahead, plowing slowly through the waist high drifts. He had made them stay well behind him. He didn't want them stomping on any tracks. When they had arrived at the crest where Thistle had found the parka, they had found nothing to help their search or to indicate why Miriam might have taken the parka off. The snow had continued falling overnight, and now the snowdrifts buried everything. Looking around, Ben had realized her body could be lying just a few feet away beneath the ocean of snow, but he had forced himself to put it out of his mind. Warwick had seemed hopeful, and it was easier to graft his misgivings onto what seemed like baseless intuition than to despair.

The threesome had only been able to get out of their shelter early that morning because of Warwick's forethought, once he had half sobered up over the coffee and dinner Roderick had provided them in Thistle's pack. Warwick had found a canvas under one of the cots and had tied it from the overhang of the roof to two pegs in the ground in front of the door to keep the snow away. In the morning, Warwick and Ben had been able with brute force to wedge the door open wide enough for them to slip through and tunnel the rest of the way out of the snow.

The mounds of snow had not shaken the tracker's confidence one bit. "I'll find her for you," he had said. "No need to kill me yet. If she stayed in the next shelter, she'll still be stuck in there. It took two of us to get past our door this morning. Even if she did get out, who could go anywhere in this without leaving tracks?"

The day was beautiful. The heavy clouds had blown over, leaving a bright blue canopy. The sun glared on the snow and forced Ben to squint, but it took the edge off the crisp wind and made him feel happy in a drowsy sort of way. Poor Thistle—he hadn't thought much about her personal tragedy in all the excitement. He tapped her on the back. "You all right?"

"I don't feel sad enough," she replied.

"You haven't had time to think."

"I cried for three days when my parents died. Then I just stopped."

"How long ago was it?" Ben asked absently. He remembered Miriam telling him, but events had cluttered in his mind.

She thought for a moment. "Two weeks."

"Don't blame yourself. Grief is a funny thing. I think it has stages."

"I'm in the angry stage then." She stopped in her tracks and heaved a deep sigh.

"You have a lot to be angry about."

"Miriam has never admitted that she thinks my grandfather had my parents killed. Warwick pretty much said it last night, didn't he? I guess I've needed to hear someone say it out loud."

"You think he had them killed?"

"It made me furious that she wouldn't say it. Why wouldn't she say it?"

"She didn't believe it."

"She was trying to protect me."

Ben put his hand under her chin. "She told me she didn't believe it. Warwick was talking about something that happened a long time ago. Your grandfather changed."

"Why protect a person who saw her very own—" She broke off and started walking again. "What is there left to protect?" she muttered.

Ben called after her, "There's plenty to protect, Thistle. You have a child's heart, no matter how hard it feels right now."

She walked a few paces further and stopped. She turned around slowly, her eyes glistening. Her lips trembled, but she said nothing.

Ben wiped his nose and folded his arms around his aching rib. He stretched out a hand toward her. "You have a little child's heart," he repeated.

She backed away from him, shaking her head, her eyes burning. Ben glanced over her at Warwick, a small smudge on the grand vista, down the trail. He was waving furiously up at them to come. Thistle noticed the shift in Ben's gaze, turned, and headed down the hill. Warwick squatted and crept like a spider to some holly bushes. He turned toward them again and signaled with his hands to stay low. Ben wondered what good it would do half way up the mountainside out in the open.

He caught up with Thistle. "If we're going to save Miriam, remember, we have to play our parts well."

Thistle nodded her head, still gazing straight ahead of her.

"Do you think you're brave enough to stay with the tracker while I go down to the shelter?"

She nodded.

"Just say something about the Chisel if he tries to pull anything."

They crept silently down to where Warwick hid and huddled next to him.

"Look there," Warwick said, "the roof of the shelter." Ben could see nothing but snow drifts. The tracker pointed. "Look left of those rocks, about ten yards. See the eave?"

"Amazing," Ben said. "You know your work. I never would have seen it from here."

Warwick nodded enthusiastically. "I'm not a murderer, but I am a tracker. Now remember. I've led you here, but I want no part of this."

"How do you know she's in there?" Thistle said. "I can't see. Hold me up."

The tracker picked her up. "Look, no tracks leading out. She's stuck in there unless she died before getting here or something else happened to her. I still don't understand the parka."

"Do you know if all the shelters are built the same way?" Ben asked.

"Identically," Warwick said. "I've been in this one. It's the same as the one we stayed in."

Ben swung his pack around to the ground. He untied the string and dug inside. "The two of you stay here and don't make a sound. I'm going in." He pulled a dagger out and laid the blade against the palm of his hand.

Thistle and Warwick stared at it, mouths open.

Warwick suddenly grabbed his wrist, his eyes intense. "Don't you fear the Lord of Grace?"

Ben looked at him steadily. "Does this mean you'll try to stop me?"

Warwick released some of the pressure on his wrist, but still held onto it. "I came to this moment—twice I came to this moment yesterday—I couldn't bring myself to kill the princess."

"You're a coward. That's plain enough."

"Don't you know that failing my mission meant certain death? My cowardice was telling me to kill her."

"And doesn't it still mean that?" Ben looked at him curiously. A floundering courage was beating its way into the tracker's face. Ben almost loved him for it.

"You're a senator." Warwick's words tumbled out in a rapid flurry. "You have as much authority as the Chisel. There are other options. This is the king's daughter. The king is the forearm of the Lord of Grace, so the priests say."

"So the princess is what, his finger?" Ben laughed as haughtily as he could muster.

"That's no answer," Warwick said. "Don't you fear the Lord of Grace?"

Ben rolled his eyes. He spoke slowly, feeling the weight of politics settling into his voice. "If the Lord of Grace exists at all, and if he were the creator of justice, he would not have lifted one man to rule over others without their consent. A king is just another name for a tyrant. I cannot believe that the true God would ordain such a thing. It amounts to slavery."

"Yet it is what the priests say of the Lord of Grace."

"They're wrong."

"How can you talk with such authority? The priests are the voice of the Lord of Grace!"

Ben's anger burst out. "When it comes to matters of belief, I submit to nothing but my own conscience. I despise blind authority."

"And yet you would lord it over others!" Warwick said. He pointed at the dagger. The conversation had turned in a direction that stabbed the real Ben, not the murderer he was pretending to be. Never mind that he wasn't planning

116

to use this dagger in his hands; the last words he had uttered had sprung from years of conviction. Did he not believe this anymore? A man's conscience had to be sovereign. How had he ever submitted to Clovenhoof's sacrifice? How had Roderick's religious rhetoric taken him in? Who were these to guide him? It had all been forced on him too quickly. He would wake up from this dream soon enough. Then what would he find that he had done?

"There was a moment yesterday," Warwick said, "when I thought I had shot the princess. You don't know how relieved I was when I found my arrow."

"So you did shoot at her."

"I'll never do it again."

Ben shook his arm free of the tracker and shoved him to the ground. "So this is where your loyalty lies."

"Please," Warwick said. Terror had rushed back into his face. "Please, I've led you to her. I've done what I was hired to do. Not everybody is a murderer."

Thistle gazed at Ben with genuine fear and bewilderment. His performance had nearly convinced her.

Ben thrust the dagger in the heel of his boot. "This won't take long." He scurried out and plowed down the hill. When he came to the shelter, he had to dig through to the door. He called out as he kicked snow away, "Anyone in here?" The work strained his rib to the breaking point. Several times he saw Warwick's head peering over the holly bush, and he motioned for him to come down and help him, but to no avail.

When Ben finally reached the door, he knocked on it and yelled, "Come on, I know you're in there. Make this easier for me." And then a bit more quietly he added, "My rib's killing me. Please." He heard a faint sound, then footsteps. Someone shoved against the door, but it wouldn't budge. "Frozen," Ben said. He took his dagger and hacked at the cracks around the door. "Shove it again," he said.

Ben heard a sigh and then the sound of something dragged across the floor. After a strange silence, a splintering crash jarred the door and swung it open. Ben dove out of its way into the snow bank. A cot dangled on the door latch for a moment and then clattered to the ground. Ben glanced up the hill and saw Warwick's head pop up from the holly bush. He slid his arm down his leg and withdrew his dagger, making sure Warwick saw its glint in the sunshine. Then he peered around the door, but no one emerged. He crawled over the top of the cot and inched along the mattress, trying to see into the dark interior of the shelter. The sky and the snow had been so bright outside that his eyes couldn't adjust.

Suddenly a small fist reached out from within the threshold and dragged him in over the edge of the cot onto the floor. The two tumbled over twice, Ben doing all he could not to stab the girl with his outstretched knife, until they came to rest in pitch darkness.

"Miriam?" he said, but instead of answering, she broke a bottle over his head, and he knew no more.

It might have been several hours before Ben awoke. He couldn't tell, but had the sense that time had passed. His head throbbed with pain. Something cold was biting into his head, something wrapped too tightly around his jaw.

His pulse beat against it. He turned over, and the ache in his rib stabbed him again. Ben groaned and felt his head with his hands, his eyes still closed. A folded up cloth filled with what—icicles—was tied to his head. It burned. He had to get it off.

"Welcome back," Miriam's voice said from somewhere in the room. She came and sat on the cot where he lay. "I'm so sorry I had to bash you over the head like that—and your rib already hurting you too! I wasn't sure it was you, your voice all muffled behind the door, and I couldn't see any other way. Why did you have that dagger out if you weren't going to use it? Murder is not your line of work, Senator. I think you should stay away from it from now on."

He opened his eyes and saw her in dim candlelight. The door was closed, the cot leaning up against its frame. "I never intended to murder you, Princess, but this bump is making me reconsider," Ben said.

She stared at him for a moment. "So you know who I am."

He acknowledged her words with a faint smile. "Where are the other two? How long have I been out?"

"Two? I only saw one, and I think he's long gone. Our fight scared him off. I saw him running away, carrying something, when I went out to drag the cot in and close the door. I couldn't help you with that door hanging wide open inviting someone to shoot an arrow through it. He was the same coward that's been tracking me since yesterday morning. I can't shake him, but he won't come

119

close enough to have it out. I guess you caught up to him at the last shelter."

"I convinced him I'd murder you for him."

"But who's the other one?"

Ben closed his eyes. "Thistle."

"Thistle?" Panic swept over her face. "How could you bring her? I left her with Roderick so nothing like this would happen. "

"I needed a new page," Ben said stupidly.

Miriam grabbed the collar of Ben's shirt and shook him, forgetting his wounds. "You stupid, stupid boy. You can't even follow orders."

Ben groaned with the pain, his head swirling with nausea.

"Oh, your wounds!" Miriam cried and dropped him back onto the bed.

Ben breathed quick, light breaths. He wiped his mouth with the back of his hand. "I had no orders to follow. I had a letter from a cowardly schoolgirl who was too afraid to travel with me. She thought it was too dangerous, if I remember right. I think I have it here somewhere." He tried to reach into his pocket, but she took hold of his hand.

"I'm sorry," she said. "You're right. I never told you who I am, but Roderick, he should have known better." She stomped a foot.

"I don't recall that you told him either," Ben said. "We never expected to run into you and your trail of murderers."

"It was not an innocent decision on his part," Miriam said, nearly crushing Ben's hand in rage, and then throwing it down. "My father used to tell me about Roderick. He has a history of sending folks directly into the most precarious places on purpose."

"He didn't send us after you. He tried to talk us out of following you."

"That's what he does. He talks you into it and then makes it seem like it's your decision."

"But your father sent you to him. He must have trusted him with your life."

"My father didn't send me!" Miriam burst out. "He thinks I'm hiking with a friend in the Svaaglen Hills."

"He didn't send you? Then what are you doing here?"

"I don't know. What am I doing here?" She stood up and paced the room. She pulled on her hair above her ears. "How did I get myself into this? How did I get that poor little lamb into this?" She flopped back down on the cot across from Ben and stared at the wall.

Ben found himself watching Miriam, enjoying the flicker of pain in her eyes. They were beautiful, brown eyes, richly dark like her hair. He hadn't really examined her before this. It had been at night with too much happening. Her nose might be a little long, he thought. Ben rarely took note of such things, but Roderick's insinuation that he cared for Miriam was tickling his mind.

"What are you looking at?" she asked self-consciously.

Ben lowered his eyes. "That tracker seemed like a nice fellow, actually."

Miriam furled her brow and looked at him incredulously. "He seemed like a nice fellow? He was out to kill me."

"But he didn't, though he had more than one chance. He was coerced into tracking you. Up there on the hill, he tried to talk me out of killing you. Don't laugh at me. I'm telling you, he seemed like a nice fellow."

"I don't want to hear this," she said fiercely. "He's a hired tracker in the service of the Senate."

"So we don't trust anyone in the Senate?"

Their eyes met, hers cutting into his.

"Would you?" she said. "Honestly, would you?"

Chapter 8
Abdicate

Ben sank back into the cot and stared at the rafters above him. Miriam fidgeted with her hands, sitting in the cot across from him. Several times she started to speak, but checked herself. Finally she gathered her boots and began working at some knots in them. Ben's head seethed with anger. Why should she not trust him? For that matter, why should he trust her? Surely, she was here on a mission to overthrow the Senate and restore her father's rule. Yet in her present fury, she struck him for the first time as—was it some old romantic notion springing up like a late flower inside of him—as elegant, like a princess. People who firmly believed in democracy could be swept into tears at the story of a lost princess.

"When I found your parka," he said, "and I thought you were dead—"

Her head jerked up. "You found my parka?"

Ben nodded. "Thistle did, actually. It wasn't until the tracker saw it that I knew it was yours. When I thought you were dead—"

She stood up suddenly, her face white even in the candlelight. "Where did Thistle find it?"

"Clinging to a tree on the mountain, as we came over the second rise, I think. Why did you take it off?"

"I traded it." She leaned over, dug around under the cot, and dragged out an ancient, matted, wool coat with loose and thready seams. "I traded it for this coat. I was sick of that tracker following me, and a storm was brewing."

"But who did you trade it with?"

"Oh, just a mountain woman I met on the trail. She was a bit crazy in the head. But I was giving her a good deal. Roderick's parka was worth far more than this old thing. We traded boots too. You never saw the ones Roderick gave me, but I assure you they were nicer than these. I pointed at the gathering clouds and told her I was in a hurry, and she seemed to understand. I wonder what happened to her."

Ben closed his eyes.

"What is it?" Miriam asked.

"You can't guess?"

What do you mean?"

"Didn't the thought occur to you that the tracker might shoot her?"

"I told you he never came close enough to shoot me. She was in no danger, I assure you."

Ben shook his head. "He told me he thought he had shot you once."

Miriam let out a little laugh. "He was bragging then."

"Maybe it wasn't you he finally took a shot at. Maybe he finally stirred himself up to do it, and it was the wrong woman. He said he was relieved when he found his arrow."

"So he must have missed her."

"Something about the way he said it made me think he didn't. There was a kind of intensity in his eyes. I need to go back and make sure."

"What about Thistle?"

"I don't think the tracker would hurt her."

"Though you do think he shot that woman?"

"How can you be so devil may care about her? Don't you feel culpable at all? If she died, it's because you gave her the parka."

"And if Thistle dies, it's because you left her in the hands of the enemy."

They stared at each other.

"A few moments ago I had the impression I was someone you couldn't trust," Ben finally said.

Miriam blew her hair out of her eyes. "You're worried about the woman, and I'm worried about Thistle. Maybe we should just go our separate ways, not that I would have any chance of rescuing her from him. I spent all yesterday eluding him; I can't turn around and go chasing after him. Ben, he thinks you're on his side. If you could catch up to him, he would trust you."

"I suppose that's what Roderick meant by dying to you," Ben said more to himself than to her, "I should let you go on by yourself."

"What are you talking about? Dying to me?"

"I had a dream about you, and I was Clovenhoof. Roderick said it was the Lord of Grace telling me what to do through Clovenhoof, a convergence."

"What did he tell you?"

Ben shifted his weight on his cot. "I'm embarrassed to say."

"If you want me to trust you—"

"I have to let you go." Roderick had been right. He had tried to protect Miriam from the tracker, and it had only resulted in losing Thistle. If he and Thistle hadn't waked him up, Warwick would have slept on in his drunken stupor and would still be stuck in the last shelter. Now he would let Miriam go, let her walk alone into Eddisford to whatever danger awaited her. The Lord of Grace would have to protect her. As for Thistle—

Miriam was smiling, curling a strand of her hair around a finger.

"What?" he asked.

"You want to protect me then?"

"I guess so," he stammered. He felt his face redden. "Of course, now that you knocked me out with that bottle—"

She laughed. "Listen, Ben, I'm going to tell you what I'm doing here and trust that you'll keep it to yourself as long as I need you to."

"I'm not a Royalist," Ben said.

"You don't have to be right now, so long as you don't want to kill me like your friends." She bit her lip. "Would you at least listen to me if I told you why I'm here? I have to have someone on my side when I get to Eddisford.

126

Otherwise it's pointless even going. I can't do this alone."

"I'm listening."

"You know that my father abdicated forty years ago. He believed in a republican form of government as much as you do, maybe more. It's one thing to seek to become a senator; it's quite another thing to give up being king to allow others to become senators."

"You're saying that he wasn't forced to abdicate, that he wanted to because of his own convictions? That's not how I've heard the story."

"Yes and no. He and Clovenhoof had studied political science at the university together. They had been dreaming of a republic for a long time, but never as something that could be created quickly and on a purely secular basis. The Lord of Grace had instituted the monarchy. They had always agreed that nothing could be done without a special revelation from the Lord of Grace—a convergence—but Clovenhoof changed after his father—"

"Did his father really give his life for your grandfather?"

"So the professor told you that. Did he also tell you how bitter he was?" Miriam tapped her finger on her lip. "It wasn't long after his father was sacrificed, maybe a year—this is all second hand, so I don't have it straight in my head—that Clovenhoof sat on the Traitor's Chair and demanded a republic. I assume that part's in your history books."

"You think he did it out of resentment?"

"I suppose you've been taught to think how daring and self-sacrificial he was in taking the chair, but think about it.

Anyone who sat on the Traitor's Chair had to be convinced of the policy he proposed because the king would have to either execute him or adopt the proposal as a just cause. That's how the chair worked. Clovenhoof asked for a republic. It left my father with two choices, to execute him or abdicate. He couldn't execute his best friend. He couldn't ignore Clovenhoof's demand either. The chair was always an integral part of the monarchy. It was a check on the king's conscience, and every one of my ancestors believed in it."

"You're talking about it as if it's a thing of the past," Ben broke in.

Miriam had been waving her hands around passionately as she spoke; now they hung in the air before her as if a string inside her had unwound. "The chair still exists?"

"It sits on the senate floor next to the moderator's chair."

"I had no idea it would still be in use."

"Well, I don't know how long it's been since anyone's sat on it. A Borlock rebel sat on it to demand the release of prisoners during their uprising, but he wasn't really taken seriously."

"You mean nothing happened to him?"

"No, they executed him. I mean he didn't have a just cause. The vote was unanimous. But what you're saying about Clovenhoof is another thing. You're turning one of our greatest founding fathers into a mere manipulator."

"One of our greatest founding fathers? I didn't hear that sort of rhetoric in any of your campaign speeches. See, that's the weakness in a republic. A senator is so worried about losing power, or gaining power that he easily twists the truth for his own purposes. A king doesn't have that pressure, does he? Secure in his position, he can speak the truth."

"Secure in his position, he can abuse his power too."

"My father despised the abuse of power. In fact, he left the country because he thought that if he stayed, people would continue to look to him as the authority even with the senate. People loved him. It's not as though there was rejoicing in the streets when he stepped down. People were disappointed; his advisors were furious. It became clear who the power-hungry were. Some of those same advisors ran for office and won. They were people-pleasers to begin with, so it wasn't as hard as they thought it would be. They treated Clovenhoof like a hero and convinced him to run for office. Once the election took place and the senate convened, my father slipped away. Nobody expected it; he just slipped away quietly."

"That's nice to know," Ben said. "I thought for a moment you were going to tell me the Senate secretly forced him into exile."

"It was the night of the ball commemorating the new Capitol." Her face lit up as though the lights from the Capitol were shining on her as she spoke. "A hundred of the newly formed senate guards surrounded the building."

"And none of them would admit to seeing him leave or helping him," Ben said.

"They didn't. He swears they didn't."

"Did he ever tell you how he did it?"

Miriam fumbled in a pocket and drew out a key. "This is how." She smiled mysteriously. "I've asked him a hundred times, but he's never told me what it went to. He likes to tease me like that. Finally I stole it from him; he thinks he lost it a few years ago, but I took it from him. The joke is on him now. Your little act of slipping out the window at your election party was nicely done too, by the way."

"Did you see me?"

"No, you were there and then you weren't. I had been about to come over and romance you out onto that verandah anyway. You saved me the trouble."

"So where did your father go?"

"Vinland, Roskilde, Hedeby, Traprain, Uulantep, Holdmark, everywhere. Do you know that in Roskilde, humans have no property rights? Inheritance of the land passes from ram to ram. But in Uulantep sheep don't voluntarily give themselves to be sacrificed. A priesthood of men secretly chooses who will be sacrificed next. Sheep live in a kind of terror. In Holdmark there are no sacrifices. They talk of the Lord of Grace during the harvest festival, but it's just a tradition.

Papa visited all these places. He never felt freer in his life. In one way I think he wanted to soak up life all he could before he returned. In another way, I think he wanted to drive himself as far away from life as he could so he could come running back to it as if it were a lost mother. Do you know what I mean by that? He had very little money, enough for train fare and boarding in the cheapest places. He was a vagabond, working every kind

130

of menial job, building calluses and coarse hands, learning this trade and that."

Miriam grew more animated as she talked, waving her arms. Ben admired her. He could never talk about his own father like this. His own father—the betrayal stabbed him afresh. When would his father find out about the Sacrifice? Had Clovenhoof turned up missing yet?

"He laid bricks in Hedeby, assisted a plumber in Vinland, cleaned crates at a fish market in Nandakke. Whatever he did, he refused advancement and gave away most of his money. He always remembered that he was a king in self-imposed exile. If he wanted a better life, something to hang onto, he could return to Redland and claim his throne. Everyone here seems to have forgotten that the republic is provisional, but he never has.

"He went on like this for twenty years, always keeping abreast of politics and goings-on in Redland, always longing to return but keeping away. Whenever he got homesick, he channeled that feeling into a new wander lust, put his pack on his back, and struck out for a new country. I can only dream about all the places he's been!"

"But he must have settled down before you came along," Ben said.

Miriam smiled at him. "This is the best part of the story. At forty years old, he thought himself a confirmed bachelor. Marriage was like advancement or money. He had thought it meant gaining something for himself, acquiring, so he had always set himself against it. He had just arrived back from a fishing trip in the North Falslip. His boat had been skirting the shores off the Uurkunla

Peninsula, dodging chunks of ice and reeling in tuna, herring, all kinds of large fish—I don't know what else. He wasn't captain of the ship or first mate or anything of course. He had these fishy hands. He could never get the smell off of them, even with the strongest cleansers. In bed at night the smell on his hands would wake him up." Miriam held her hands together against her cheek to illustrate.

Ben nodded. "So he was ready for another job change."

"Right, but he wasn't in any hurry. He had to spend the money he'd earned on the trip first. They'd had a great catch. He was eating dinner, sitting by himself in the feasting-hall of a cheap inn in Svegeby. The candlelight in the room shone very dimly, and outside the window, the snow fell in thick flurries."

"You're describing this as though you were there," Ben said.

"Well, of course I wasn't there then, but I have been there," she said. "It was late in the Fall. Suddenly, waves of homesickness overwhelmed him. He hadn't felt this way in years, though he'd suffered pangs all along. He left the borsch he had been eating there on the table with all the cash he had in his pocket. He had enough money stashed away upstairs to get him back to Redland where he had untold riches as king, so what did it matter now?"

"Assuming they welcomed him back," Ben said.

"Like I said, he never doubted that. Papa rushed up stairs, flung the door open to his room, and gathered his things quickly into his pack, sweeping them with his forearm off the dresser and tables. As a lark, he left a pile

132

of his money under the mattress for someone to find. He was skipping down the hall—if you can imagine a forty-some-year old man doing that—when he burst into a waking dream more vivid than any sleeping dream he had ever had before. It was as though the world we live in were a package wrapped around another world more real than ours, and he had been a drawing on that package, and he had suddenly been able to burst through the paper. That's how he describes it, as if we're crawling around on the surface of things, but the real world's within, far richer than we can imagine.

"In this dream, Papa stood in the same hallway, but he was lower to the ground, and when he examined himself, he found that he was Ramsportion, Clovenhoof's father, the ram who had given himself for his father. You see, it

was a convergence, just like yours. At the end of the hall, a door swung open, and light poured through. Papa clomped forward and looked out the door. There lay all of Redland—as we know it, not as it would be in the dream. A voice suddenly sprung from behind him, but he was too fat to turn his head around and see who made it. Papa says it was a voice like autumn air. He'd never heard a voice so beautiful in his life. The voice said, 'Bury the seed, Ramsportion. Bury it if you want it to grow into anything.' And then suddenly the wrapping enveloped the dream again and he was himself standing in the hallway."

Miriam laughed and bounced to her feet. "This is the best part."

Ben became conscious of smiling at her. "You said that before."

"It's the best part of the best part," she said. "Be quiet and listen. Remember he was in the hall and the dream had just left him. A voice from behind him, a shadow of the more beautiful one in the dream, said to him, 'Sir, are you ill?'

"He turned around and stared into the eyes of a young Fortimeian woman. She had a slim face with high, bony cheeks and a wide smile. The coarseness of her face seemed softened by suffering somehow. Her eyes wore a shy sadness. Her hair was long, dark, and straight."

"She must have been your mother," Ben said.

"Why do you say that?" Miriam smiled playfully.

"See there?" Ben said. "That's the very smile you described."

"It was my mother. She would teach him to bury the seed. 'You were standing there staring into space,' she said. 'Are you ill?'

134

"'Yes,' he said. 'I was daydreaming. I'm sorry. Let me allow you by.' He stood flat against the wall so she could get by him.

"She leaned against the opposite wall. 'But where were you headed?'

"Each time he heard her speak, he heard echoes of the more beautiful voice in his dream. 'Where was I headed?' A sudden clarity pierced him as if physically, and he reeled with it.

"She grasped his shoulders. 'You seem ill. Can I help you?'

"'I need food,' he said, 'excellent food and wine.' He smiled and stood up straight; his weakness seemed to have popped like a bubble.

"She looked into his face and saw a king, or at least a man like one."

Ben interrupted. "So what was the sudden clarity?"

"The sudden clarity. Yes." Miriam tugged on her lower lip thoughtfully. "Papa realized that all these years when he had kept himself free of the world, he had done it so he could hang on to Redland. He had never relinquished his hold on it in his own mind. The voice in his dream told him to let go of Redland, to bury it, and it was the perfect voice of the beautiful woman in the hallway. He thought that only she could be the instrument the Lord of Grace would give him to help him forget. I'm not sure you could assume things like that, but he did. He showed her the money under his mattress and took her to the finest restaurant in Svegeby that evening. They ate Uulan salmon with asparagus and drank red wine.

"She fell in love with him. Her name was Rietka. She was the daughter of a fish packer in Svegeby. Imagine that. She had been a fish packer herself for the past ten years. 'We'll be packing your tuna over the next week, Reinard,' she said, laughing. Her father rented a flat above the bakery next door to the inn. They were allowed to use the attic above their flat, but there was no way into it from their living quarters. She had to climb up through a drop ladder in the hallway in the inn, walk through the attic, and open a door to get to their attic. While Papa had stood entranced in his dream, Mama had lowered the ladder, climbed down it, and put it back up. She had wondered at this strange man standing there in the hallway as though he were in a trance. She had wondered if he had just received some terrible news, as though some intense sorrow had pierced his heart.

"When she found out what his sorrow was, she couldn't believe it. 'You're a king, and you go fishing in the North Falslip?'

"'I'm not a king. I abdicated.'

"'But you could go back and be a king if you wanted to?'

"'Yes, but—' and he told her about the dream and her voice.

"She was intrigued by the Sacrifice and the Lord of Grace. You know that the Fortimai have no god, unless you can call fate a god. They spend their lives running from it as though it were a beast hunting them. Yet here was a god who loved her, who invited her to his home, however bloody the means. She felt as though someone

136

was calling her from far away when he spoke, and he had such conviction and authority in his voice. No one had ever fallen in love with her before either, and he kept looking at her in that strange way. Girls notice these things. It can be very unsettling." Miriam smiled at Ben playfully.

Ben looked down at his hands and picked at a scab.

"She took him to see her father, and they got on together like the wind and the rain. A few months later my father and grandfather were eyeing each other across the Carom table. The old man had won three games in a row. Papa said, 'If I win the next one, will you let me marry your daughter?' She wasn't there; she had gone out to the vegetable market.

"The old man said, 'Just what are you planning to do with your life?'

"Papa said, 'You couldn't argue with what I plan.'

"The old man said, 'Why is that? I suppose you want to make my daughter queen of Redland, and it won't make any difference to you whether I see her again in my life or not, though she's my only joy.' Papa says he wore a fierce animal expression on his face when he said this, like a bear when its cubs are threatened.

"Papa looked at him and said, 'No. I want to pack fish. How can you argue with that if it's the path you've chosen for yourself?'

"Grandpa was dumbfounded. They played the game, and Papa lost again. He rose to leave, dejected, but grandpa threw the Carom board aside and grasped his arm. 'You'll be my son, Reinard, flesh of my flesh, bone of

137

my bone.' When Mama returned, papa twirled her around the room and asked her to marry him."

"Did he really pack fish? It's just so inconceivable." Ben mused. "You should hear what I've said about him in speeches."

"I have heard." Miriam laughed. "Clovenhoof sent me to hear what you were saying to the miners in Chirbury. Ben, at one point I had to go outside to laugh at you. It's not just you though. Why does everyone here demonize him?"

"I've always thought of your father as a secretive, conniving sort, ready to pounce on the republic from the distant shadows."

"Secretive, yes—conniving, no." Miriam played with a piece of loose gauze near Ben's ear. "Ready to pounce, maybe, if need be. Of course, I got a bit of a head start on him. I felt like someone needed to scout out the land first, and was I ever right?"

"But didn't your father let go of Redland like the dream told him to?"

"Yes, at least until my mother died a year ago. Mama always said that the Lord of Grace gives when you release." Miriam tugged on the gauze a bit, enough to bring Ben a tinge of pain. "Life's all about giving and receiving, never about earning or clutching or hanging on. I don't know how many times she said that."

Ben stared at Miriam. "I've been trying to remember what Clovenhoof said at the end—his blessing on me. Those were his very words."

138

"Really?" She bit her lip in thought. "He was quoting me then. How I loved and pitied the old professor."

"So the king wants to rule in his old age," Ben said.

"He's sixty-five years old, Ben. He's been away for forty-five years. All his forefathers died in Eddisford, even King Russell who was a scoundrel and assassinated. All his forefathers are buried in the Abbey at Warmouth. Of all the kings of Redland—I'm saying this objectively, not just as his daughter. Of all the kings of Redland, he gave the country its greatest gift. And he gave it freely, of his own accord." She paused. "King Reinard the Republican. That would be an appropriate title for him. The Senate is the fruit of his reign. If only it would embrace him when he returns."

Ben closed his eyes. "Even if I did believe you, I'm new to the Senate. I don't think there's much I can do. The Chairman would have your father thrown in prison if he returns. The letter he sent me made his position very clear. Royalists are enemies of the state."

"He's revised history in people's minds."

"And you're sure that it isn't your father who's revised it for you?"

"If I can't even bring you to believe me—do you think I'm here to overthrow the Senate?"

He studied the rafters above them for a long time before he answered, mulling her story over in his mind. "I'm meant to turn my back on you," he finally said. "It doesn't seem to matter much."

"First the professor, and now you," she said. "Maybe I'm trying to force things. I had this crazy idea that if I could win the professor over, he could introduce me to the Senate, and I could speak for my father, clear a path for him. It was all coming together until he decided to offer himself for you, and then I thought you were meant to be the one. Now everything seems to be against me, even the Lord of Grace."

Ben reached over and touched her cheek. "If it makes any difference, I want to believe you," he said.

For a moment it seemed that she might lean over and kiss him, she looked at him with such gratitude, but she turned abruptly and swept her coat up. "Follow your dream then," she said. "The Lord of Grace will go with you. I've told you all I can tell you, and I've already waited too long if I'm going to try to help Thistle." Gathering the ragged coat around her, she walked to the door, opened it, and kicked it shut behind her.

Chapter 9
Casualty

Ben woke slowly from a drowsy sleep. He had wanted to leave as soon as Miriam had left, but dizziness had forced him back onto his cot, and then he had fallen asleep. He felt warm and comfortable in spite of his wounds. If he lay without moving, it was as though he were a dandelion seed floating in the afternoon air. The orange parka tumbled through his mind's eye. It rolled in the wind, this way and that, its hood flapping violently. Snow beat against it, pinned it to a tree on a mountain ledge. Ben stared into the darkness of the rafters above him. Why was the parka clinging to that ledge? If the tracker had killed the mountain woman and discovered that she was not the princess, wouldn't he have left her where she was or buried her with the parka on her body? Why would the parka be flying around in the wind? Had she tried to take it off and lost it in the wind? He couldn't put it together, but somehow it made more sense to him to think that the woman must still be alive.

Holding his ribs, Ben gathered himself up and went to the door. He unfastened the latch and stepped out into the sunshine. The sun crawled westward above his head, promising a few hours of daylight before it hit the sharp mountain peaks. Water streamed from the eaves and tree branches. Ben gathered his things and trudged back up the mountain, the way he had come. The snow had melted a great deal during the day, but it was still above his ankles, and the trek hard going. He paused at the bush where he had last seen Thistle. Two sets of tracks led around the side of the mountain. No doubt Warwick's would double around in some way and eventually lead Miriam to Eddisford. Perhaps he would accomplish his mission better with Miriam following him than the other way around. Of course he couldn't carry Thistle all the way to Eddisford. What would he do with her when he got tired?

He had to keep his focus on the mountain woman. The new bandage that Miriam had wrapped around him while he was knocked out braced his ribs tightly. Ben was grateful for it. He could breathe fairly comfortably as he climbed. All around him the drip, drip, drip of melting snow formed a chorus. By the time he reached the crest where Thistle had found the parka, he felt cheerful and optimistic. He had only to discover his role in the grand scheme of things step by step. He looked around for the mountain woman, but there was no sign of her. Where would the parka have flown from? Which way had the wind been blowing the night before? Up over the crest at their faces? He scanned the terrain. To the north of the path the mountainside sloped around, and a smattering of boulders cluttered the arch some fifty yards below. There in a rocky cleft, he saw a smudge of darkness, the mouth of a cave.

Ben trudged down to take a closer look. The snow near the cave and on the rocks lay unevenly as though someone had stumbled past. He was climbing over the rocks at the entrance when he stopped cold. His hand hovered above a dried blotch of blood. Another blotch, smeared by a handprint, colored a rock ahead of him. He paused. This is what he had expected after all. The danger had surely gone with Warwick, but Ben slipped his knife from his belt just to be sure. The prospect of seeing a corpse made his stomach churn. He placed his hand on the rock above the blood splotch and hoisted himself up.

An angry, feline snarl suddenly ripped the air directly above Ben's head. He swung around and found himself face to face with a snow-leopard cub, its features strung tight with terror. Ben froze, his knife poised for attack. He couldn't kill this small, frightened creature, but where was

its mother? The chill wind tugged at the cat's fir. It squinted at Ben. He waited, but no mother materialized. With a steady motion, Ben reached into his pocket and tossed a scrap of dried meat to the cub. It drew back from the offering, sniffing, confused. It inched forward, still sniffing. Ben sat down, leaning back on his palms, and looked out over the mountain range, ignoring the cub. The sun balanced on the tip of a jagged peak to the west, its red rays spilling out over the valley. The cub licked the meat, dragged it back to the mouth of the cave, and ate. A few minutes passed, and Ben felt the cub brushing against the back of his arm.

"Let's go see what's inside," Ben said softly. He rose slowly and stepped into the cave. The cub followed, brushing the back of his leg with its head. Then it bounded ahead into the darkness and jumped up on something. As his eyes adjusted to the darkness, Ben made out a woman lying under a heap of furs. She struck him at first as an old woman who looked somehow young, but on looking at her for a moment longer, he decided it was the other way around. Something about her young face wasn't right. She lay on a bed of straw strewn over a great slab of rock that jutted out of the cave wall. A similar slab jutted out beyond the bed a little higher, and served as a table, littered with a few plates, cups, and eating utensils.

The cub curled up by her side. The woman's eyes opened, and she drew back. "Are you the Chisel?" she asked, her voice filled more with wonder than fear. "He said you'd come."

"I'm here to help," Ben said.

144

"He said you'd find him and kill him." She reached out as if to clutch his jacket, but missed and let her arm dangle over the edge of the slab she lay on.

"Are you hurt?"

"The hunter shot me," she said with an innocent smile vacant of understanding. Her speech lay thick in her mouth as though her tongue were smothered with honey. "He found me prancing," she said, "and he shot me."

"Are you bleeding?" Ben asked.

With a great effort, she folded the furs back from her shoulders. An arrow had pierced through her side. She had patched the bleeding in the front with some dirty rodent skins, but hadn't been able to manage her back. She had lost a lot of blood. Ben foraged in his pack and produced some linen strips Roderick had tucked in for his head. He removed the skins and wrapped the linen strips around the woman so that they covered both wounds.

She lay back and fell asleep, exhausted. Ben sat by her side, wondering if she would ever wake again. How had this poor half-witted woman wandered into the way of such danger? It seemed so senseless. Who was this Chisel whom Warwick feared so much? How close was he to the Chairman of the Senate? He had the note to prove Barkloin's involvement. The scar on Warwick's neck flashed through his mind, and he shuddered. Everything led to more confusion. He had started his campaign with such a trust in his political party, such a respect for the Chairman, such a pride in his own role; now it had all eroded away. The leopard cub curled up by the woman's feet and watched him with curious green eyes.

145

Ben was dozing off himself when a groan echoed from deep within the woman. He smoothed her hair back gently. It was coarse and matted, and clung to the side of her face. She wept loudly, the tears streaming down the ridge of her nose and along her cheek.

"Are you in pain?" he asked.

"My side hurts. The hunter pulled the arrow from me. He was cruel." Her words burst from her mouth in spasms as the tears flowed. "Why didn't he kill me on the spot?"

He stroked her hair and whispered, "It's over now. Lie still."

Her body tensed further, and she rose on one elbow to speak, but couldn't for gasping. Blood spotted her bandage afresh.

"You must stop straining like this. Lie back." Ben took her shoulders firmly and laid her back down.

She resisted for a moment, then sank in his grasp, groaning from deep within. It was as though her deepest sorrow had suddenly been unlatched from the hollow of her chest and now burst out in an anguished bellow. Her lips moved, but formed no words.

"Don't talk," Ben said.

Her breathing slowed as she relaxed and closed her eyes again. Ben took a bowl to the mouth of the cave and held it under a dripping icicle. He dipped his handkerchief in it. Though the cold burned his fingers, he held the handkerchief cupped in his hand until it warmed. Then he dabbed it gently on the woman's forehead and cheeks, cooling her and rinsing her tears away.

146

She smiled, her eyes still closed. "The hunter called me a princess—" She spoke with a sudden clarity. Her tongue seemed to have withered from its swollen size. Ben watched her in wonder. He wiped off some phlegm that leaked out of the corner of her mouth. She remained silent for a long time, her breathing growing fainter. "—until he saw my face up close." Her lips quivered. "I've always been ugly, but she had said how lovely I looked in the parka. She had said I looked like a princess." Her eyes opened and looked longingly into Ben's. "I thought so too."

Tears came to Ben's eyes. "I'm sure you did," he said.

She nodded ever so slightly, and then the light left her eyes. For the second time in only a few days, Ben stared into the face of the dead. "Miriam, how will I ever tell you?" he whispered. He reached his hand out to the leopard cub, but it wouldn't advance. It seemed to feel the sense of death in the cave.

Ben closed the woman's eyes with his fingers. He couldn't leave her here in the cave to rot. She had suffered enough indignity in her life. He had a latrine trowel in his pack, but how long would it take to dig a hole large enough for burial in the winter soil? He could cover her with snow, mark the spot, and come back later to bury her. No, he would bury her, no matter how long it took him to dig the hole. He took his trowel outside, found a flat spot of dirt away from trees, and jabbed it in the ground. The digging brought fresh pain to his rib, and it was long after the moon had crept over the treetops before he finished. The cub watched the ordeal to the end, sitting silent a few yards from the spot with a stoical curiosity. When Ben hiked away the next morning, he saw that the cub lay with its back to the marker, fast asleep.

Chapter 10
Introductions

The City of Eddisford lay stretched across the horizon like a painting on a canvas. Ben had never seen anything like it. The barley fields with their scattered late autumn haystacks rose in a gradual slope to the city walls. The poplar-lined roads that wound through them were littered with people and sheep in a bustle of cheerful excitement.

Ben stood on the crest of a hill still ten miles or more from the city, unwinding the bandage from around his head. He didn't want everyone staring at him and asking questions when he arrived. He pulled his hair down gently over the wound to cover it as much as possible.

"So that's the capital," he said, gazing at the city. He sat down in the tall grass and ate some cucumber slices and bread, unwilling to go any further. A few nights before he had been so full of passion, so sure of himself, as he wandered through the crowd at his victory party, picking at the olives and pickled plums among the hors d'oeuvres. Since then, he had been pulled this way and that like white taffy. Seeing the city, he felt his old patriotism rise in his heart, yet it was like a parchment in the wind with no place to land. A restless urge to join the happy people he saw and lose himself in the city for a while overwhelmed him. Who knew? He might get a glimpse of Thistle. After seeing the ruthlessness of Warwick's handiwork, Miriam's concern had come to make more sense. The senate wouldn't convene until the following afternoon; he had a little time.

Ben threw his leftover scraps near a prairie dog hole where little heads had been peeping out at him. He hoisted his pack gently on his back and set off. Once the pack was tugging on his shoulders again, he changed his mind. He would take the quickest path to his office, where he could unload it. He needed to find a doctor. He needed to sink into a steaming bath. He needed to lie on a soft mattress and drift to sleep. The bump on his head wasn't so bad as long as he didn't touch it, but he needed something desperately for the pain in his rib.

Ben considered throwing his pack in a ditch several times before he reached the city gates. The sun was very near setting behind his shoulder now. His sagging shadow stretched out before him like an aging snake. He took a deep breath, and smiling a little out of embarrassment at the necessary protocol, stepped up to the Yeoman of the City Gate. "I'm Senator Benjamin Edmundson. Sir Yeoman, will you show me to the Houses of Senate?"

The yeoman saluted him stiffly. "Your wish is my duty, Sir. Welcome to the capital."

Ben saluted in return. "Please drop the formality, Sir Yeoman, and walk with me rather than ahead of me."

The yeoman beamed. "Thank you, Sir. It's an honor, Sir. I'm sorry for asking, but didn't anyone come with you? Most senators arrive with a few pages if not a whole entourage of them."

"I can't seem to hang onto my pages," Ben said. "I've lost three in the last two days."

The yeoman took Ben's pack from his shoulders and put it on his own. Ben nearly fell over with relief.

"Shall I cry your arrival, Sir? It's tradition and your privilege."

"Please don't," Ben said, rolling his shoulders around to release the stiffness. "I've gorged on vanity enough for a while. Would you point things out to me as we go?"

"I'll be glad to, Sir." The yeoman shook his head and smiled. "It's strange to think I won't be seeing the old professor again. I think I got to where I rather enjoyed his abuse."

Ben furrowed his brow. "His abuse?"

"He had a way with sharp words, if you know what I mean?" The yeoman started walking, and Ben plodded along beside him. He pointed back at the gate they had just passed through. "The Mouth of Bread," he said. "We call it that because most of the grain in Redland comes through this gate to be milled. There are other mouths, but we won't see any on our way. Down this street, Sir." He turned down a cobblestone street fringed with shops of all kinds—vegetable stands, clockworks, shoe repairs. Ben read the signs in wonder.

"There's one of Senator Jacobson's furniture stores, Sir. You'll become familiar with that place, I'll guess."

151

"Why so?"

"You don't know? He's a pillar in your party. He represents us here, the capital city."

"And he owns a furniture store?"

"People don't know whether he's a senator or a merchant. I suppose if you're a serious Republican, you'd be both. They say his money won him votes, and now his votes are winning him money. Being such a craftsman, you might say he made the stool he stands on, literally and figuratively." The yeoman slapped his knee and laughed heartily. "I just made that up, Sir. I guess that's a first rate joke."

Ben frowned.

"He's a craftsman, see. He makes furniture. He's always whittling on something. Some of the men in the guard, they call him the Chisel in an affectionate way." He laughed again. "You'll get to know him, sure. His suite is right across from yours, and both of you—" The yeoman broke off. "What is it, Sir?"

"They call him the Chisel?"

"As I said, Sir, only in an affectionate way. They mean no disrespect. No doubt they'll be calling you something soon. Is something wrong, Sir?"

"I think someone mistook me for him."

"I don't see how that's possible," the yeoman said. "He's a head taller than you, a big hulking fellow, and not like you at all."

"Not like me?"

"He's the sort that always seems like he's looking for a brawl, if you understand my meaning. That's why the men

152

in the Guard like him." He laughed. "He makes a good senator, I guess. He can get a bill passed by sheer will. I may be a mere yeoman of the guard, but I'm a thinking man. I've spent some of my free hours in the Senate Gallery and seen what goes on. If I wanted a bill passed, I'd get a fighter like Senator Jacobson on my side. Sure, the two of you will probably be fast friends a week from now." Here the yeoman winked. "You've been kind letting me rattle on walking right next to you all friendly like, but I see your eyes and ears are wide open. It must have taken a shrewd mind to oust old Professor Clovenhoof."

"He didn't intend to win, at least not at the end."

"What?" The yeoman looked at Ben in disbelief. "Senator Clovenhoof turn down a fight?" He shook his head. "You're being modest."

"He took on a greater fight," Ben said. He hesitated for a moment, but this was as good a time as any to try out the truth. "He had to overcome his will to live. He offered me his life in the Sacrifice."

The yeoman stopped. "He's dead then."

"By my hand." Ben could see the questions careening through the yeoman's head. With everyone he would meet, this is what he would face. "Come," he said. "Are we almost there?"

"Right around the corner," the yeoman stammered.

They rounded the next corner and came out into a courtyard. A wide cobblestone lane circled a lawn lined with trees and benches. Though the courtyard was large, it seemed hemmed in as high buildings surrounded it on three sides. The yeoman swept his hand across them.

153

"These are the Senatorial Suites," he said. "I'll lead you to yours. And there's the Capitol." He pointed to the far side of the courtyard, where a domed building stood, veiled by every kind of tree Ben could imagine, no two alike.

"The trees!" Ben said, his mouth hanging open.

The yeoman laughed. "If that exclamation doesn't reflect the image of the old professor within you, I don't know what will. I believe he did give his life for you, Senator. How the old professor loved those trees!" The yeoman yanked on Ben's arm and led him to a huge conch-shell horn mounted on a stone. "Stand right here behind me," he said. Then he gripped the horn, took a deep breath, and blew it. A rich, loud note rang out and echoed from the walls around the courtyard. Ben started to speak, but the yeoman put his finger to Ben's lips. From all sides of the courtyard, windows opened, and heads appeared, silent and expectant. The yeoman cried, "Eddisford welcomes Benjamin Edmundson, Senator of Redland, true representative of Blackwater Valley. Give him due honor, for he speaks for his people." The folks in the windows hollered and clapped and stamped their hooves, and then disappeared back inside as quickly as they had emerged.

The yeoman led Ben around to the east side of the courtyard and into one of the buildings. The hallways were spacious, with high ceilings and tall windows on each end. As they walked down the hall, Ben noticed that each door was engraved with multiple names, some as many as ten or twelve, all representing the senators that had occupied the suite. The yeoman stopped in front of the last door, set his pack down, and handed him a key. "Here we are, Sir. I'll leave you here and bid you a good day."

"Thank you," Ben said.

The yeoman turned and walked back down the hall. Ben stared at the door. It bore only two names, Helfroth Clovenhoof and Benjamin Edmundson. Tiny wood shavings were still lodged in his own name. On  impulse, he drew his pocketknife to pick them out, but as he was opening the knife, the door next to his opened and a young ram stuck his head out. The sheep wore a checkered vest and bow tie, and a large monocle circled his right eye.

The sheep stared for a few moments. Just when Ben decided he wasn't going to say anything, he burst out, "You must be Benjamin Edmundson. I'm Colonel Forager."

"Are you in the army?" Ben asked.

"No, that's my name. My father thought it might inspire nobility, heroics—" He waved a hoof to indicate more honorable traits.

"Has it worked?"

"I don't suppose so," the Colonel said. "It's memorable though. That probably helped me get elected. There were quite a few candidates when I first started campaigning."

"Are you new to the senate this year?"

"No, I've been here a year and a half. I'm mid-way through my first term." He laughed. "Not that I've done anything significant. None of the issues seem important. It's been downright dull. You probably have a hard time believing it, just starting out as you are, but I wouldn't expect too much excitement."

Ben smiled, but found no adequate reply.

"Here, I'll show you into your suite," Colonel said. "Professor Clovenhoof said you'd probably win the election. I think he was tired of all the bickering; he'd gotten pretty cynical toward the end. Everything in the suite is of course yours now. He would have taken anything he really valued."

Ben unlocked the door and stepped in. The room felt stifling with the distinct scents of an aged ram. Colonel pushed past him and opened the windows, inviting the early evening air in. Stacks of parchments lined shelves from floor to ceiling on the wall to the right. The wide low couch made to accommodate sheep sat against the wall on the left, and beyond it was a low table with wide benches. Two doors opened on the left, one to a stone-floored kitchen and the other to sleeping quarters. In spite of the stuffiness, the room was clean.

"Care to join me for dinner?" Colonel asked. "I was just headed out."

"Maybe I could join you tomorrow," Ben said, easing himself into a chair. "I just want to rest right now."

"Tired from the trip?"

"Yes, and my rib is killing me. I'll probably want a doctor in the morning."

"Did you hurt yourself? I saw you favoring it, and I noticed something under your hair there."

"I got into a few tousles on the way, up in the mountains."

Colonel opened his eyes wide. "Bandits? I've heard of robbers along some of the mountain passes."

Ben paused. Had he already said too much? He couldn't walk around hiding the pain in his chest. People were bound to notice. He needed a story.

In the silence, a voice came from the open doorway. "Curious."

Ben turned his head to see a huge man, well over six feet tall, with a wide smile on his face. "Hello," he said, "I'm Warren Jacobson. My suite's right across from yours." The voice did not match the man; it came out like a thin whistle, as though the diaphragm could not bear the burden of the lungs and the air had barely slipped past the throat.

As though he were reading Ben's thoughts, the senator took a chisel from his pocket and carved the remaining shavings out of Ben's name in the door. "Welcome to Eddisford, Senator Benjamin Edmundson. So glad the Colonel has made you feel comfortable. There's a tub full of water in your kitchen that the Chairman of the Senate arranged for you, if you'd like to take a bath. It just needs heating. I overheard him asking someone if you'd arrived yet this afternoon, but I guess you're too tired to see

157

him—and did you say injured?" A look of deep concern swept over his face.

Colonel chipped in, "Bandits, I think. He was about to tell me the story."

"It isn't anything worth mentioning," Ben said. "I suppose I should write the sheriff back in Blackwater about policing the Runcorn Pass better, but I don't see how he could with so much open land and so little resources."

"I've heard of other attacks," Jacobson said. "Just the other day a friend of mine came across a little lamb wandering around in the foothills—said her party had been attacked and she had run away and gotten lost." His eye met Ben's. "It's a dangerous place, those mountains."

There was no hiding the alarm that surged through Ben, but he could at least hide it from Colonel. He winced and held his chest as though a fresh pain had stabbed him.

"Let me check on your bath water and light the fire under it for you. You just rest," Colonel said, and clopped into the kitchen.

Jacobson licked his lips and continued staring at Ben as if he were waiting for an answer. The sound of a crackling fire soon filled the silence.

"I lost a little lamb myself a few days ago," Ben said slowly. "I wonder if she could be the same one."

"I could introduce you to my friend," Jacobson said.

Colonel came back into the room before Ben could reply. It was a relief. He couldn't think on his feet like this. He didn't have his bearings. The thought of Thistle enduring another night of captivity, whatever form it took, ground at his feelings, but he couldn't truly help her unless he knew what he was about. Apparently "the Chisel" planned to use her as some sort of leverage, so she seemed safe enough.

"I think maybe tomorrow," he said, "after I see the doctor and feel settled. We have the morning free before the opening session, right?"

Jacobson all but sneered. He wasn't fooled. Ben stood up and ushered Colonel to the door. The huge man stood aside to let the sheep by.

"I'll recommend a doctor for you," Colonel said.

"Thank you," Ben replied. "You both have been most—" He paused just for a second to throw Jacobson another carefree glance "—helpful." Then he closed the door on both of them and went to tend to his bath.

Chapter 11
Mistrust

When the coals under his tub had turned to ash and Ben stepped into the water, it was at first so hot that he could hardly move, but it soothed the pain in his chest. A mild dizziness fell over him in the vapors of the bath. A cleansing sweat dripped down his face. It was his first chance in three days to relax and ponder out what all had taken place. He remembered Roderick's words. He was a believer now, and needed to act on universal principles.

He wondered if Barkloin and Jacobson knew about Clovenhoof's conversion. He suspected not, but he would never again hide the sacrifice that Clovenhoof had made for him. Would a confession of the Sacrifice immediately connect Ben to the Royalists? The Sacrifice and loyalty to the king were part and parcel, or at least he had always supposed they were.

For himself, the religious conversion had come before the political one. Now that he came to think of it, a tiny bitterness had been scratching at the back of his mind. He had been coerced into both. Clovenhoof had pressed the

Sacrifice upon him so suddenly that he had killed the old ram before he had much thought about it. Likewise, Miriam had been in such danger and so trusting that he couldn't help but fall in with her. Would he have made either conversion without the pressure of crisis? He didn't think so, yet he couldn't deny that he had sincerely converted in either case. Clovenhoof had given his life for Ben, and consequently he trusted in the Lord of Grace. Miriam had put her life in his hands, and he had believed the story of her father's sincerity. These things still felt like clothes you could put on and take off; they were only slowly seeping beneath the skin into his true self.

And then a hoof tap sounded on the door to his suite.

Holding his side to support his diaphragm, he called, "It's open."

He heard the door swing open and the clomping of heavy hooves, then a pause.

"Be out in a bit," he said. He sat still for another moment, soaking in what he could of the coveted warmth and listening. Apparently the visitor was waiting patiently. Ben lifted himself out of the bath, dried off, and put some fresh clothes on. The clean clothes brought back his senses somehow, and he felt more alert than he had in a couple of days. He opened the door to find not one, but two visitors, both elderly sheep.

One of them clopped forward. "So glad to meet you," he said. "Ribald Barkloin. Did you get my recent letter? When I heard about your unfortunate accident—well, this is Dr. Bolstrum, the finest doctor in Eddisford." He sat on his haunches and gestured toward the other sheep.

161

Dr. Bolstrum stepped forward. "What seems to be the trouble, Sir? Could I have a look at it?"

Ben grabbed a chair from the kitchen table and sat down in front of the doctor. He fought off an immediate dislike for Barkloin. He thought of the note in his pocket. Still, bringing the doctor was a welcome present. "It's my head and my ribs," he said. "I really appreciate this. I'll have to get word to Senator Forager that I've been taken care of."

"No need," said Barkloin. "He's the one who informed me of your arrival. I told him I was bringing Bolstrum here myself."

"Lower your head so I can get at it." The doctor tugged at Ben's hair to better see the head wound. "Badly bruised," he mumbled. "Cut's scabbed nicely. Ooh, but there's still a bit of glass. Let me get that." He fished a pair of tweezers out of his bag, and wedging them adroitly in his jaw, tugged the piece out.

Ben flinched.

"Dizzy spells?" Bolstrum asked.

Ben shook his head.

Bolstrum wet a cotton swab with a dark red ointment and dabbed it on the bleeding cut. Ben flinched again. "Medicinal herbs, my own concoction," the doctor muttered. "Now let's see the ribs."

Ben pulled his shirt up gently over his head.

"It's a good sign that you can do that," Bolstrum said. "I'm warning you; I'll have to prod a bit."

Ben eyed the doctor's hooves. His own doctor in Blackwater had been a human with soft hands.

"He's the gentlest doctor in town," Barkloin said. "You shouldn't hesitate to trust him, Senator."

"Trust is a concept that's lost all meaning to me in the last few days," Ben said. "When I received your letter—"

"No politics yet," Bolstrum broke in, "not till after I'm through. I want you to let your breath out and hold it for a bit. Can you do that?"

Ben nodded and let his breath out. The doctor nuzzled his muzzle softly under Ben's diaphragm and rolled the top of his nose and forehead against Ben's chest, first on the left side and then on the right. Ben yelped with pain as the forehead came against a rib on the right side. The doctor probed the area gently with his forehead.

"Might be cracked, but I don't think so," he said. "Did you hear a pop? It's not out of position. Not too swollen either. Did you have ice? Someone's taken good care of you."

Ben wondered if this information was the purpose of the doctor's visit, to find out the circumstances behind his injuries. After all, a murderer had either turned up dead or missing. If Warwick didn't have the imagination to connect him to the incident, Barkloin did. The Chairman was smiling at him as if he could read his thoughts. Ben made a decision.

"As a matter of fact," he said. "She was incredibly capable—very surprising for a princess."

The doctor brought his head up so quickly that his muzzle bumped Ben on the chin. "I'm so sorry," he mumbled, trying to regain composure. "It's true then," he said, looking over at Barkloin.

"Very wise," Barkloin said. "The truth is always your ally, whatever your position." He squinted and picked at a piece of something in his teeth. "And I wonder what that position is? Strange rumors find their way over the mountains, things that are hard to piece together."

"I'm glad you see it that way, Chairman," Ben said, "because I can't put it all together myself, and I was hoping you could enlighten me on some of the things that have happened to me. I admit I'm fresh and inexperienced. A little guidance would be most welcome."

Barkloin chuckled. "I'm starting to like you, Benjamin Edmundson. You tell me your experiences, and I'll tell you how to think about them. How about that?"

"It's important to me that we are honest with each other," Ben said. "I still believe in our republic, and I want to continue to do so."

"Didn't I tell you he would be an idealist?" Barkloin said, looking at Bolstrum.

"And I said to tie your politics to your tail and sit on it," the doctor huffed. "And I'll say it again. I'm in the middle of an examination here." He turned to Ben. "Nothing much you can do even if it is cracked," he said. "Wrapping it will help with the pain, but I'm guessing you could also use some pain powder." He retrieved a bag of powder from his pouch and dropped it in Ben's hand. "You won't regret taking this," he said. "One spoon after breakfast and one before bed as needed. Don't be lifting anything heavy or bumping into things with that rib. Keep the head wound clean even if it hurts to wash it. I'd keep it open to the air from now on—no need for the bandage.

That's all. Now you can quibble all you want about politics." He turned abruptly and walked into the kitchen. "Any grasses left in the pantry, perhaps a few sprouts Clovenhoof might have left that you won't care for?"

Barkloin climbed onto one end of the long low couch and motioned Ben to sit at the other end. The couch creaked under Barkloin's weight. The room was growing dark, so Ben lit a lamp and sat down. He found it hard to meet the Chairman's eye, but he forced himself to look directly at him.

"Professor Clovenhoof sacrificed his life for me," he said.

Barkloin stared at him for a moment before answering. "A senseless death. We grasp for meaning when we grow old. It's a great temptation." He shook his head sorrowfully. "And the young are so vulnerable to the aged."

Ben ignored the patronizing slight. "Was there ever a time when you believed in the Sacrifice, Sir?"

"When I was young, I dreamed of it—throwing my life away for someone—it's very romantic. But look what I've done with my life. Look what we've built. That's a sacrifice too, and beneficial to far more people, don't you think?"

"I don't think you could quantify eternal life, even if it were just one person's."

Bolstrum's laugh floated in from the kitchen. "He sounds like a believer, Barkloin. He's beyond your powers already. My guess is the princess is a pretty one."

Barkloin grunted. "I respect your religious beliefs, Ben. I myself believe in the Lord of Grace. I don't think I would be Chairman of the Senate if I didn't."

"So you don't think I murdered Professor Clovenhoof?"

"If the republic is to survive and work properly, we must accept a pluralistic view of things. While I don't believe that the Sacrifice secures anything for you in the world to come, I would never judge you for practicing a deeply entrenched part of your religion."

"Where does that leave you?" asked Ben. "How do you personally feel about Professor Clovenhoof's death?"

"Clovenhoof spent his life struggling against his father." Barkloin chuckled and shook his head. "We're all bent that way psychologically. It keeps things even. An idealist is replaced by a pragmatist, who is then replaced by an idealist. Too many idealists and we all kill each other. Too many pragmatists and life becomes dull."

"Guess which one the Chairman is?" Bolstrum shouted from the kitchen.

"After I sacrificed Professor Clovenhoof," Ben said, "I went back to my election party. I couldn't bring myself to tell my father what I had done."

Barkloin nodded. "It's very honest of you to tell me. I suppose we're all the same deep inside."

"Are we?" Ben asked. "Before you arrived, I was thinking how I feel changed, though I'm not sure it's any of my own doing or how deep it is. At the party I met someone I never expected to meet."

"The princess," Barkloin said.

"No, a little lamb. She had been told to put herself in my care."

Barkloin looked at Ben curiously, cocking his head.

Bolstrum emerged from the kitchen, nudging a wheeled tray that held a few carrots, a pile of celery sprouts and cumin. "Look what I found, compliments of the late professor. There's plenty to go around."

"And who was the little lamb?" Barkloin asked.

"You don't have any idea?" Ben asked.

"Should I know who it was?"

"Her parents were killed by men with senate insignia on their sleeves."

Barkloin sat up straight and furrowed his brow as though he was reconsidering something. He yanked a mouthful of celery sprouts from the tray and munched on them pensively. When he had finished, he said, "I didn't realize a lamb was involved. Is it a little ram or ewe?"

"She's a ewe," Ben said.

"I feel for her," Barkloin said. "Children shouldn't have to get caught in the middle of these things."

"Did you order her parents' death?"

"I ordered their arrest."

"They were murdered."

"They resisted arrest."

"That's not how she tells it."

"She described it to you?"

"Well, not exactly to me." Ben stood up and grabbed a carrot from the tray. He felt its rough skin in the palm of his hand, coarse and cold. "She described it to the princess. They were killed on the ramp to their basement after hiding their child."

"And you believe the princess," Barkloin said. "They were traitors, of course, secretly plotting to overthrow the republic."

"Everyone deserves a fair trial," Ben said.

Bolstrum chuckled to himself. "Neither one of you will ever know the truth. I suggest you make peace."

"We're talking about murder here," Ben said vehemently.

"Someone might well say that about Clovenhoof's death," Bolstrum said.

Ben walked into the kitchen with his carrot. He threw open some drawers, looking for a peeler. If a sheep had carrots, surely he had a peeler, but he couldn't find one; he slammed the drawers shut. He was a senator. He had to be diplomatic if he expected to have any influence over the Chairman. He came back out into the living room. "I'm sorry about the outburst," he said.

"I check people's background before I hire them to do a job," Barkloin said. "Then I have to trust their report when they finish it. I may very well have been misinformed."

"Can anything be done?" Ben asked.

"If it went to court, it would be the word of a lamb against the word of two officers of the Senate Guard," Bolstrum said.

"I'm afraid it would only be one officer," Ben said.

Barkloin chuckled, raised his head as though he would say something, and then chuckled again. "Two mysteries are solved," he finally said. "Our friend gave you your wounds, and you hit him over the head with a shovel."

168

"Close," Ben said. "He did give me this chest wound, but it was the princess who hit him with the shovel."

"You were fighting valiantly for the princess."

"No, I thought he was after me. You had warned me about Royalists, so I assumed he was one. If he had declared himself and said he was there to arrest the princess, things might have ended differently for him."

"But why were you with the princess?"

Ben put his carrot back on the tray with the others. "She was Clovenhoof's page. She was helping me bury him."

Bolstrum let a half-eaten cumin sprout fall from his mouth. "She was what?"

Barkloin didn't seem at all surprised.

"Clovenhoof didn't know who she was at first," Ben said. "She wanted to earn his trust and then have him introduce her to the Senate."

"Only he had other plans," Barkloin said.

"You mean the Sacrifice?" Ben asked.

Barkloin nodded. "I suppose the news of his son's death set him over the edge. Who wouldn't long for death?"

"According to the princess, he had already decided."

"Really? I'd like to hear that from her lips myself."

"Maybe you will," Ben said. "I know she'll want to meet you."

"You have such trust in her," Barkloin said. "You don't think that's a little dangerous?"

"Apparently it is," Ben said. "Your friend tried to murder her a few nights ago."

"There you go using that word again."

"I assure you he didn't announce that he was there to arrest her. Listen, Chairman, this conversation is not reassuring me one bit. If the republic has to hire murderers to secure its strength—"

"They were not murderers! Our security officers are not murderers!" Barkloin nearly leapt off the couch, a surprising feat for his size, and paced back and forth across the room shaking his head in agitation. He stopped in front of Ben. "They were not sent to murder," he said.

Ben stared into his eyes. "Chairman, if you didn't send them to murder, they acted on someone else's orders."

"Or their own," the sheep said, his small eyes darting back and forth in thought.

"How is Senator Jacobson involved?" Ben asked. He shivered, realizing that the warmth of the bath had worn off. He reached for his shirt and slowly eased it over his head.

"Jacobson?" Something flickered in the Chairman's eye. Was it fear, defensiveness, or amusement? It was certainly some sort of recognition, as though he had been expecting the question, but the flicker disappeared before Ben could analyze it. "What would he have to do with it?"

"I caught up with your second officer in the dark," Ben said. "He was afraid someone called 'the Chisel' had sent me. He seemed to think I was going to kill him for botching the job."

Barkloin chuckled. "That would have been Warwick."

Ben nodded. "That's the man. He told me his name."

"Best tracker in Redland, but the biggest coward in the world. Someone must have planted a seed in his brain about Jacobson. I don't see how killing the princess would improve the price of beds or feasting-room benches though, if you know what I mean."

He glanced at Bulstrom, who smiled knowingly.

"Before you came tonight," Ben said hesitantly, "Senator Jacobson paid me a visit. He indicated that the lamb who had been with me, Professor Clovenhoof's granddaughter, was in his care, and she had been with Warwick last I saw her. It seems reasonable to me that either Warwick reported to Senator Jacobson, or Senator Jacobson caught up with Warwick as he feared."

Barkloin shook his head. "Well, I can't figure it out." He chuckled again. "I didn't even know your lamb had gone missing. Why didn't you say so sooner?" He leaned over the tray and swept a mouthful of sprouts off of it. Chomping on the sprouts with a wide grin, he let out a sigh as if to indicate that the whole thing was a mystery but that he was sure it would all come out straight. "Bolstrum—" but his words were cut short.

The window to the courtyard suddenly shattered, and an object hurled past the doctor's ear. It bounced on the floor and rolled to a stop against the door. Ben sprang up and rushed to the window, only to see a dark, human figure sprint out of the courtyard on the far side. Shouts sprang from various corners of the square, and booted feet followed the figure.

Bolstrum laughed heartily, surprise pasted over his face. "Nearly took my ear off!"

The Chairman picked up the object in his mouth. It was a rock with a piece of paper wrapped around it, secured with a knotted string. He started to pick at the string, but Bolstrum stopped him. "You shouldn't be opening other people's mail," he said, breaking into a laugh again. He smiled back and forth at Ben and Barkloin as though they were missing the joke. "Politics," he said. "Such an exciting life!"

Ben unwound the rest of the string and smoothed out the paper against the wall. He read it aloud. He had chosen his course to be straightforward and open with the Chairman, and he would stick to it.

"Hand over the princess. We know you have her.
Long live the King!"

Ben and the Chairman eyed each other.

"Is this message for you or for me?" Ben asked.

Barkloin raised an eyebrow. "You tell me, Senator."

Bolstrum snorted, and a bit of cumin flew out of his nose. "I'm watching history!" he said.

A knock came at the door, and Bolstrum opened it. A tall man in a military vest and knickers clicked his heals and bowed. Ben noticed the senate insignia on his

172

shoulder. "We apologize, Sir," the officer said, his head still bowed. "I don't know how the intruder got by us. No excuses, Sir."

"Don't let it happen again," Barkloin snapped.

"No, Sir." The officer continued to stand in the doorway with his head bowed.

"Be at rest, Commander," Barkloin said. "This is Senator Edmundson." A hint of sarcasm entered his voice. "He is one of us now, under your protection."

The man relaxed and looked up. He examined Ben from head to toe, then extended his hand to him. "Glad to meet you, Senator. Welcome to Eddisford. Roland Stanch, Commander of the Senate Guard."

Ben shook his hand. "Glad to meet you," he said, a little uneasily.

"Senator, your security is our first priority," Stanch said. "The constitution gives us full authority to protect you wherever you go during your term of office. Don't be shy about asking for security when you feel you need it. Sometimes new senators—"

Ben cut him off in a friendly way, "I think I could have used you already, Commander."

"Tonight's intrusion was highly irregular," Stanch said. "I trust it won't happen again. We'll be on a higher alert from here on out." He looked apologetically at the Chairman. "Was it a Royalist, Sir?"

"It was," Barkloin said. "Now I suppose you'll heed my warnings more seriously, Commander? I'm glad it was only a stone this time. I gather you have a man tracking the culprit."

"Yes, Sir, I sent the best man we have."

"Your best man?" Ben asked. "And is anyone following him?"

"Sir?" Stanch cocked his head.

"Just a little humor," Barkloin said, easing Stanch toward the door. "Back to your duties, Commander. I'll be heading out in a moment."

Stanch saluted, and closed the door behind him.

Barkloin faced Ben. "I guess we'll find out which one of us has her," he said.

"Or if neither of us has her," Ben said.

"Anymore house calls tonight, Chairman?" Bolstrum asked cheerfully.

Barkloin unlatched the door, and the two sheep left the suite. Ben checked on his bath water, but it had grown tepid. He came back out in the living room and swept the broken shards of glass into a pile under the broken window. Then he sat down with the rock, turning it over and over in his hands. It seemed to him quite likely that Barkloin had snatched Miriam.

Chapter 12
Rescue

Ben stood in a large, vacant room. All before him was a dim haze he could not see through, but he had the sense that walls surrounded him. No air stirred. He sniffed at the stuffiness. The room needed airing out! There was a chair behind him. His tail was brushing it. He could not feel its contours, just one tiny bit of surface where his tail brushed it, yet he knew it was a chair and that he must walk away from it. He took a step. His hoof clopped loudly on the marble floor. He paused.

Someone else had taken a step off in the distance, perhaps in another room a long way away—had stepped on something like glass. Ben listened intently. "Who's there?" he asked. His voice seemed to fold into space and come around a corner. He twitched his ear one last time and sat bolt upright in bed.

A figure stood in the doorway, moonlight illuminating black baggy clothes. A knit mask with eye holes covered the figure's head and face. "I need your help," whispered a muffled voice.

"Who are you?" he asked.

The figure tugged on the mask, and Miriam's head emerged. "I couldn't do it, but you're tall enough," she said. "We could change clothes, switch places, and you could get her out."

"Miriam!" Ben threw the covers aside and rushed to her. "You're alive! No one's hurt you!"

A warm smile spread over her face. "Hi Ben," she said weakly, her voice losing all edge.

On impulse, he cupped her cheeks in his hands and kissed her.

She stared at him, her cheeks flushing in the moonlight. "You kissed me."

"I'm sorry." He found his hands still holding her cheeks in his palms, released her, but wanted to kiss her all over again. "I'm sorry," he said again.

"It's good to see you too." She smiled at him. "Have you always been this impulsive?"

Ben lowered his hand. "It's like I've taken everything and tossed it into the air and I'm just watching where everything lands," he said. "Miriam, I—"

She put her hand over his mouth and shook her head. "Quick, change clothes with me. These are way too big on me, so they should fit you just fine." She dodged into the front room and shut the door.

He stood alone in the moonlight, dumbfounded. He would have told her he loved her. He would have told her that he would never let any harm come to her. Did she not want him to tell her that? She had returned his kiss. What kind of idiot was he, kissing her like that? Did he have any clue what he was doing? He could hear her taking her clothes off. In a moment, the door cracked open and her hand emerged, holding the black clothes she had been wearing. When he didn't immediately grab them, she shook them. "Come on, Ben, there's no time."

He slipped off his pajamas and exchanged them for her clothes.

"Are you putting them on now?" she asked.

"Yes," he said. He could smell her scent, a feint woodsy freshness, as he slipped the shirt on over his head. "What is it you want me to do?"

"I've found where they're keeping Thistle."

"I thought they'd caught you too," he interrupted. "Someone threw a rock through my window."

Miriam laughed. "That was me."

"You?"

She emerged from the bathroom. "You looked a bit too cozy with the Chairman for my liking. You're so trusting, Ben."

"You were trying to drive a wedge between us?"

"He wants me arrested. I haven't done anything wrong."

"But you came back. Aren't you worried someone's following you now? They sent someone after you."

"Some friends of mine dropped a bag over his head. He's in their custody now."

"So you've linked up with some Royalists."

"Actually, no—well, to be honest they weren't friends—though, yes, they were Royalists." Miriam climbed into Ben's bed and pulled the covers up to her face. She heaved a sigh that ended in a tremor. "I spoke with one of them this afternoon, but he didn't know who I was, at least I didn't think he did until later. I was just trying to find out where everyone stood. I'm not here to start a revolution. No one seems to understand that. They want me to be their pawn, Ben."

"So if you haven't joined them, why did they drop a bag over Warwick's head?"

She smiled and bit her lip playfully. "I arranged it. There've been two of those so-called Royalists following me. They thought it was me coming around the corner. If Warwick hasn't made too much noise, they might still think they've bagged me, but it's not likely. Now put your mask on."

Ben draped it over his head, easing it gently over his wound, and lined the holes up with his eyes. "I feel ridiculous."

"You'd make a good thief," she said.

"And you know where Thistle is and think I can rescue her?"

"Yes, you'll have to pay attention because it's a bit complex."

"In the meantime, you're going to lie here and pretend to be me."

"No, I'm not pretending anything. I had to wear something, and your pajamas looked warm. Now listen," she said. "One of the Senate Guard will pass by your window at some point in the next few minutes. Count to ten slowly after he does, then roll out the window and run as straight as you can across the courtyard. Don't stop to look whether anyone sees you or not. You only have seven or eight seconds to get across."

"Won't there be security guarding the building on that side?"

"Yes, but they will be on the far side of the building at that point. They're too much like clockwork. That's something we'll have to fix when my father comes back. Once you're on the other side, slip behind the row of holly and crawl along the building toward the Senate House."

"I'm a senator, Miriam. Why do I need to sneak out? Why can't I just tell these guys I'm going for a midnight walk?"

"Because they will take it on themselves to guard you, and you'll never get free of them. And don't forget who killed Thistle's parents—friends of these people."

When she had given him the directions, Ben slipped into the other room and peaked out the window from the edge of the curtain. A cool breeze played with some leaves in the courtyard. Nothing else stirred. Then softly at first, but getting increasingly louder, he heard the clop clop of hooves coming closer. He ducked under the window until the sound was right in front of him. Then he counted, "One, two, three. . . ." When he reached ten, he rolled over the window ledge and sprinted between the trees across the courtyard. His rib throbbed with every footfall. He was aware of how vulnerable he was. An arrow would pass through his heart any moment.

To Ben's surprise, he reached the other side without event. Now to crawl along the building until he heard the other security officer. How had she worked all this out? And there was the definite tread, as she had predicted, this time the boots of a man. Ben held his breath until the man passed by, humming something leisurely to himself. Then he counted to ten again and broke out of the bushes. The courtyard lay empty now in the moonlight, this time as he had come to expect. He walked steadily toward the Senate House in the footsteps of the last watchman and turned the corner.

On the far side of the Senate Suites opposite his own, Ben veered into an alley and began to negotiate the maze that was the heart of Eddisford. The buildings were tall and cramped together, mostly three stories or taller. Few windows were lit. The moon flashed into sight occasionally, but quickly hid itself behind the next building. The darkness might have scared another man, but Ben felt an enclosed security in it, as though he were kicking through the womb of the city. So many sleeping bodies stacked in so many rows, all trusting that all was well.

Somewhere around the next corner, a tiny lamb lay in a storeroom. Was she asleep, or did she huddle in fear with the memories of her parents' murder and the realization that she was in the hands of those who killed them? As he was checking his bearings, Ben heard a noise behind him, a small gasp and a scuffling of feet as though someone had tripped. "She always underestimates her enemies," he thought. He ducked into the shadows of an awning. If he remained still, he would blend in with the store items stacked in sacks against the wall.

Two men padded by, then stopped at the corner.

"Which way did he go?" one of them whispered.

The other one put his finger to his lips and shook his head. He motioned for his partner to go one way and him the other down the cross street.

Ben jabbed a hole in a sack beside him with his pocketknife and felt a stream of grain pour out. This was the feed store on the corner. He was in the right place. He pocketed some of the grain in case Thistle hadn't been fed in her captivity. Then he crawled along the porch under the awning until he came to the corner. He looked each way quickly; both men were turned the other direction. He stood up and climbed onto a pile of the sacks, then hoisted himself up onto the awning and lay flat on his back for a moment. The edge of the awning had caught his rib. He breathed lightly in a measured calm until the pain receded.

Then Ben crawled back along the awning until he reached the other edge. He stood up, though it was difficult because of the slope, and braced the wall, one hand gripping the corner of a window and the other the corner of the building. Holding on tightly, he leaned toward his right hand until he could see around the corner. The space between the buildings was at first pitch dark, but gradually his eyes adjusted, and he could see what Miriam had meant. Somebody taller was needed. After a space of about four feet, a window ledge jutted out enough for someone to stand on. She had tried to stretch her leg across to it, but couldn't quite make it. Ben nudged himself as close to the corner as he could before trying. Looking across the gap, he shook his head at her bravery.

"All right," he said, and counted to three. On his first try, he realized he couldn't hang onto the corner of the window and reach the ledge with his foot. He would have to slide his hand along the wall and catch the corner of the building to keep from falling out into open air. He took a deep breath and lunged.

For a moment Ben was suspended in air. Then seemingly all at once, his chest caught the corner of the building, he yelped, and his foot landed safely on the ledge. He froze, clinging to the corner of the window,

 hoping that no lamps would be lit behind it, hoping that the men around the corner were out of earshot. They weren't. He heard them sprinting back. They had just come around the corner of the building when a door in the next building over swung open, and a shaft of light streamed out. A man held up a lantern and stuck his head around the door. Ben held his breath. His heart seemed to have lodged itself against his swollen rib, beating ruthlessly against it.

The two men caught in the shaft of light stumbled, bewildered for a moment, the senate insignia burned onto their sleeves. They suddenly leaped forward, drawing swords, and rushed at the man in the doorway. He called something back into the building and slammed the door before they could reach him. The first to reach it yanked on the handle. To his surprise, it burst open, knocking him and his partner back off their feet. Three men tumbled out of the doorway onto them. In the scuffle, the lantern was jarred loose, smashed, and extinguished, leaving the men in a black confusion.

Neither group had seen Ben hovering above them. He slid his feet along the ledge until he came to the other corner of the building, where he saw that he could step across onto a second floor verandah on the building from which the men had emerged. According to Miriam, they were keeping Thistle somewhere on the second or third floor. Ben jumped the breech, but as he did, a bit of moonlight between the buildings flung his shadow on the brawling men. One of them saw it, stared up toward Ben and would have alerted the others, but a dagger plunged through his chest, and he breathed his last.

Ben shook himself out of his shock. The noise of the brawl cloaked his movements. He rattled the latch on the door to the verandah, and to his relief found it unlocked. He slipped into the room and shut the door behind him. He listened intently for the sound of breathing. Nothing. He slipped through the room, out a door and into a dark hallway. A light flickered from below a ramp on the right, but no sounds rose from the first floor yet. He had to be

183

quick. He opened the door directly across the hall and listened again.

A movement in the far corner caught his attention, a small rustling. Stacked furniture—chairs, stools, tables—all in ordered piles, obscured his view. He dropped to his knees and crawled cautiously forward. As he drew near, he could hear a labored breathing, and an odd, tiny squeak. He inched his way around the furniture, and there she was, a dark little form tied up in ropes. She was tied to a footstool, tangled up with it in such a way that she could hardly move, but she was patiently rubbing the ropes that held her fore-hooves against the corner of a desk.

"Thistle," he whispered.

She stopped rubbing, twisting her gagged face up to peer into the darkness.

Ben crawled forward and tried to take her into his arms, footstool and all. She squirmed, resisting, a look of terror in her eyes.

He peeled his mask off. "It's me, Ben."

Her eyes went wide. Relief shuddered through her little body in a series of convulsions.

"It's going to be all right," he said softly. "Don't cry now." He tried to untie the knots, but they resisted stubbornly. "There's no time to untie you. I'll have to take you as you are. Do you trust me?"

She nodded her head.

He scooped her and the stool up and crept to the door. The hallway was still dark and empty, but now he could hear voices rising from the ramp to the first floor, an argument.

A first voice: "It wasn't my fault! How was I to know they were part of the Guard?"

A second: "You don't kill someone before you know who he is!"

And yet another, more urgent but softer: "We can sort that out later. We have to clean this up."

The first: "But why were they out there? Who informed on us?"

Ben slipped across the hall, into the room he had originally entered, and back out onto the verandah. He paused for a moment. He could make the first jump with Thistle in his arms, but not the second around the corner. He examined the spot on the rope where she had been filing. "Good thing you didn't wear all the way through these ropes," he whispered. He stuck his left arm between her forelegs and the stool and slung her as gently as he could over his shoulder. He felt her wince. "This will only take a few seconds," he said, and jumped to the ledge on the other building. Moving quickly, he edged along the ledge, and then without a moment's hesitation, jumped back around the corner, grabbing the window and the corner of the building as he had done on his way up. His timing was better this time, and though his fingers scraped the wall precariously, he hung on. Thistle let out a muffled bleat as the stool flapped her against his back.

"Just a bit farther," he said. He crawled the length of the awning and gently lowered her onto a high stack of grain sacks. He lay still for a moment, listening. "All right." He flipped himself down from the awning.

Fumbling with the gag first, and then the ropes, he untied her.

"Thank you," she whispered. "Is Miriam safe?"

He nodded. "We'll talk in a bit. Let me carry you. Your hooves—" He considered leaving the stool, but smiling to himself, thought better of it.

Three blocks away, he set her down. "I think we're safe for the time being; we can talk now. I don't think we should take the shortest way though."

"Where are we going?" Thistle asked.

"My place in the Senate Suites."

She stared up at him. "I thought you might have joined the Royalists."

Ben chuckled. "That's what I said to Miriam, but she hasn't joined them either. There doesn't seem to be a good side to join right now. She says the Royalists want to start a revolution. Of course that's what I've always been taught about them."

"But the Senate had my parents killed."

"Those people who were holding you hostage had your parents killed. Did you hear them arguing when we passed through the hall? They were talking about how they had just killed two Senate Guards outside. The Senate isn't all one faction." Ben took a few steps and beckoned her to come with him. "We need to keep moving," he said.

They walked in silence past a statue of a ram with a sword in his mouth, along a narrow canal, down another street. Thistle craned her neck from side to side, taking in the midnight city in obvious wonder. Ben felt his own head getting heavier. How much sleep had he gotten

186

before Miriam appeared in his doorway?

Thistle broke the silence. "Did the two guards come with you? Were they your friends?"

"No," Ben said. "They were following me. I'm not sure, but I think they thought I was the guy who broke my window."

"Someone broke your window?"

"Miriam broke it." He laughed. "I'll explain all that, but I want you to tell me what's happened to you. Start from where you saw me disappear into the cabin up in the mountains."

Thistle looked up at Ben curiously. "Did Miriam hurt you? Because you didn't come out, and I would have thought that—"

Ben interrupted her. "It wasn't a fair fight. I didn't mean to hurt her, but she didn't know who I was, see. She hit me over the head with a bottle."

Thistle snorted.

Ben kicked her playfully. "Can we get on to your story now?"

"Well," Thistle said, "the tracker said we should get away quick because things had gone wrong. I said I didn't want to, but he said he had a lot more experience in this sort of thing. I figured you were in good hands—" she snorted again— "even if you had been knocked out. And I didn't want to give myself away. I didn't know what would happen to me, but I started to think about that tracker—" She broke off, and they walked in silence, the clip clop of her hooves the only noise in the night air.

Ben shifted the stool from one shoulder to the other. "So did he trust you?"

"He was as scared as I was. Each time he had caught up with the princess, someone had killed his partner. He was sure you had been murdered. He said the Royalists are brutal and wouldn't blink at killing a senator. But now he had to report to the Chisel that his mission had failed, and that seemed to scare him just as much. When we got to Eddisford, we didn't go right away to the furniture store where we were supposed to meet the Chisel. The tracker was too scared, the coward. He dragged me to a pub, but I wasn't allowed to go in because I'm too young, so I had to sit outside. Sitting there on the stoop of the pub, I thought about running away, but the sun was so warm and I was so tired, and where did I have to run to? I still thought maybe I could find things out for you. Boy, that was a big mistake. It took him about an hour before he came staggering out like a boat in a storm. 'To the Chisel!' he cried, and dragged me down the street, everyone hopping out of our way. I hated him, the stupid, cowardly drunk. He hurt me. Everyone was staring at us."

A sob suddenly rolled out of her throat. "I hated him. I didn't care if the Chisel killed him. And I hate him more now." She stopped walking and hung her head.

Ben leaned down and stroked the sides of her neck. "Thistle—" but she shook her head in a silent rage and backed away from him, breathing heavily. He wanted to take her in his arms, to force her sorrow out of her. She hung her head again and rooted something from a crack in the cobblestone.

"Come on then," he said. "My suite isn't far from here."

They walked in silence again until he could hear that her breathing had calmed. He looked down at her tentatively. "We have to sneak back through the courtyard. Do exactly what I say."

She nodded her head.

He smiled. "It'll be like we're burglars."

"Why do we have to sneak in? Can't you go anywhere you want if you're a senator?"

"I don't particularly want them to know I was out and about."

"Don't they already know?"

He shrugged his shoulders. "I don't know what they know. Maybe those two guards haven't turned up missing yet. Maybe they were the only ones who saw me. I don't know. It's just best that we're not seen."

They walked to the next corner and looked around it cautiously. "Follow me, and don't talk," he whispered. "I have to count to do this properly. Even then it might not work."

They crept across the street, and into the bushes, waited for the guard to pass, counted, slid around the building, waited for the guard to pass—all as he had done coming out. The clockwork precision of the guards baffled him, yet someone must have seen him coming out. When he dropped Thistle and the stool into his window and tumbled in after her, he was more relieved than he had imagined he would be. The sprint seemed to have cheered Thistle up. She lay on the floor breathing heavily, her eyes sagging and a weak smile splayed across her face.

"We are spies, aren't we?" she said.

"According to Miriam, we may be the only ones truly for the king," Ben said, clutching his chest. "When my rib stops hurting, I'll go wake her. We have a lot of planning to do."

"Can I wake her up?"

"She'd love that."

Ben stood up slowly and went to the pantry to see if there was any more food, as Thistle clopped into the other room. He rummaged through bins of spinach and Brussels sprouts until he found a tin of crackers. He tried one, but it was stale. He emptied the tin into the trash bin. He held another tin up to the window to see more clearly and found it was smoked salmon. "Miriam will like this," he muttered.

"She's not here."

"What?"

Thistle's little form stood alone in the doorway. "Where have they taken her?"

Ben rushed past her into the bedroom. The bed was made neatly, his pajamas folded on the pillow.

Chapter 13
Craftsmanship

Ben woke to the peace of the sun caressing his face. The air filled his lungs with morning. Thistle's soft voice floated in from the other room like a tiny feather rising and falling on unseen currents.

"There is an orchard far beyond
the purple hills of Redland's shores
and when I wade the wildest pond
I'll taste the fruit of all its stores"

He smelled coffee and drifted back to sleep. "All is not well in Redland," Clovenhoof's voice whispered in his ear. Ben sat up and looked around, but the room was empty.

In the other room, Thistle sang on.

"The broken ropes of every bond
untangled on the mossy floors . . ."

She saw him through the open door and broke off. "Good morning, Sir. Will you have coffee and toast?"

Ben smiled at her formality. "Please." She bounced toward the kitchen as he staggered out of his pajamas and into his clothes. He shook his head at her resilience. Where was Miriam? He had calmed Thistle's fretting the night before, tucking her in between blankets on the couch and shushing her questions for which he had no answers. "Things will look brighter in the morning," he had said, and now apparently they did.

As he re-wrapped the bandage around his chest, the image of the man who had been stabbed the night before flashed before his eyes. The morning sunshine suddenly felt like a lie. The man had been looking at him in one kind of alarm when the dagger had pierced him, and a wholly different kind of alarm, terror, had swept over him. How many people had been killed in the past few days? Ben needed to keep track to keep it in perspective. Was it four? The archer at the fire, the mountain woman, the two guards. Six if you counted Thistle's parents.

Thistle brought his plate between her teeth and slid it onto the table beside his coffee. "Sir," she said, climbing up on the bench across from him. "I'm ready to tell the rest of my story. I couldn't go on last night, but I'm ready now."

"Thistle, if there are things that are too painful—"

"In a nutshell, Sir," she plowed on, "Warwick took me to the Chisel's furniture store. I think he's a senator like yourself, Sir."

"I've met him," Ben said. "Go on."

She gave him a curious look, but he ignored it, dipping his toast in his coffee. If she wanted to say "Sir" and "Yes, Sir" to him and treat him like her superior, he would amuse her.

Evidently encouraged by his silent authority, she continued in a hushed, important tone. "Warwick blundered in and told him everything. I had guessed it already back at Roderick's—I knew, but I didn't want to know I think—the tracker, he was one of the murderers who killed my parents." She took a deep breath to gather herself. "The way he described it was just the way I remember it. They were hurrying down the ramp to the basement yelling, 'Hide!' 'Hide!' when the arrows pierced them. When he described it to the Chisel, I couldn't think to hide my surprise. And anger! And horror! That evil man took one look at me and he knew.

"'Whom do you suppose they were yelling to?' the Chisel asked.

"'Each other?' the tracker said.

"'Blockhead!' the Chisel said.

"By then I was backing toward the door, though I knew it was useless. He set his men on me. They tied me to that stool, and they were going to carry me upstairs, but the Chisel wanted me there while he interrogated Warwick. He said he was more likely to hear the truth that way.

"Then he took a dagger from inside his boot and held it up to Warwick's neck where his old scar was throbbing in and out, he was so scared. And he said, 'You know who gave you this scar?'

"Warwick could hardly nod his head because of the dagger. I think he tried to say, 'Clovenhoof,' but it just came out like a small puff of air.

"'Do you know who gave it to you?'" the Chisel shouted this time. His face was right up in front of Warwick's. I thought the tracker's eyes were going to pop out. And then I saw that the dagger had already drawn blood, and it was dripping down Warwick's neck. The Chisel pointed at me. 'It was that little sheep's grandfather. That's who it was.'

"The tracker was still too stupid to understand. He turned his eyes toward me—he didn't dare move his head—as though he were asking for help.

"The Chisel relaxed his hand and pulled the dagger out of Warwick's skin. 'You killed her parents.' He said it with a smile, looking back and forth at us, enjoying himself. He was sinister. I hated him then more than I hated Warwick.

"He pushed the tracker down in a chair and said, 'Talk.' Warwick told him how the murderer hadn't come back from the campfire. His name was Herengist if that's helpful."

Ben soaked the name in the pool of his mind for a moment. "Herengist." He hadn't thought much about the man as a real man, someone with dreams, hopes, maybe even a family. It had been dark, and the struggle had been quick and violent.

Thistle continued, "Warwick told him how he had followed the princess, how you and I had caught up to him and how we had joined forces to find her, and how you must have been killed by Royalists. The Chisel looked at me hard after he said that. I didn't see any reason to pretend anymore, and I hated both of them so much. I yelled out, 'Ha, that's what you think!'

"Even at that point, Warwick seemed confused. 'He was on her side all along, you coward!' I shouted it at his

194

face. Then I spat at the Chisel. 'And you'll never catch her!'

"The Chisel came over to me and smiled at me. He said, 'You have the same feisty spirit your grandfather has. If he were still anybody important, I might have thought about keeping you alive and handing you over to him.'" Thistle put her chin on the table and sighed again.

Ben caressed the side of her face with the back of his hand. "Whatever folks think of him, it seems that he didn't have anything to do with your parents' murders."

Thistle smiled weakly. "As angry as I was, that thought didn't come into my head until later. Then someone banged on the door, and a voice cried out, 'Announcing the Chairman of the Senate of Redland, the Honorable Ribald Barkloin.'

"The Chisel leaned down into my face. 'If you have any desire to live, you'll keep your mouth shut.' Then he opened a closet door, and they threw me inside. I think they would have taken me upstairs, but there wasn't time. The Chairman's men were opening the outside door as the men were still closing mine. I was stuck underneath the stool, something was jabbing me in the back, and I felt like I could hardly breathe in that stuffy closet, but I kept my mouth shut.

"The Chairman wanted to know right off how the tracker's mission had gone. The Chisel was scared of the Chairman—I could tell that. He wasn't about to let Warwick do any of the talking. 'Things didn't go quite as planned,' the Chisel said. 'First, the Royalist sheep resisted arrest and had to be killed.' He lied just like that. He made it up on the spot."

"I don't think he made it up on the spot," Ben said. "I think he meant to have them murdered all along."

Thistle furrowed her little brow. "You may be right. The Chairman was furious. 'Where's that imbecile Herengist? I specifically instructed him to take them peacefully. I wanted their trial to set an example!'

"Before the Chisel could say anything, the tracker— well, I couldn't see, but he must have thrown himself at the Chairman's feet. He was blubbering like a baby that he hadn't killed them. The Chairman was yelling at him, 'Get up, Warwick! Get up, you pathetic piece of slime! Where's Herengist? I want to talk to him!'

"'That's the next thing that went wrong,' the Chisel said. Then everyone was silent for a minute.

"'Was he killed?' the Chairman asked. Somebody must have nodded his head. 'By whom? How did it happen?'

"The Chisel spoke up. 'Warwick didn't see who. Someone was with the princess when they caught up to her. It might have been some Royalist that she hooked up with, but I have my own theory.'

"'And that is?' the Chairman asked.

"'I need to verify some things before I make any accusations.'"

Ben smiled. "He suspects the truth, of course—that it was me. That's why he told me about finding you, why he wants to talk to me today."

"There wasn't much else," she said. "The Chairman seemed eager to leave once he had his information, and

196

the Chisel was happy to see him out."

"Thistle, you've been a wonderful spy. How could you doubt yourself?"

She beamed. "Will you keep me as your page?"

"At least until Miriam's out of danger, assuming things ever come to that point." Ben finished his toast and took the last swig of his coffee. "And we'll have to make these rooms work for both of us," he said. "I was going to replace some of the furniture with more people stuff, but there's no reason we can't have both. I hate to say this, but we probably need to visit a furniture store soon."

Thistle stared at him for a moment in feigned alarm, and they burst out laughing. Before they had regained themselves, someone knocked at the door. Thistle jumped up to answer it, but Ben stopped her. "Go in the kitchen for a bit. If it's the Chisel—and you better call him Senator Jacobson from here on out—I might find something out before he sees you."

"Yes, Sir." She smiled and clopped into the kitchen, humming softly to herself.

Ben opened the door.

"Hello, friend!" Colonel Forager stood smiling in front of him, his monocle shining in the morning sunlight. "How's the wounded warrior?" He peered up at Ben's head. "Still nasty looking, but your hair covers most of it."

"Come in. Come in," Ben said. "I was just about to ask my page for something more substantial for breakfast. All I've had is toast and coffee. How about some clover? I'll have eggs. I think I saw some of both in the kitchen last night."

"I'd be delighted!" Colonel walked in and gasped, "What happened to your window?"

"Bit of an accident. Look here, this is my page, Thistle Clovenhoof."

Thistle, who had just entered from the kitchen pushing the cart with two fresh cups of coffee, bent her forehooves in a formal bow.

"Delighted," Colonel said, pressing his muzzle down on the wider cup meant for a sheep. "A bit young for a page." He frowned. "Clovenhoof, huh? Any relation—"

"Granddaughter."

"Seems very capable." He took a sip of his coffee and sat down on the couch. "She makes good coffee. You need to hang onto this one."

Encouraged, Thistle pushed the footstool from the furniture store up to his feet.

"Don't mind if I do," Colonel said. He tried to stretch his legs to rest them on the footstool, but found them too short to reach it. "It's not really meant for sheep." He laughed and slid himself further down so his rump came to rest on it. "There." He leaned up on one fore-knee, half on the stool and half on the couch, looking very uncomfortable, but totally unconcerned. "Somebody mentioned clover," he said, and Thistle scurried into the kitchen. Smiling at Ben, Colonel asked, "When did she arrive?"

"Middle of the night."

"I was going to ask if you got a good night's sleep."

"Just a mild disruption, and I put her to bed quickly."

Colonel's eyes canvassed the broken window. "Someone didn't throw her through there, did they?"

Ben laughed. "The Chairman came by with your friend Bolstrum last night. Someone threw a rock through the window at the Chairman."

"Now there's a job I wouldn't want," Colonel said. "Glad you've seen a doctor though."

"Thank you for that."

"You didn't look so good. I sent my page over to the doctor the moment I left, and he must have been available. He's never come so quickly when I've needed him. Speaking of pages, I've never seen a sheep handle eggs very well. You sure you trust yours with the job you've given her just now?"

"How are you doing in there, Thistle?" Ben called. He could hear some shuffling around and the sizzling of oil in a skillet.

"Uhh," Thistle's small voice inched around the kitchen door.

Ben rose to see how she was doing, but a knock on the hall door stopped him. "I wonder who that could be," he said, and opened it.

Senator Jacobson stood smiling, his large body bulging at the seams of a new, maroon velvet vest. "Here as I promised," he said, his voice the thin whistle that Ben still couldn't get used to, "ready to take you to my friend and your lost item."

"Come in, Senator," Ben said. "We were about to have breakfast, eggs of some kind, I believe." He ushered the large man in and guided him to the other side of the couch

199

from where Colonel was reclining precariously.

"Good morning, Jacobson," Colonel said. "I see you're spiffed up for the opening session." He clamped a hoof to the edge of his monocle and breathed on it.

Jacobson lowered himself onto the couch in swaying motions like an alligator sliding into a lake. His self-satisfied smile broadened as he greeted the sheep. "Senator Forager, I think today we'll find—" but suddenly he broke off, the smile wiped from his face.

Colonel fixed his monocle back over his eye and regarded him curiously. "Something the matter?"

Jacobson was staring at the stool.

Colonel became self-conscious of the way he was lounging and pushed his rump up onto the couch. "Care to have the stool?" he said. "Doesn't do me much good with these short legs." He smiled back and forth between Jacobson and the stool.

Now Ben knew that Jacobson had not yet been informed that Thistle was missing. It was even possible that the guards hadn't discovered her absence yet. "I'll take the stool," Ben said. "I just acquired it second-hand yesterday, as a matter of fact. It was such a steal, I couldn't pass it up." He picked it up and turned it upside down. "See the carving on the legs? It's excellent craftsmanship. Isn't that your line of work, Senator Jacobson? Look, though—" and he pointed at some marks on the legs— "It's a real shame. The last owner must have tied it up in a move. See the marks where the rope chafed at it?" He held it up to Colonel's face.

The sheep cocked his head and examined it politely, but before he could say anything, Ben called into the kitchen, "How is breakfast coming, page?"

"Two plates and a trough coming up," Thistle called.

At the sound of her voice, Jacobson rose to his feet. He stood in a frozen confusion looking back and forth at Ben and Colonel, apparently trying to decide if Colonel was in on the joke.

Colonel turned himself over and crawled off the couch. "Eggs prepared by a lamb," he said playfully, "this will be interesting."

Suppressing a smile, Ben turned his chair around and sat at the table. Colonel clambered onto the bench across from him. Jacobson walked slowly over to the table. He did not sit down. He stared fixedly at Ben.

Ben considered another comment on furniture and a couple on ropes, but before he could settle on one, Thistle pushed the door open and walked in, bearing Colonel's trough. She placed it in front of him. "I mixed in some parsley, and it's topped with cumin—senator's special. Two more on their way." She turned to go, but seeing the Chisel looming dangerously over Ben, she stopped and bowed. "Good morning, Senator," she said curtly, and walked back into the kitchen.

A reckless impulse grabbed Ben. "I'm curious, Senator Forager. There are some issues that Senator Clovenhoof and I never debated in our campaign, and I could never get a handle on what he believed."

Colonel sniffed his food longingly. "He was very opinionated about most everything," he said.

"I was particularly curious about the Sacrifice," Ben said.

"Now there's an issue I stay away from," Colonel said. "No political capital there."

Thistle returned with Jacobson's plate in her mouth and set it at his place. Seeing that he hadn't sat down yet, she tugged his bench back before returning to the kitchen. He sat down slowly, still wearing a quizzical look that he couldn't seem to shake.

Colonel continued, "Clovenhoof was firmly against the Sacrifice. He was against anything that smelled centrist, whether it had to do with God, king, or man. The idea that a sheep's life would be forfeited to a man's—I mean, it puts man at the center, doesn't it?"

Ben toyed with his fork. Thistle backed in the door with his plate in her mouth and set it before him. He jabbed his fork in the eggs, then froze, his eyes closed. The motion had brought it back to him—the feel of Clovenhoof's flesh beneath his knife, the sudden burst through the skin and the tug of muscle and tendon.

"You're scaring me a little," Colonel said.

Ben realized that the others were staring at him. "I'm just wondering what changed his mind."

"Changed his mind?" It was the first Jacobson had spoken since hearing Thistle's voice.

Ben put his fork down on the table and looked up at Jacobson first, and then Colonel. "He asked me to sacrifice him."

Now Colonel seemed as stunned as Jacobson, his mouth hung open like a tent flap. "And you're going to do it?"

Ben hesitated. Thistle stirred behind him. "I've already done it," he said, "three nights ago, the night I was elected."

Jacobson pushed his chair back from the table and gaped at Ben.

Colonel's eyes seemed to slide past them to some point on the wall, as if he could see through it into eternity. "So he's buried and gone. He was always kind to me—well, not always kind, but—" He fumbled with his monocle, and Ben could see that his hooves were shaking.

"Not quite buried," Ben said, resting his eyes squarely on Jacobson. "I was interrupted." Ben could see the chains in Jacobson's head tugging it all together into one pile. The last log would fall in place at any moment. Herengist and Warwick had come upon the sacrifice of Clovenhoof. If the princess had been Clovenhoof's page, then. . . .

A loud knocking shattered the silence, and before Ben could answer the door, a young man about his own age burst in. "I'm so sorry," he heaved, "but I thought you should know. The whole senate is astir." He bent over to regain his breath.

"Who are you?" Ben asked.

"I'm sorry. This is my page, Benedict," Colonel said.

Benedict straightened up. "The king's daughter has come to Redland, and she's sitting on the Traitor's Chair!"

Chapter 14
Precarious

Colonel Forager clopped up the steps to the Senate on all fours, Ben at the back of his heels. Colonel had offered to accompany him, show him the ropes, and Ben had agreed, thinking it would force him to remain calm in the face of the present crisis. Miriam's plan seemed rash to him—she could be executed—though it had a certain logic to it. If the republic began peacefully with the chair, maybe it could end peacefully with it. Roderick would probably love the symmetry in it, see some spiritual truth in it. She was safe on the chair, at least until the senate voted on her proposal. Ben had a fairly clear idea what that proposal would be, and at this point he couldn't see that it would lead to anything but her death. What was she thinking, throwing her life away like this! If it came to that, he would rescue her. He was already devising plans in his head. He would need help. But there was no one to trust. He felt a cold sweat beading up in the small of his back.

When Colonel's page had delivered the message about the princess, all three senators had gaped in wonder at him. Jacobson had excused himself with a quick, curt bow, the humiliation of having lost Thistle behind him in the wake of the news. Thistle's officious air had suddenly drained from her. She had plopped down on the floor in a state of worry beyond anything Ben had seen in her in the short time he had known her. He had given her a job. "Wash up the breakfast things and wait for me here." After donning his own boots and vest, he had met Colonel in the hallway.

Now Ben saw that a group of twenty or so men and sheep, presumably fellow senators, were all gathered in an uproar in the lobby of the building. Jacobson stood in the middle of the group, shouting in a futile attempt to make them listen to him. As Colonel and Ben pushed the door open, the noise exploded in their faces. Ben could hardly catch a word of what they were saying.

Colonel gave Ben a wry look and mouthed, "Welcome to the Senate. Those I believe are all members of your party."

Ben smiled. The two pushed through the throng and opened the heavy oak doors into the huge domed chamber where the Senate met. Ben's mouth dropped open. The room wore an aged freshness like a forest. The walls, the columns that supported them, and the furniture were of a dark oaken wood. Sunlight streamed from windows high in the dome to illuminate the podium. At the end of one shaft of light, sat the princess, so regal that Ben could hardly imagine that she was the same girl he had met in the forest. Had he really kissed her the night before? The back of the ancient chair stretched high above her head, a deep carving of a sheep and a man holding a scroll etched in its grains. Ben couldn't make out what the scroll said from where he stood. He caught Miriam's eye for a panicked moment, and then her gaze floated past him as though there had been no recognition. When the doors had fully shut behind him, Ben felt the hush of the Senate Chamber. Men and sheep whispered to each other in small clumps around their desks.

Miriam sat still as a statue. A jeweled tiara crowned her head, and a purple velvet mantle with a white fur collar was draped over her shoulders. Beneath it, an elegant blue gown flowed to her ankles, which were crossed and tucked to one side under her chair.

Ben leaned over Colonel's shoulder. "Where did she get those things?"

Colonel swung his head toward a door to the side of the chamber. "The crown jewels and robes are all displayed in an ante-chamber off that way," he whispered. "She must have burgled them. It would have involved smashing some glass cabinets. I'm surprised she isn't wearing any of the jewels."

"Maybe we can't see them."

"They're big."

"She probably didn't like the way they looked on her. She's not the type to like ornate things."

Colonel stopped and readjusted his monocle. "You know her?"

Ben pushed past him. "Come on, show me my seat."

Colonel followed, shaking his head. "Clovenhoof asks you to sacrifice him, the Chairman of the Senate comes to see you on your first night here, someone throws a stone through your window, and now you say you know the princess. Making friends with you is going to prove the biggest mistake of my career. I bet there's no walking the middle ground with you."

"I wish there were, but things keep happening to me," Ben said. "None of it comes by choice."

"You're going too far."

Ben turned and found that Colonel had stopped a few yards behind him. Each senator had a section of the room to himself, surrounded by a fence-like barrier about three feet high. Narrow aisles ran along all four sides of each cubicle, and a gate swung out of the two sides. Colonel was holding one of these gates for him with his forehead.

Ben entered the gate and sat down at the desk. It still had the wide, low bench meant for a sheep's haunches and hooves.

"We'll get that switched for you," Colonel whispered. "Look at me. I'm over here." He crossed the aisle to Ben's left and into the next area. "This is my spot," he half whispered, half called.

Ben nodded. Colonel lifted the top of his desk and started foraging inside it. The distinct smell of ginger wafted Ben's way. Ben checked inside his own desk. He had half expected to find some mysterious communication from Clovenhoof, but it was empty but for some tufts of grass in the corners. He peeked over the raised top to see if Miriam might be looking at him, but she had lifted her eyes to the ceiling and was apparently examining the dome. Every minute or so, the door to the foyer opened and Ben could hear snatches of the argument. It was actually more coherent when he got it in small snatches like this.

"The chair doesn't mean anything anymore. It's an old tradition." . . . "The constitution protects her." . . . "She's a traitor." . . . "She has his cheekbones." . . . "Would the Royalists retaliate?" . . . "Should we call out the Guard?"

There was nothing to do. Ben closed his eyes. He imagined his father and mother walking through the door and seeing him here in the Senate Chamber, pride beaming in their eyes. He had painted this scene in his head many times during the campaign. Now the paint smeared into confusion. If his father knew the truth, would he even look at him? His father—the brooding strength of the hemlock towering above him—would he ever step out of that shadow?

The door swung open again behind him, ushering in the tumultuous noise of the arguers, but this time the noise swept into the room in a sort of dying roar. Ben swiveled around on his bench and saw the large pack of senators and their pages flocking in, the Chairman of the Senate in their lead. Barkloin wore a bright green pinstriped vest with a red scarf that seemed to shine in the dull light of the room. He smiled confidently at everyone as he passed. He nodded to Ben, blinking his eyes in an affectionate way.

The senators branched out to their own seats as Barkloin climbed the ramp to the podium and propped himself up on the bench behind the lectern. He waited until all was silent, his eyes roving the chamber to each point where whispering lingered.

Miriam shifted herself in her seat and fixed her eyes on the Chairman. Her hands grasped the ends of the armrests. Other than her initial glance, it was the first sign of nervousness Ben had noticed in her.

Barkloin sighed and chuckled. "The new session doesn't open until this afternoon, and yet here we all are. I myself would have liked to finish my laundry this morning. I had to leave it by the river when one of Senator Egbertson's pages came flying up to me with a message of what he termed 'extreme urgency.'" Nervous laughter fluttered around the room. Barkloin cleared his throat and sighed again. He glanced at the princess, and the corners of his mouth rose ever so slightly.

Nothing seemed to faze the chairman, or at least he could successfully project the image that nothing did. His glance made the princess seem like an insignificant supplicant, nothing to cause such trouble.

"Now that you've chosen to sit on the chair, I don't suppose you are going anywhere, my dear?"

Miriam shook her head in a manner that implied neither subservience nor defiance. Ben found himself smiling in admiration at her, but still she wouldn't glance at him.

Barkloin acknowledged her with another chuckle. "In that case—"

A voice from the floor interrupted him. "The chair is a remnant of the monarchy."

Another one chimed in before Barkloin could answer. "She's a traitor to the Republic."

Still another cried, "The Royalists are behind this."

Barkloin stood up. He forked the gavel in his hoof and brought it down with a thud that closed all mouths. His nostrils flared. "This is not a crisis," he said, his manner relaxing even as he said it. "A citizen of our country has placed herself on the Traitor's Chair. Following the laws of our constitution—check it yourselves if you need to, gentle sheep and men—the senate will hear her plea in our opening session. Until then, she will remain in the chair under the protection of the Senate Guard." He steadied his eye for a moment on those who had spoken, and then stepped down from the podium, walked up the aisle, and left the room.

The door hadn't closed behind him before two guardsmen marched in and stood at attention on the floor in front of the chair. The chamber returned to silence. For a moment no one moved. Miriam's eyes drifted back up to the domed ceiling.

Ben looked over at Colonel.

"Are you sure she knows you?" Colonel whispered. "She hasn't given you a glance since you walked in."

"She knows what she's doing. She has her own mind." Ben pointed at the bump on his head. "She gave me this, you know."

"Really?" Colonel said. "All that about bandits on the Runcorn Pass then—"

"Those were your words. I didn't particularly want to bring the princess up at that point."

"Protecting her then? You know, the way you were smiling at her a few minutes ago, I was beginning to think you might have some romantic feelings for her."

"Let's go get something to eat," Ben said.

"You don't want to keep watch over her, huh?"

"Come on."

Other senators and their pages had begun filing out of the chamber. Ben tugged Colonel into the aisle. "I'll tell you anything you want to know about my crazy, mixed up last few days, as long as you promise to stick with me."

"By 'stick with me,' I hope you don't mean politically," Colonel said. "I vote my own mind, which is to say, whatever way prolongs my career. Now, I will gladly stick with you if you are talking about going out and finding some food. This excitement has made me hungry again."

"It's nice to know you're a true friend," Ben said.

They emerged in the open air, blinking in the sunlight. Aside from the dispersing senators and their associates, the courtyard was empty.

"The Royalists really must not know what she's done," Colonel said.

"She doesn't want to have anything to do with the Royalists," Ben said. "The last thing she wants is bloodshed. It's better for her that they don't know. Why would she sit on the chair if she wanted to create a revolution?"

Colonel tugged on Ben's sleeve, and they headed toward the side street Ben had crept down the night before. "If she isn't going to ask for a return to power, what is she going to ask for?"

"Right now she just wants to bring her father back to his homeland in peace."

"As king?"

"He decreed the Senate into being. He doesn't see why the Senate wouldn't welcome him back."

"There's a thing called power, isn't there? No one wants it threatened. Would he want to reign?"

"If he had the right to reign, would you oppose it?"

"That's the question, isn't it?" Colonel stopped walking for a moment, removed his fogged monocle to wipe it with his handkerchief, and dabbed at his brow. The sun seemed to be getting to him. "I've read the constitution. I know that it makes provision for the king to return and assume his throne if he chooses. A constitutional government is a strange thing if you asked me. It presupposes that the will of the generation who wrote it have the right to govern the will of those who come after them. The constitution becomes the inspired scripture that no one can question. What if some of its contents are fundamentally flawed?" Colonel broke off. He put a fore-hoof on Ben's leg and twisted his head around in every direction. "All this is off the record of course. Politically incorrect, I think."

"Where are we headed, anyway?" Ben asked.

"There's a little café just this side of the river, The Crane's Neck. It's not the best place, but they have this thick potato soup with alfalfa sliced into it. I'm craving it at the moment. You might even like it." Colonel turned down another side street shaded by weeping willows. "It's at the end of this street," he said. "I keep my belloret there."

"You play the belloret?"

"I have to relax somehow, and sometimes people put money in the bowl." Colonel smiled. "I don't think some of the regulars know I'm a senator."

Ben found himself ducking under the leafy strands of the willows or parting them to keep up with Colonel, who had no trouble walking under them. A breeze had picked up, and Ben could see glimpses of the river shining through the sweeping veil. He was hungry.

The Crane's Neck was a dilapidated stone building with windows hung askew, but it offered a nice view of the river, and a delicious smell of sautéed onions and garlic hovered around the entrance.

"Good place to get away," Colonel said. " If you're going to do something stupid before the sun sets—and I

213

have no doubt you will, considering your record over the last few days and the way you were ogling the princess—you need a quiet morning to gather your wits."

"I'm not planning on doing anything stupid," Ben said.

"At least not until they vote to execute the princess. Then you'll be a hero. For now, I want you to relax and let your mind wander."

They ducked into the café. Ben seated himself on a cushion beside one of the low tables where morning light was streaming in from a window. Each cushion was a different shade of green and seemed to float like a lily pad on the rich blue carpet. Colonel clopped over to a corner of the room and picked up a reeded instrument with a slide. He blew a couple of soft notes, and some of the other customers turned their heads. Then he blew a long low note that swirled into a river of soft melody, each note a ripple of longing. A waitress in a bright orange, flowery blouse came out from behind the counter and smiled at him, tapping one of her hooves to the beat. Ben closed his eyes and let the music coat his worries.

When Colonel finally seemed to ease the river into the ocean, an old sheep wrapped in a dark blue blanket dropped some coins in front of him in a tin, and a few customers clapped. Colonel acknowledged them with a gentle nod and set the instrument down. He joined Ben at the table and waved a hoof cheerfully toward the waitress. "Dandelion, my friend needs a menu."

Ben picked up a toothpick and rolled it between his teeth. The waitress came with the menu, flicked one of

Colonel's ears playfully with her muzzle, and retreated into the kitchen.

Colonel smiled and winked at Ben. "Nice ewe, that one. Do you think she likes me? Maybe you shouldn't set your sights so high. A princess—"

Ben chuckled. Another waitress was seating three other senators at a neighboring table, two sheep and a man in pressed scarves and vests. Ben recognized them as some of those who had been arguing in the lobby of the Senate Hall.

Colonel twisted around and looked at them. "Defeats my whole purpose!" he said, loudly enough that one of them turned his head.

Ben put his finger to his lips. "I want to hear what they're saying."

"No, I'm sure you really don't," Colonel said, but fell silent in a brooding scowl. The volume of the conversation at the other table was rising into an animated discussion.

"How do we even know she's the princess?" one of the two sheep said. He had a sagging look to his eyes and seemed thinner than a healthy sheep ought to look.

"You called her a princess. Are you saying there's a king?" This came from the human, an older man who kept pointing at the others when he talked.

"You know what I mean. Let's say she's the daughter of the man who used to be king—"

"Would it be worse for her to be the princess, or to be an impostor?" said the other sheep, an eager smile lighting his face.

"She's an impostor either way. We'll hang her at dawn," said the first sheep.

Ben winced. Colonel shook his head and snorted as if to indicate that Ben should blow it off.

"Maybe she's insane," the old man said. "Maybe she thinks she's the princess, but really isn't." He nearly poked one of the sheep's sagging eyes out as he spoke. "Then we wouldn't have to hang her."

"How would you prove she's insane?" asked the fatter sheep.

"Sitting on that chair is insane," cried the old man, laughing and jabbing at his friends as if they didn't understand his joke.

The senators talked on with a disengaged humor that sickened Ben. He rubbed his eyes with the palms of his hands. His fingers grazed the bruise on his head. The spot no longer hurt except to the touch. His rib, on the other hand, still dealt him a small jolt with every breath he took. Even so, he could forget about his rib for hours and then suddenly feel it leap into his conscious mind. The senators seemed to own no sense of Miriam's life, or even their own for that matter. A person could go along like this, ignoring the pain of reality, talking about insanity and hanging and death as though they were all part of a big joke. Clovenhoof's last squeal burst into Ben's ears, and he lifted his hands to them unconsciously.

"These guys are all talk," Colonel said. "You don't have to worry about them. They don't have any real power."

Ben looked up at Colonel. "It's not real to them."

"To the insane the sane are insane," Colonel said. He raised his eyebrows. "You hear what they're saying. Your friend is insane because she believes in what she's doing."

"And they don't," Ben said. "It's just a game to them."

"As it is to me," Colonel said, suddenly serious.

Ben stared at him.

"If you refuse to relax, maybe you need to be stirred up," Colonel said. "Why are you sitting here just listening to them? They're going to kill the girl you love. It'll be easy to be heroic later when there's a rope and gallows, but it'll be too late then. Now is the time for action. Do you believe you're a senator of Redland?"

"Nice speech, dear." The waitress had returned and was smiling at them around a piece of parchment in her mouth. She set it down on the floor. "Will you go out and fight for me the day they want to hang me?"

"I'll be here eating my potato soup with alfalfa," Colonel said.

The waitress stamped her hoof on the parchment and turned to Ben. "And what'll you have, sweetie?"

"I'll have the corn soup with onion slices and carrots," Ben said.

The waitress winked. "Colonel here, he would lay his life down for me—" she paused and tweaked his ear again "—if it would earn him some votes. He's a senator through and through, and I love him for it. You go on and talk politics. I'll be back with your soup."

When she had gone, Ben leaned over the table intently. "I thought you didn't care what happened to Miriam, and now you're trying to talk me into doing something dramatic."

"I don't care what happens to Miriam," Colonel said. "I'm sorry. That sounds very callous, but I'm just being honest with you. I don't know the princess personally, and what she's doing is very dangerous to the Republic. You on the other hand do claim to care, so on that basis, I'm giving you good advice."

Ben rubbed the palms of his hands against his eyelids. "It's so hopeless. If I went over there and said that the king has a right to return—"

"They would think you're insane."

"Yes."

"You need to get used to this feeling, if you're going to last long as a senator. Find the angle where you won't seem so insane. Where's your common ground? Campaigning was easy wasn't it? You just had to prove the other guy wrong to other people. Now you have to prove him wrong to himself. Now you have to persuade him to vote in a way that he may have promised others he would never do."

Ben leaned back and stared up at the ceiling.

"If it helps any," Colonel said, "you were doing a pretty good job of persuading me on the way here. Just talk sense. Don't make speeches. Mean what you say."

"What do you think my chances are?"

"Saving the princess? Slim, but not so slim that you shouldn't have a bite to eat first."

As if on cue, the waitress came with their soup. Ben burned his tongue trying to eat it too quickly. He was a senator. He had precious little time in which to act.

Chapter 15
Persuasion

The three senators looked up from their meals curiously. A piece of parsley dangled from the sallow sheep's mouth. He slurped it in and said, "No, sit down. Join us. How about your friend?"

Ben dragged another cushion to their table, retrieved his mug, and sat down with them. Colonel motioned that he would stay at his table. He had never said he would give him moral support, but Ben had hoped he might accompany him. He felt betrayed.

"I couldn't help overhearing your conversation about the princess," Ben began. "I'm Benjamin Edmundson, the new senator from Blackwater." He nodded to each of them.

The old man folded his arms and raised his eyebrows. The sallow sheep grunted a greeting.

The other sheep nodded to him. "I'm Morton Ramswidth. I represent the Mudbirth Bog area." He twitched his ear toward the first sheep. "This is Philastrus Fullwithers." He waved toward the old man as if to introduce him too, but something in the old man's eye stopped him short.

Ben filled the hollow of the awkward pause. "I didn't expect to find something so enormously important on my first day here," he said. "Truthfully, I'm nervous about it."

"Do you think it's that important?" Ramswidth asked.

"As comfortable as the Chairman looked this morning, I know that he sees the Royalist threat as a real crisis," Ben said.

"Nice to know," Fullwithers said, raising his eyebrows cheerfully. "You realize you're talking to three Socialists right now. If his administration can't handle the situation, all the better for us." He exchanged a smile with the old man.

"But then you are assuming there's no real threat," Ben said.

"Royalists have always been with us," Fullwithers said. "Can you see the country returning to a monarchy? I can't."

"Under one condition I can," Ben said.

Fullwithers snorted incredulously. "What's that?"

"That you offer the Royalists a martyr."

"A martyr?" Ramswidth seemed to choke on something deep in his throat. He looked at his fellow senators, but they didn't seem impressed.

"I don't see how a lunatic can be a martyr," Fullwithers said.

Ben leaned forward. "Assuming she is a lunatic, is upholding the law worth putting her to death?"

"Life without law is anarchy," the old man spoke up.

"Do you really believe that?" Ben asked. "Because if so, you can't take a vote like this lightly and pretend to yourselves that someone who appears very sincere is crazy just so you can hang her out of convenience. Let me assure you that I believe she is the princess and that she has a legitimate constitutional right to ask of the congress what she is going to ask."

The three senators exchanged embarrassed glances.

Ben leaned back. "I'm sorry. I came on too strong just now. I'm new at this."

"So what do you know that we don't know?" asked Ramswidth.

Ben took a deep breath. "She's going to ask for her father to come back and live out the rest of his life in Redland."

"As king?"

"Yes, but I don't believe to overthrow or even undermine the Senate in anyway."

"I don't see how you can have a kingdom and a republic all in one," the old man said.

"Remember, he was a Republican, the original Republican."

"Well," the old man said, "you could argue that Clovenhoof was the original Republican. He forced Reinard's hand."

"You say his name like you knew him," Ben said.

The old man smiled. "There aren't very many of us left who knew him. Of course Clovenhoof is gone now, but there's still Edgetho Haroldson and Brosius Boldmuzzle."

Ben looked into the old man's eyes. "It's someone like you, who remembers the king, who might find a compromise and keep us from a civil war."

The three senators exchanged smiles again.

"Civil war?" Ramswidth snorted.

The old man stood up and stretched his arms into his jacket. "It's not unusual to get a little dramatic when you're starting out, Mr. Edmundson. Don't let it bother you if we're not impressed." He turned to Ramswidth. "Did you say you were paying for this meal?"

Ramswidth foraged in his vest pocket for some coins and counted them as he dropped them on the table. He nudged Fullwithers, who was licking pieces of grass from the edges of his trough, and they followed the old man out the door.

Ben ran his hands through his hair. "That was a waste of time," he said.

Colonel shuffled over from the other table and plopped down on one of the vacated cushions. "It probably was, but at least you gave them something to think about. And on a different day, you might have been able to convince them." He nudged Ben's mug toward him. "Don't you want to drink this?"

Ben pushed it away and stood up to go, rummaging in his pockets for change. Then he thought better of it, sat back down, and quietly emptied his mug, staring ahead of him and saying nothing.

"If it makes any difference, you convinced me of your point of view," Colonel said. "I'm not saying I'm going to vote in her favor; don't get me wrong. I'm just speaking

223

from a purely idealistic point of view."

"If only we had more time," Ben answered. "For my part, the soup here was delicious." He rose and stretched. "Come on, let's get going."

Ben waited on a bench in front of The Crane's Neck. Dandelion had detained Colonel on his way out, whispering something in his ear and nudging him toward the kitchen. The cool breeze that rustled through the willows worked fruitlessly at calming Ben's nerves. He tried to let his eyes rest on the swaying limbs of the trees, but the picture of Miriam swaying from the gallows kept forming in the shadows. Far down the street, he could hear the commotion of the city, see the legs of people hurrying to unknown places. The peace of this street was an illusion.

Colonel finally clopped out of The Crane's Neck, all business again. "Best be on our way," he said, "only an hour until the session starts," and he started off down the street.

Ben followed him silently.

"Where do you suppose all those people are headed?" Colonel suddenly asked. He jabbed a hoof toward the street ahead.

The legs below the willow branches were all hurrying in the same direction, toward the Capitol, some walking fast, some running.

"An uprising!" Ben gasped. He broke into a run, the willow limbs lashing his face and arms.

"Wait," Colonel called, clopping after him. "Do you think it's safe?"

"They'll form a mob! Everything will be ruined!"

"And you're going to stop them? Who's they anyway?"

"I don't know, Royalists? We have to do something."

"Getting killed won't help! Could we please stop and talk it over?"

Ben stopped. A tangle of willow branches draped themselves around him. He fought out of them and sank to his knees. "She did not inform the Royalists," he raged, "but that is what every senator will think."

"Every senator except two," Colonel said.

Still panting, Ben unclenched his fists a little.

"Unless we die," Colonel said. "Then it will be every senator again."

"We don't have much time. If they are forming a mob, would they recognize you as a senator? I think I'm safe enough. No one knows me yet."

Colonel took his monocle from his eye and stuffed it in his pants pocket. He unbuttoned his vest and slung it into the ditch. He loosened his belt a few notches until his pants hung around his haunches. He turned up his collar and yanked on his scarf until it hung crooked. "I need my Belloret," he said and headed back to the Crane's Neck.

Ben followed him. "My father's been warning people about Royalist uprisings for years. I never thought it could really happen."

"This one has certainly caught me by surprise."

"We might have to fight."

Colonel managed a laugh through his hurried panting. "Do you mean against each other, or together against the Royalists?"

"I meant against the Royalists, but if you try to stop me from saving Miriam—"

"Trust me, you won't have to fight me. The worst I might do is trip you while you're rushing out of the Senate Chamber with her. Even that sounds a little too daring for me."

Colonel banged the door of the café open and rushed in. Ben waited outside, leaning over and gathering his breath. In the reprieve, a thought thudded into his mind as though someone had heaved a stone onto a sandy beach. He was a believer now. Why shouldn't he pray? He looked up and down the street. Nothing stirred but the breeze in the willows. "Lord of Grace, keep her safe." He listened to his voice speaking the words with the curiosity of an eavesdropper. The words twanged like the string of a foreign instrument. "Keep her safe." Nothing followed— no vision of light, no flood of quiet peace—but he was surprised at his own sense of expectation. That itself was a welcome change.

Colonel hurdled out the door before Ben could analyze himself any further. "Carry this and look purposeful," he said, handing Ben the belloret case and tucking the instrument itself under his arm. "Loosen your collar a bit like mine. We're musicians, see? We'll look like we're on our way to a gig. We'll be surprised at all the commotion, but we have somewhere to go."

They headed back down the street, Ben ducking under the willow branches with the instrument case on his shoulder. When they reached the thoroughfare, they turned casually toward the Capitol Square and walked along purposefully, stepping out of others' way as they rushed by. A block from the Senatorial Suites, they skirted the square and came around the back of their own building. No one had given them a second look. In fact, the focused intensity of those rushing toward the square alarmed both senators.

"If this doesn't end in violence, I'd be surprised," Ben said, scooting out of the way of five young rams with lead pipes in their mouths.

"I can't believe this is Eddisford," Colonel said. "How does a peaceful city suddenly turn violent like this? It makes you question our inner nature." A man with a pitchfork careened around a corner and collided with him. Colonel tripped over his horn and yelped.

"Sorry!" the man shouted, and sped off.

"It's dented," Colonel said, fingering the bell. He shook his head.

Ben could now see the side door to their building. Four nervous looking guards stood post in front of it. "Our suites haven't been taken at least. Let's find out what we can from Thistle and Benedict and then see if there's a safe way back to Miriam."

As they approached the door, the guards all eyed them warily, their hands clenching their weapons more tightly. "What business do you have here?" one barked, but then another relaxed and smiled. "It's Senator Forager and his belloret, Sir. I've heard him play it at The Crane's Neck."

Colonel smiled broadly. "Quite a day, isn't it, gentlemen? Have you met your newest charge? This is Senator Edmundson."

The guards shook his hand and welcomed him. He could feel the sweat on their palms and the tension in their fingers.

"I'm sorry, Sir." The first guard bowed curtly to Colonel. "I mistook you for musicians."

"You were meant to, or at least they were." Colonel waved his hoof toward the courtyard. "Has Commander Stanch issued any orders regarding all this?"

The door swung open even as he asked the question, and Commander Stanch emerged. "Why are you standing out there where you're so vulnerable?" he asked. "Come inside, quickly."

He yanked on Ben's arm, and Colonel followed them into the hall.

"My best unit of men is positioned in the lobby of the Capitol. If the rabble becomes violent, my men can hold them back. I believe the Chairman and most of the Senate are safe inside. The Senatorial Suites on the other hand are indefensible—too many low windows. I suggest you pick up anything you wouldn't want to see in the hands of Royalists in the next few minutes and disappear for a while."

"But if there's a coup—" Ben began.

"It won't come to that," Stanch said. "I feel sure it won't. I've seen—" The glass window in the door behind them suddenly shattered into bits, and an arrow pierced the wall behind Colonel's ear.

The door opened, and two of the guards clambered in and crouched beneath the window. "Get back," they cried. "A Sniper's on the roof of the Capitol."

"The roof? Then he has to be our man!" Stanch began examining the arrow, but quickly jumped back when another whizzed through the window. "Who's he shooting at?"

A knock sounded low against the door, and one of the guards cracked it. A guard who had remained outside stuck his head in. "He's shooting at us, Sir. I don't think anyone in the courtyard has even noticed him."

"The last thing I want to report is that we started the violence," Stanch said.

"He's one of us, Sir. I got a good look at his uniform."

"Have you got a good angle on him?"

"I think so, Sir."

"Shoot him."

The man ducked out, and the door closed.

Ben leaned against the wall, stunned. "You might know the man," he said.

Stanch stared at a spot on the wall, his eyes glazed for a moment. "This cannot turn violent," he said. Then he snapped into action and gave the two senators a shove. "Go quickly, get what you need, and we'll see you out of the building in a few minutes."

They walked briskly down the hall to their doors, the commander in their wake. "And stay away from the windows," he added. Even as he spoke, the volume of the shouting seemed to increase outside.

Colonel had already opened his door and gone in when Ben turned to Stanch. "Do you suppose I could find a safe way into the Capitol?"

"Don't be ridiculous," Stanch said. "The more senators I have away from all this the better."

Ben fumbled with his key, but his hand was shaking so much, his stabs at the keyhole went awry.

Thistle's small voice called through the door. "Is that you, Sir?"

"Yes, let me in."

The lock rattled and was still.

Ben tried the latch, and it opened. He stepped in cautiously. Thistle stood before him with her hooves planted solidly on the floor and an iron candlestick in her mouth, ready to swing it at his legs.

"It's me," he blurted. "Don't swing."

She dropped the candlestick and smiled up at him in relief. "I didn't know what to do."

"No, I think that was the right thing," he said. "You're a brave sheep." He glanced around the room. "You had some furniture delivered."

"Benedict told me we have an account with the Senate that we can put expenses on, so I didn't need money. I was so nervous about Miriam and had nothing to do. I didn't think you would mind."

"And the window is fixed."

As he said it, they heard a window shatter somewhere nearby, and then another. Boots trampled down the hall outside the door.

"Not for long," Thistle said.

Ben scrambled into the kitchen and grabbed his medicine. He scanned the room for anything else he might need. How long would he be gone? He had no idea.

Where would he go? He couldn't just walk away and leave Miriam in that chair. Now that violence was breaking out, the senate would condemn her to death. If the Royalists managed to force their way into the Capitol—would she leave the chair? Anything might happen. He threw his jacket over his shoulder and opened the door.

Commander Stanch was talking in a low, hurried voice to Colonel and Benedict down the hall. Benedict was turning a sword over in his hands as if he were trying to get the feel of it. "All right then," Stanch finally said, Colonel nodded, and they rushed up the hall to where Ben and Thistle were standing.

"Change of plan," Colonel said. "We're surrounded, and things have turned violent." Stanch fished a key ring from his pocket, chose a key, and opened the door across from Ben's.

Ben followed them in. "This is Senator Jacobson's—"

Stanch cut him off. "Be quiet and shut the door behind you."

More windows shattered.

"Is anyone here?" Thistle asked.

"I said be quiet," Stanch whispered furiously.

He and Benedict lifted two corners of an elaborately designed rug on the floor and folded it over, exposing a trap door. Stanch lifted the door and motioned them in. The shouting in the hall increased. It sounded like someone was smashing furniture across the hall in Ben's suite. A steep ramp led into the darkness below the floor.

"Hurry," Stanch whispered.

The doorlatch behind them rattled. Ben picked up Thistle and plunged down the ramp. He heard Colonel backing down it carefully behind him and Benedict and Stanch fumbling with the carpet and the trap door. Ben descended the ramp until it ended, he guessed, a few stories below ground. He stopped there and put Thistle

down, suddenly aware of the heaving pain in his chest. She nudged against his left leg. The air around them was thick and dank. It smelled of roots. He felt the walls and found them dirt on three sides. The fourth side was presumably the beginning of a corridor.

Colonel bumped into him from behind. "Excuse me."

"Should we wait?" Ben asked.

Above them, Stanch and Benedict were still fumbling with the carpet and the trap door. They could hear Stanch's indistinct curses streaming down with the shifting bits of light. Then a loud crash splintered the darkness. All was still for a moment.

"They're in!" Stanch cried. "Draw swords!" For a moment everything went black. Then the trap door was thrown open wide, and swords clashed. "Run," Stanch cried again, "I'll deal with these blackguards!"

Again swords clashed between muffled voices.

"I'm not leaving you," Benedict cried. "Look out!"

It was infuriating to watch from the bottom of the ramp, the figures all a blur. Ben put his hand on Colonel's back. "I don't know where this tunnel leads, but take Thistle further in and hide. I'm going up to help." He wriggled past Colonel.

The fight above Ben had grown more intense. He tried to make out what he was seeing as he rushed up the ramp, but it was all a flurry of arms and swords. He had nearly reached them when a body tumbled down the ramp and bowled him over backwards. He rolled with the body in shock, reaching for anything to grab hold of, hitting his back, his head, his knees, his shoulder, rolling over again and again until they came to rest at the bottom, the body on top of him. Was it Stanch or Benedict? Ben's own body was a sea of aching pain, and out of it rose the monster of his searing rib. "Just breathe," he thought.

Then the fighting above him abruptly ended.

Silence.

A voice said, "Drag him out," and after a bit of shuffling, "Now there's a prize. You've killed Stanch!"

"Who?" Another voice, a bit higher and more winded than the first.

"The Commander of the Senate Guard. You should be proud of yourself."

"I didn't want to kill anyone."

"Is the other one dead?"

"Dead or soon to be." This was a third voice. "I caught him up under the ribs. I'll bite my shoe if I didn't pierce his heart."

Ben suddenly felt sick. It was Benedict who lay on top of him—dead? Was he breathing? In his panic he couldn't tell. Three figures shifted in the small light above him, apparently peering down into the darkness. He remained still, the wind caught in his chest.

"What if he's still alive?"

"Nothing's moving down there."

"Where does it lead?"

"Probably nowhere. It's just a hideout, I suspect. Here, we'll close it up, drag that cabinet over it and be done with it."

"But there could be others down there."

"They'll be out of the way until the revolution's over, right? We'll come back and check on them then."

The men backed out of the opening, and the light narrowed until it disappeared altogether. Then Ben heard the scraping of the cabinet across the floor. Trapped, and for how long? He breathed, heaving Benedict's body with his battered chest. He waited for the pain to subside. He wouldn't have the strength to throw the body off himself. He took another breath and rolled on his side. A warm liquid trickled down his arm. A wave of nausea passed over him. He closed his eyes. Was Benedict dead?

With another heave of his chest, he wriggled out from under the body. On his hands and knees now, he took long slow breaths and waited till the dizziness retreated down his spine. He found Benedict's wrist and felt for his pulse. "Lord of Grace, please!" He felt nothing at first and moved his fingers. There it was, a gentle throb. Alive! But he had felt blood. He had to stop up the wound.

234

Confound the darkness; he couldn't see anything. He remembered seeing a handkerchief in the pocket of Benedict's jacket. As he felt for it, he became conscious of Benedict's breathing, thin and rasping. Perhaps the sword had pierced his lung. He found the handkerchief, pulled the jacket apart, and ripped the shirt open. He could feel blood oozing slowly from under the rib. He stanched it with the handkerchief and held it firmly in place. The effort was difficult. He couldn't get into a comfortable position, but he dared not release the pressure. He switched hands several times.

In all this time he had heard no noise from down the dark corridor. He called into the darkness, "Colonel, Thistle, are you down there?" but no reply came. How long could the tunnel be?

Suddenly Benedict coughed, gasped, flailed an arm, and tried to lift his head.

"Lie still," Ben said. "I'm trying to stop your bleeding, but you can't move around."

Benedict became still. After a moment, he sputtered a thin whisper, "Thank you."

"Conserve your breath," Ben said. "I should be thanking you. You and the commander saved our lives."

Thick, silent moments passed. Ben became increasingly aware of the dampness in the air, the smell of roots and soil and rotting timber. Finally he felt that he could release the pressure on the wound long enough to unwind the bandage from his own chest, wrap it around Benedict's chest, and hold the handkerchief in place. Managing it in the dark, he suspected that the bandage was filthy, dragging soil each time it passed under Benedict no matter how hard he tried to keep it clean. He couldn't just wait for someone to stumble on them. They had to get Benedict out of here.

He leaned close to Benedict's face. "Just lie here and breathe as easily as you can. I'm going to find Colonel. We'll be right back."

Benedict found his hand and squeezed it.

Ben stood up slowly and felt his way into the darkness. The tunnel stretched for what might have been a hundred yards with several turns, and as he went further in, the air grew thicker and ranker with earth. "Thistle, Colonel, are you there?"

Then very faintly, he heard Colonel's voice.

"Through a tunnel burrow deeper
Find your mother's infant sorrow
Feed it to the heartless reaper
He will comfort you tomorrow."

The song broke off. "Here, taste this. It was growing right out of the wall. It's elm root. It'll comfort you. Don't you worry. We're all going to be fine."

"Thistle, Colonel?" Ben called.

Colonel's choked voice replied, "Is that you, Ben? Everything all right?"

"I'm coming to you," Ben said. The tunnel rounded a bend and then another. "Colonel?"

"We're right here."

His voice was so close to his feet that Ben jumped backwards.

"I've got a scared little one here," Colonel said. "Seems she doesn't like dark, underground places."

Ben knelt down beside them and reached out to touch Thistle. She was quivering from muzzle to tail, huddled against Colonel's underside.

Ben patted her softly behind the head. "No one's going to hurt you now." He took her gently into his own arms, and she burrowed her muzzle into his armpit. "Benedict is wounded," he said. "He was stabbed up under the rib, but it's missed his heart. I think I stopped the bleeding, but he'll need care soon. We've got to get him out of this hole."

Colonel rose to his hooves. "And Commander Stanch?" he asked.

Ben hesitated. The silence itself communicated the truth. He felt the bundle in his arms knot into a rock. "I'm sorry," he said.

Colonel sighed.

"They've shut the door and put a cabinet over it." Ben said. "We're stuck in here for who knows how long."

Colonel's hooves clopped back and forth on the floor as though he were trying to decide between two courses of action. "Well then," he said. "You two stay here. That's best for Thistle's sake. I'll be back in a few minutes." Colonel pushed past him, heading back up the tunnel toward the ramp.

Ben leaned his back against the wall and concentrated on breathing slowly. Now that there was nothing to do, the pain in his rib grabbed his attention again, and he sensed a dull throbbing in his head as though someone were beating a drum in a cave a long way away. He pulled the bag of powder out of his pocket and choked some of it down.

In the quiet, Thistle's body lost its tension, and finally she crawled off of him and lay with her back to his leg. "What's going to happen to us?" she asked.

"I suppose, when all the excitement's over, someone will come along and wonder why there's a cabinet in the middle of the floor. I wish I knew what was going on up there. The session ought to be starting pretty soon if the mob hasn't broken into the Capitol and—and crowned the princess."

Thistle let out a nervous laugh. "Would she let them?"

"She makes a beautiful princess," Ben said. "You should have seen her tiara."

"Do you love her?'

"What? We just met a few days ago, Thistle."

"I'm worried about her."

"I would do anything to save her right now."

A long silence followed. The happy thought was apparently enough to cradle her. He closed his eyes and napped. There was nothing to do but wait.

He might have slept for a minute or an hour. Colonel was kicking him in the leg and talking a mile a minute into his face.

"I couldn't find the commander's body. Where is it? You didn't tell me they dragged it out. I can't believe this bad luck."

"What are you talking about? Yes, they dragged him out."

Colonel clambered over his legs and headed deeper into the tunnel. "We're stuck," he said. "There's no way out."

Ben got to his feet and followed him. "Why is this suddenly a revelation to you?"

Colonel didn't answer. He walked a bit further and stopped. "Feel this," he said.

Ben stepped up beside him and put his hand out. A damp, rough metal like iron blocked the way. He brushed his fingers to a corner and felt a crack, then down the crack, and his wrist hit a doorlatch. He tried it, but of course, it was locked.

"Commander Stanch had the key," Colonel said flatly.

"We weren't just hiding then," Ben said.

"He was taking us into the Capitol. I don't know how long Benedict will last. I assumed—"

Ben slid his back down the wall until he was sitting on the floor. He leaned his head against the door and chuckled to himself. "Have you tried knocking?"

"Nobody answers," Thistle said. "We tried when we first got here."

"We're still way below ground," Colonel said.

Then a thought struck Ben. Was there any chance? "I wonder if this is how the king slipped away."

"The king? You mean however many years ago, when he disappeared?"

"This is how he got out of the Capitol unseen. It's brilliant."

"Though not a lot of help to us now," Colonel said.

"If I had Miriam's key, I bet anything it would fit this lock."

Thistle suddenly sprang up next to him. She wriggled around in circles trying to reach something in her knickers with her mouth. Several times she bumped into Ben and excused herself to Colonel.

"What are you doing?" Ben asked.

"I have a key," she said. "I found it in those black clothes you were wearing last night while I was cleaning up this morning. Miriam must have left it on them when she changed clothes with you. Maybe it's the one you're talking about."

She wriggled around some more and then stopped, panting. She said something indistinct, and Ben gathered that the key was in her mouth. He put his hand under her chin, and the key fell into it.

It took a little doing to jam the key into the rusted lock, but once Ben got it all the way, it turned easily and clicked.

Chapter 16
Ambivalence

The iron door groaned on its hinges. A cloud of dust curled around its edges. Ben fell into a fit of coughing, and the two sheep backed away from the door, choking on the soot.

"It probably hasn't been opened in years," Ben said.

"Commander Stanch had a key to it," Thistle said.

"I would think that the less you use something, the fewer people know about it, and the more useful it is in a crisis." Colonel laughed wryly to himself. "Don't I sound like a seasoned spy."

"We're all going to be seasoned spies before this is done," Ben said, "if we live through it."

He groped into the space beyond the door. About two feet in, he bumped into a ladder that extended straight up the side of a brick wall. The rungs on the ladder were slender iron bars.

Ben sighed. "I don't think either one of you can climb this. I might be able to carry Thistle up, but not Benedict. I'll have to go up and bring back a doctor for him." He backed away to let them examine it.

241

"It's like a chimney," Thistle said. "Only it comes down rather than up."

"Sheep can't climb this," Colonel said, "I guess I'll have to stay down here and miss all the action. Assuming re-election time comes again, at least I won't have to explain why I voted one way or the other today."

"You'll have a heroic story about being stuck in a tunnel," Ben said. He handed the key over to Colonel. "Here, in case they come looking for you, but haven't found the key on Commander Stanch. You can cram yourself in here and lock the door behind you."

"I won't be leaving Benedict's side," Colonel said. "If he dies, I won't be able to live with myself. He served me so well—and to think, I never once considered offering him my life."

"I'm sure you would have some day," Ben said. "You're still young."

"No," Colonel said sharply, "a sheep can't say that so easily. We have this choice every day, to offer ourselves in the Sacrifice. If you never did, you can't say you would have because, see, you could have. It's a simple matter. I didn't just put it off; I never considered it. Two years making my breakfast, footing my messages, and suddenly one afternoon he's on the verge of death."

"Is there a doctor in the Capitol?" Ben asked.

"Not that I know of," Colonel said. "But you must find help somehow. I need to get back to Benedict."

Ben knelt down with his back to Thistle. "Lay yourself across my neck. It's a few flights up, be still as I climb. Here we go."

242

He stood up cautiously, clutching the ladder. Then he climbed rung by rung. As they rose, the air grew less damp and smelled more like a building and less like a cave. He had to adjust Thistle's weight several times, grunting with the pressure on his rib. At last, Ben reached out for another rung and there was none. He felt above him and encountered a ceiling of wood. He felt a brick wall to his left side. He kicked out behind him and encountered brick there as well.

"Hurry," Thistle whispered.

Ben felt to his right. It was wood. He felt all around for a doorlatch, but the search was futile. He pushed against it, but it didn't move. He felt Thistle slipping from around his neck. He kicked out against the wood. Still nothing happened, but he sensed a slight give. If it were a door, perhaps the hinges were close to the ladder. He leaned back and kicked it further away from the ladder. The door resisted for a moment, then flew open into a dark room. Ben stepped in and sat down. Thistle rolled off his back.

They were in a closet. Ben steadied himself to stand up and knocked over a mop. It clattered against a bucket and fell among some brooms. A crack under a door a few feet away let in some light. Ben found himself squinting in the dark. Beyond the door, things seemed in a pandemonium. He could hear shouts, running feet, the dragging of furniture, and behind that, the roaring chant of thousands, "Death to the Senate! Release our princess!"

"Do you think they've gotten into the Capitol?" Thistle asked.

243

"I'm pretty sure they haven't. We'll have to listen at the door," Ben said. "There's no sense in giving ourselves away if they have. We'll have to sneak out somehow. The main thing is getting a doctor for Benedict, but we've got to think about Miriam too."

He put his ear to the door and listened. It was hard to distinguish between one voice and another for several minutes, but finally someone quite close yelled, "Mind the door to the garden! They're over the garden wall! Shove that cabinet against it!"

"They're still outside. Come on." Ben shoved the door open, and he and Thistle emerged into the hallway that circled the Senate Chamber. Near them, five guards pressed against a door while others dragged a cabinet with a glass face full of medallions up behind them.

"Come on," an officer shouted, "we just have to secure the door on the south side now. You four stay here in case there's a breach."

Ben stooped down to Thistle. "Find a doctor among the Senate Guard. They're bound to have medics among them. I've got to see what's happening in the Senate."

She looked at him apprehensively.

"If you see any of the men who held you captive, steer clear of them," Ben said, "but they'll be on the job, so you shouldn't have to fear them. When you've found a medic, bring him here and send him down the ladder. If he won't believe you, bring him to me, or come and get me. Can you do this?"

Thistle nodded her head.

"One more thing. The passage has to be kept a secret. We may need it to get Miriam out of here. If he doesn't seem trustworthy, don't take him into the passage. You'll just have to make that determination, but Benedict's life depends on us getting him help."

Resolution filled Thistle's eyes. "You can count on me, Sir." She turned and trotted down the hallway.

Ben walked briskly in the opposite direction. Though it was midday, candles on sconces lit the way. There were no windows on the first floor, probably as a security precaution for just such an occurrence. When he came to a side entrance into the Senate Chamber, Ben stopped for a breath. The climb up the ladder had taken more out of him than he had wanted to show Thistle. Without the bandage, his heart seemed to be pounding madly against the injured rib, and even his head was starting to throb again. He had to keep his focus.

Ben cracked the door and slipped into the Senate Chamber. He stood just inside for a moment to establish his bearings. The door he had slipped through stood in the shadow of the balcony. The room was strangely silent. None of the noise from the mob outside penetrated the walls. Every few minutes a page peaked out into the hallway to report to his senator on the security of the building, and the noise rushed through in a sudden burst that snapped silent when the door shut again. Senator Jacobson was making a speech on the platform, his imposing body all but enveloping the lectern. Behind him in the moderator's seat, the Chairman lounged, chewing on a green onion, looking as though he couldn't be more bored with the proceedings. Miriam sat more tensely than before in the Traitor's Chair, her gaze fixed on Jacobson as he spoke.

"The Senate Guards have successfully secured the building for the time being," he wheezed, "and the army is surely organizing a force to apprehend this mob as we speak. We might even look at this whole episode as a godsend. The faceless Royalists now have faces. Once we round them up, we will know who they are. I find it interesting that some of our own number are absent from the Senate Chamber this afternoon." His gaze swept the room slowly, resting on several empty seats, including Ben's.

Barkloin stirred behind him. "Surely you aren't accusing everyone absent from this session of being a Royalist. My good fellow, there are often empty seats in our midst."

"I only mean to call their loyalty into question," Jacobson said. "I make no accusations. The princess has claimed that she didn't raise the rabble. Though her words hold no sway with me, it is possible that someone else might have done it on her behalf to scare us into accepting her proposition and sparing her life."

A murmur of agreement rose from the Senate floor. Jacobson's interpretation of events made sense. Ben could feel defiance creeping through the room. He took advantage of the senator's dramatic pause to leave the shadow of the balcony and make his way to his seat. He could not have timed his entrance more effectively. Jacobson had already opened his mouth to spit out his next word when his eyes fell on Ben. Seeing Jacobson's bewilderment, all eyes turned toward Ben and followed him across the room. Ben became self-conscious and tripped over his boots. Recovering himself, he stole a glance at Miriam. As before, she was not looking at him—in fact, she may have been the only person in the chamber not looking at him—but something in her manner had transformed, as though a new strength had seized her. His presence encouraged her; he fought back a smile.

When he had seated himself, Ben looked up at the Chairman. Jacobson had not continued his speech; everyone seemed to expect Ben to say something, but he wasn't sure where to start, or if it was even appropriate to speak.

"I'm sorry for the interruption," Ben spluttered.

Barkloin chuckled. "We're glad to have you join us, Senator Edmundson. Senator Jacobson has implied that you might have joined yonder rabble, but I'm glad to see you haven't."

"I apologize again," Ben said. "I don't know the protocol yet. Senator Jacobson appears to have the floor, but I have some news, a matter of some urgency."

"You may speak so long as you do not interrupt the senator who has the podium," the Chairman said. "If you wish to take the podium, you may send a page to my clerk here to sign your name on this list."

Jacobson wasn't talking yet. Ben plowed ahead. "I would like to speak on the issue at hand, particularly if my loyalty to the Republic has been questioned, but my page is searching for a doctor among the guard right now. In our attempt to get here, Commander Stanch has been killed, and Senator Forager's page has been severely wounded. If anyone in here has practiced medicine—"

A pall fell over the room. He could almost taste the respect that each man held for the fallen commander. That respect mingled with fear. Men and sheep gaped at him with mouths open.

"So the bloodshed has begun," Barkloin said ominously. "Do we have a doctor among us?"

No one replied for a moment. Then a sheep in a ruffled shirt and rolled up sleeves spoke. "There are a few medics among the Guard, Senator Edmundson. Rest assured that your page will be led to one of them."

"Then we will proceed with the matter at hand," Barkloin said. "In the absence of a page, you may sign your own name for the podium, Senator Edmundson."

Ben rose and started forward to the clerk's desk. For the moment, he appeared to have the Chairman's sympathy and that of most of the senators. He must not squander it.

In the meantime, Senator Jacobson had gathered himself. "Now a man has been killed and another injured. Perhaps more of the Guard have been hurt, and all in the name of raising this so called princess to power. I say the surest way of stamping out an uprising is eliminating the reason for it. We need to send a quick and decisive message."

The Chairman cleared his throat, coughed, and swallowed a portion of the onion in his mouth. "Senator Jacobson, while I admit that the sound of the rebels outside is raising the wool on my neck as much as the hairs on yours, we must not let fear influence our decision where justice is concerned. We must simply ask ourselves, 'Do we believe first that the proposal made by the princess is constitutionally justified and second that it is a boon to our society?'"

Jacobson stamped his fist on the lectern. "I can speak to both of those questions, Chairman."

Ben reached the clerk's desk and stooped to sign his name on the list. Three names followed Jacobson's, and it didn't seem like the Chisel would relinquish his position at the lectern anytime soon, especially since he felt Ben waiting eagerly to get up there and defend Miriam. It could be hours before Ben had his chance. In the meantime, a man was dying in the tunnel below the building and he had little assurance that Thistle had found help for him.

Jacobson had begun a long narrative on the writers of the constitution. "We must take into consideration the narrowness of their points of view. We cannot ignore the fact that, as wise as they were in creating our constitution, elements of the language in the document reflect a system of values that no one takes seriously anymore. The wheat must be husked and the husk thrown away. The intent of their writing must be adjusted for a more liberal society."

Ben signed his name to the list and started to turn around, but caught sight of the minutes the clerk was taking in short hand. He whispered to the clerk, "Would your record of Princess Miriam's proposal still be in short hand?"

The clerk nodded, continuing to take down Jacobson's high-pitched words in indecipherable quipped jots. Jacobson paused for effect.

The clerk smiled. "But she read it from a piece of parchment."

Ben turned his head to Miriam. She glanced at him, a flicker of a nervous smile at the corner of her mouth.

Jacobson lurched onto his next point. "A republic cannot rest in the palm of one religion. A recognition of the king by the State in any function, whether he is given power or not, would be a tacit recognition of his divine right to be there. A true republic that represents all people must eschew any tie to religion. A true republic must be comprised of officials placed in leadership by the consent of the people and only the consent of the people."

Ben could feel the prongs of Jacobson's arguments catching hold of minds in the chamber. They were rational and well delivered. A week ago he would have been listening with enthusiasm and some jealousy. He made up his mind and walked across the stage behind Jacobson to the Traitor's Chair. He excused himself quietly as he pushed in front of Barkloin, but he couldn't bring himself to look the Chairman in the eye. Barkloin merely grunted. It might even have been a burp.

Ben knelt down beside Miriam, his arm resting on her chair rest, and looked into her eyes. To his surprise, she clutched hold of his arm. Her lips trembled. The eyes of the senate turned to them. Jacobson paused and cocked his head toward Ben in annoyance. Someone in the back of the chamber chuckled, and having made his point,

Jacobson continued with his speech.

Ben whispered in Miriam's ear, "I'm sorry I arrived late, but it couldn't be helped. Can I see your proposal? I have to know exactly what you said if I'm going to champion it."

She reached behind her on the chair and handed him a folded piece of paper. He started to rise, but she held her grip on his arm. "I'm scared."

He nodded, holding her gaze. "I'm here with you, whatever happens," he said.

She leaned forward and whispered. "There's a chill in their eyes. They have no sympathy for me."

"They're scared too," Ben said. "The quiet in here is an illusion, and they know it."

"Do you think the Guard will hold the building against the mob?"

Ben shrugged his shoulders. "It depends on how many join the mob, and if Jacobson is right, how soon the army will rescue us."

Miriam managed a smile. "Rescue us, so we can hang me properly."

"I'm going to try to speak for you," Ben said.

He drew his arm from her clutch, and she let it go. Ben found his way back to his desk, aware that he was barely listening to the rest of Jacobson's speech. How could anyone concentrate in a crisis like this? Would anyone pay attention to his words when the time came? The Chisel was winding down. The substance of his arguments had passed, and he was closing with a flourish on the glory of

251

the Republic. Ben unfolded the piece of paper and read Miriam's proposal.

Mr. Chairman and honored members of the Senate, I am Miriam Elaine, Princess of Redland, daughter of King Reinard, who exiled himself for the greater good of the Republic at its inception. My father is a loyal citizen of this republic who seeks no power, but wishes to return to his homeland to finish his days and to be buried with his fathers in the Royal Cemetery. My request is that the Senate invite him back as King of Redland with safe passage and a state welcome. The Constitution guarantees this right in Article 22. This article states, "The Senate as an institution is the gift of the royal family, and should the rightful king choose to return to the throne at any point, he would have a right to do so." My father is a republican through and through. You need not worry that he will attempt to overthrow the very power that he freely gave you.

Ben nodded. It was a good speech, straight to the point. The less said, the less it gave to disagree with. She had been counting on someone else to draw out the arguments in her favor, someone else to build sympathy for her. Ben's absence must have terrified her.

Jacobson finished his speech with dripping sympathy. "It is a terrible thing to put a young woman to death. None of us, I dare say, has the stomach for it." He paused and scanned the room gravely. "But we must all have the heads for it. It would be convenient if all traitors were vigorous men with arrogant faces, but that is a romantic dream." He jabbed his finger toward Miriam. "Look at the person who sits before you on the Traitor's Chair. She's beautiful isn't she, decked out in her royal garments and tiara? Remember what those emblems stand for—a monarchy in which the state bows to the whims of a single family. She is a traitor to the Republic, and we have a duty to the people of this nation to reject her proposal. Perhaps the king sent his daughter ahead of himself. Perhaps he thought, 'Surely they would not kill a beautiful young woman in her prime.' Do not allow your sympathy to blackmail you, or you will fall as prey into the hands of your enemy."

Jacobson bowed solemnly and left the podium. The silence in the room was palpable. A sheep near Ben stared down at his desk with a determined brow. A man behind him turned a pocket watch over and over in the palm of his hand in grave contemplation. Ben could see it in their faces. The Senate was prepared to sacrifice Miriam for the greater good. Having seated himself, Jacobson swiveled in his chair and met Ben's eye, his former embarrassment gone. He didn't need to implicate Ben to win the argument. He had overstepped himself, but pulled back marvelously. His eyes seemed to warn Ben. Do not throw away your career at such an early moment. There need be no enmity between us. Come to your senses and back away from this precipice.

The Chairman cleared his throat. The clerk had handed him the list of speakers. "Senator Wardergard, you have the floor if you think there is anything further to say."

A debonair ram in black knickers, a stiff white pleated shirt, and a purple scarf stood up and clopped forward on his hind legs, his muzzle in the air. As he stepped up to the podium, he surveyed the Chairman with obvious disdain. Barkloin scooped up another green onion in his mouth and chewed it loudly, as if to say he didn't care what Wardergard thought of him. Wardergard planted his forehooves on the lectern and smiled at the Senate. He had a handsome face for a sheep. His eyes had a softness that few other sheep had, and his teeth were clean and white.

"A time of crisis," he began, "a time of crisis offers us a crisp view of our circumstances that we would not otherwise have. I don't believe, for instance, that for all our rhetoric, anybody in this room woke up this morning thinking that the Royalist threat was so great. Who suspected that such a great number would or could lay siege to the Capitol and hole us up in here this afternoon? Our temptation right now is to sprint to a place of safety—call in the army, put the rebels down, execute the young lady to my right—without pondering seriously what brought us to this juncture. Consider the policies of your present Chairman and his cronies. Consider their paltry response to our present high unemployment and perpetual low wages draped in economic rhetoric to hide their contempt for the poor. They approach every problem in the nation with a heartless, tough attitude that mocks the plight of the common worker. Who brought these folks into the streets? Was it the princess? No. Satisfied people do not riot. We need a kinder leadership."

Ben could see where this speech was heading. He remembered his father once saying, "Here's the sad truth, son. The capacity for partisan politics in a corrupted republic increases in measure with the crisis at hand. We'll be making speeches about each other as the warriors of the Fortimai overrun us."

Suddenly, the building shook. It was only a slight tremor, but it turned all heads. Wardergard stumbled on a word, cleared his throat, and resumed his speech. Several pages leaped to their feet and ran to the doors. They returned moments later, and a wave of whispers crossed the room.

"Battering ram."

Another tremor shook the building. Tension in the chamber mounted. Wardergard turned around and whispered something to the Chairman. Barkloin rose from his seat and conferred quietly with him. In the interval, whispers rose again around Ben. He heard the senator behind him ask his page if he was carrying anything that would serve as a weapon. Miriam sat steadily on in the Traitor's Chair, looking wide-eyed around the room. Ben could see that where she looked for sympathy, she found only fear. He was trying to catch her eye when the gate to his cubicle opened and Thistle rushed through, panting heavily.

"Sir, I can't get a medic to help us," she said. "Several of the Guard on the roof have been shot, and also one on the verandah. The medics won't leave them. They're all wondering where Commander Stanch is. I didn't tell them anything. They seemed too panicky. There hasn't been any sign of the army yet. There's a Captain Warbuckle in charge. He seems very clear-headed, doesn't want to hurt anyone, but some of the officers are out for blood.

They're saying that some of their own have been wounded, and that changes things. They're holding the doors so far—but did you hear the battering ram?"

"Stop for a moment. You're going too fast." Ben knelt down in front of Thistle, his hands on her shoulders. "Are you telling me that no one is here to help Benedict?"

She nodded her head. "But, Sir—"

Ben closed his eyes. He had to do something, but he felt stretched in both directions like a prisoner on a rack. If he stayed to speak for Miriam, it might be too late to find help for Benedict. If he managed to get out and help Benedict, it would be too late to speak for Miriam.

"Sir?"

Ben's eyes had drifted back to Miriam. She was watching them intently as though she had been trying to read Thistle's lips. Ben shook his head and mouthed, "No doctor." She frowned and looked as though she would rise from her seat, but seeing the Chairman and Wardergard eyeing her, she lowered herself back into her sanctuary. Ben found himself wondering if she had had anything to eat, or if they had allowed her to visit the restroom.

"Sir?"

Ben turned his attention to the little lamb. "Yes?"

"No one has tried speaking to the rioters."

"What could anyone say to them," Ben said, panic converting to bitterness, "to hold off until the Senate kills the princess?"

Thistle looked up at him scornfully. "You wouldn't say that."

"No, but while I'm telling them something else, they will be killing her."

Thistle came close to Ben and put her muzzle on his knees. She looked searchingly into his eyes. She took a deep breath and turned her head toward Miriam. "You have to do it, Sir."

"Do what?" he asked. "Doing one thing I have to do is walking away from another thing I have to do. And now you're putting another responsibility on me. Why do you think the crowd would listen to me?"

"You just said it, Sir."

"What did I just say?"

"You have to walk away from her." She looked back into his eyes and blinked. "Into the fire."

The nightmare that had woken him at Roderick's cabin billowed like black smoke into his mind. "The convergence," he whispered.

"I heard you telling Roderick," she said.

He felt the terror of the dream afresh and understood it. Walking into the fire was nothing, leaving Miriam everything. And the other dream—Clovenhoof clopping away from the chair—left him with no doubt as to the course he must take. Could he do this? He had told Miriam he would speak for her. He had seen how much she relied on him. She had told him she was scared, and he had replied, "I'm here with you, whatever happens."

Wardergard was back at the lectern. "Considering the delicacy, the fragility, of our situation—"

Another tremor rocked the building.

Ben had no time to consider the delicacy, the fragility, of the situation. "Thistle, you stay here. I'll need to know what has happened here while I was gone if I get back." He stood up, fixing his eyes on Miriam. Somewhere in the corner of his attention, Wardergard was discussing the protocol of trained soldiers attacking armed civilians. Miriam cocked her head as if to ask Ben what he was doing. Ben took a deep breath. How could he leave her like this? He mouthed, "I have to go." Bewilderment crept over her face. Her lips parted. Ben turned, opened the gate of his cubicle, and walked up the aisle to the door. He could feel her mounting fear with each step, but he could not look back, lest he lose his resolve.

Chapter 17
Parley

The battering ram thrashed the door yet again. The hallway echoed with the sound. The beams that held the doors closed were already bowed and weakening, and the cabinet that was pushed against it bounced precariously. The moment Ben emerged from the Senate Chamber, guards pushed him aside and laid a heavy oak desk on its back in front of the door.

"That will be the last senator out of that door," a guardsman said. He was a square-shouldered, dark ram—solid horns above focused eyes—with a captain's stripes. He seemed to enjoy his ingenuity. "Now, turn the cabinet on its side and lop off those weak legs with your swords. Good. Now the other cabinet—excellent! Now wedge the carpets between them."

Their work done, the guards stood back and waited for the next blow of the battering ram. When it came, the doors hardly budged. The sound that had clattered with almost a splintering give was now a thick thud. The guards sighed audibly.

"Well done. They'll shift to another door now if they have any brains," the captain said, "but we have enough furniture to plug them all if we have to. Wainwright, Bixon, and Cliveson, go around to the western door and get the others to help you dam up the door like this. Warfmanson, you and your lot follow me."

Ben caught the captain by the shoulder as he headed off toward the eastern door. "Captain Warbuckle—"

The captain turned and looked at Ben earnestly. "We're doing what we can, Senator. I'm sorry I don't have time to—"

Ben interrupted him. "No, Captain, I want to speak to the crowd. How do I get to the verandah?"

Warbuckle looked at him in wonder. "They're shooting arrows at my men up there. Are you aware of that?"

Ben nodded. "Someone has to try talking to them. This will either end in diplomacy or a massacre."

"It's my duty to keep you out of harm's way," the captain said.

"It's your duty to protect me as well as you can while I go about my business," Ben said, "which is diplomacy. Show me the way."

Warbuckle licked his lips in thought, seemed to argue with himself for a moment, and then turned on his hooves. "Follow me. How will you get their attention without being shot?"

Ben jumped after him. "I don't know. Maybe a white flag?"

The captain opened a panel in the wall that Ben had not realized was a door and clopped up the ramp behind

260

it. The joy of intrigue had flashed back into the soldier's eyes. "I'll have my men sweeping the crowd from the corners of the verandah. If anyone tries to shoot you, we'll put him down. Of course, we might not get him until he's released his shaft, but that's the risk you're taking." With his mouth, he withdrew a handkerchief from a pocket on his foreleg. "Here's your flag."

Ben grabbed it as they emerged onto the verandah. It was a large marble-floored porch strewn with tables and chairs. Ben had heard that some senators and their families watched fireworks from the verandah on New Year's Eve. It was large enough for formal dances in the summer months. In one of the far corners, close to the edge of the building overlooking the mob, a medic knelt beside a wounded soldier. When the soldier saw Ben, he suddenly flailed his uninjured arm wildly and yelled something at the medic. Ben ran over to them, crouching as he got close to the edge of the building where he could make out the faces of people and sheep beneath the trees. The colonel came behind him, motioning the few guards who had followed him up to the verandah to stay low.

"He wants to talk to you," the medic said.

"I have to talk to the crowd before they break into the building."

"It's important," the wounded man gasped.

"He needs to relax," the medic said, more to the wounded man than to Ben. "He's lost some blood, but I think I have it stanched now." He pointed at the man's shoulder.

261

Ben glanced at the area, but he had seen too much of wounds lately to stomach any more. "We don't have much time," he said.

The man lifted himself onto an elbow in spite of the medic's urging. "Senator Edmundson? It is Senator Edmundson, isn't it?" He choked, gasped, and fell back on his head.

"Yes," Ben said, "I'm Senator Edmundson," the title sounding strange in his own mouth.

The man closed his eyes and breathed in light rhythmic breaths through chapped lips. "I'm sorry," he said finally.

Ben took his hand and squeezed it, resisting an urge to hurry him.

"I leaked the news to the Royalists," he said, "about the princess, that she was here."

Ben nodded. "Why?"

"We had no idea there would be so many." He tried to rise again, but this time the medic held him firmly down.

"You can talk," the medic said. "You may not get up."

The man relinquished the struggle. "The Chisel said we could draw them out, make everyone show their cards—he said—"

"Senator Jacobson!" Ben had suspected as much, but his fury rose within him. "I suppose he's probably arranged for the army to arrive in the nick of time—no doubt when the princess has been executed—and slaughter the traitors!"

The man shook his head. He swallowed a few times before he could regain his voice. "That might have been his plan, but the Chairman sent the army away."

Ben's mouth dropped open. "Where? When?"

"Around noon, just before all this started. One of our men arrived from the Runcorn Pass, said a message came across the mountains that the king was returning. We know that the king has been courting the Fortimai. An army of their strength could—"Something gurgled in his throat, and he swallowed hard. "The Chairman suspected an invasion."

"The Chairman hasn't told any of the senators this."

"Only a few of the Guard know. We've all been so busy, and there hasn't been any communication with the outside."

Ben furrowed his brow. "What are those two up to?"

"They're trying to save the republic, Sir."

"A republic does not behave like this," Ben said.

"I don't think the Chairman knew about the leak, Sir. The Chisel, Senator Jacobson, was acting independently."

"Yet you were following his orders."

The man grimaced. He seemed genuinely ashamed of himself. New stabs of pain seemed to throb through his shoulder. He squinted and writhed into a different position.

The medic dabbed at his shoulder as fresh blood seeped out. "I just thought you should know before you spoke to the crowd. No army is going to come and rescue us. There are senators—and certainly members of the Guard—who want a blood bath. You may be the only thing standing in their way."

Ben held the man's gaze for a moment. "I understand. Tell me your name."

"Erlichson," the man replied, "Guardsman First Class."

"Thank you for your candor, Guardsman Erlichson." Ben squeezed his hand again, then crawled over to the edge of the verandah. A low wall, about three feet high shielded him from arrows.

The captain ordered his men to various points where they could take glances at the crowd and clopped over to Ben. "He's right about the mood of some of our men," Warbuckle said, "but the last thing I want is a blood bath, and I promise you I will keep my men in order. We'll do everything we can to keep the crowd calm and out of the Capitol, but if they break through the doors, I will command my men to shoot. My duty is to protect the Senate."

"I understand."

Ben took the white handkerchief and waved it over the edge of the wall. Three arrows whizzed by his arm. "I need something else to hold it with."

"Here." The captain reached around with his head and pulled a rapier from a sheath on his rib-armor. He twirled it adroitly in his mouth, stuck it through a corner of the handkerchief and dropped it in front of Ben.

"Impressive," Ben said.

"I love my work," Warbuckle replied.

Ben raised the flag. Again, an arrow flew by. He waved it in a wide sweeping motion. The commotion in the courtyard continued, unabated. Ben waved the flag more violently. Another arrow whizzed by. "This isn't any good," he said.

Then the building shook again.

"They're hitting on the Western door now," the captain said.

Ben leaned his head against the wall, trying to focus. "I have to get their attention. Do you have any rope?"

The captain nodded.

"I need quill and ink, a rope, and a chair. Send someone quick."

Warbuckle hurried over to one of his men and gave him the order. The man sprinted off, keeping his head low. Ben took Miriam's speech out of his pocket and unfolded it. He tried to wipe the creases smooth while he waited. Soon, two guards emerged on the verandah with the necessary items. Ben pointed to the western side of the building and headed that way on all fours himself. They converged just above the door as the battering ram slammed into it again. The crowd below bellowed cheers and started up a chant again. "Give us our Princess."

"I don't like the sound of that," Warbuckle said. "The door isn't secured yet. They know it will break soon. What are my men doing down there?"

Ben opened the bottle of ink and dabbed the quill in it. He spread the paper with Miriam's speech face down on the marble floor and wrote, "On the reverse side of this parchment is the proposal that your princess made to the Senate in her own hand. If you cherish her life, stop pounding on the door and listen to my words. I will speak to you from the roof of the verandah. Long live King Reinard, Senator Benjamin Edmundson." Ben dug a hole in the top of the parchment and stuck it onto one of the legs of the chair. Then he tied the rope to the back of the chair.

"Lower it over the side," he said, "right on top of them, but slowly. Don't knock anyone out with it."

The captain and one of his men gently tipped the chair over the edge of the wall and let out the slack on the rope little by little.

Boom! The battering ram hit the door again. Was there a hint of splintering in the sound? The crowd cheered again.

"They don't see it."

"Just wait."

And then, as though a swirling breeze had caught every voice and carried it away, the cheering petered out.

"What are they lowering there?"

"Look!"

"It has a message attached to it! Look!"

The crowd waited in silence. Ben held the sword up and waved the white flag over the wall. No arrow flew by. What was happening below?

A strong voice suddenly broke through the silence. "On the reverse side of this paper is the proposal—"

Warbuckle and Ben exchanged smiles.

The reader finished Ben's note and began reading Miriam's proposal. His voice, which had carried a hint of sarcasm as he read Ben's words, took on a reverent tone as he read hers. Ben was moved by the emotion. These people believed her, believed in her. If only he could make them trust him. As the reader reached the end, Ben lifted the sword and gently swayed the white flag above him.

"A white flag!"

"Up there!"

No arrows flew by.

Ben nodded to the captain and slowly rose. Though most were obscured by tree limbs and leaves, below him stood a multitude of people and sheep. He hadn't imagined so many—a group of heavily-built miners still holding the freshly cut tree trunk they were using as a battering ram, merchants in their jackets and knickers, ladies and ewes in flour-coated aprons, college students in uniforms—all peering up at him, their passion suspended.

"You have just heard the princess's plea to the Senate," Ben said, his voice echoing between the buildings. "She sits on the Traitor's Chair right now as I speak to you."

A murmur wormed through the crowd.

Ben raised his voice above it. "She is not a traitor!"

Several voices shouted, "No," in unison, and another shouted, "They are the traitors!" The crowd stirred eagerly.

Ben hardened his voice. "But you are turning her into one." He looked from face to face at those he could see between the trees. "The more you shout and pound on this building, the more fear binds the hearts of the senators. They do not want to murder a beautiful young lady, but they are willing to execute someone they see as a threat to the Republic of Redland. She has chosen a course that the constitution of our republic sanctions, even honors—a course that would bear witness to a noble personal sacrifice, if it weren't for the threat of a revolution. I beg you to drop the log, lower your bows,

267

sheathe your swords. I am not asking you to go home, but to turn your violence into a vigil. Pray for justice. I am not asking you to pray for mercy, because the princess is no traitor. Pray for justice."

The crowd had grown silent as he spoke. When he stopped, he saw men and sheep, one by one, from the oldest to the youngest, lower their weapons. Finally the foremost of the miners turned and nodded to his companions, and they lowered the battering ram.

Ben took a large breath. "Several of the Guard have been hurt in the fighting. If we brought them down and opened the doors so we could carry them to a doctor, would you allow a few of us through safely?"

Faces turned toward each other below him. The crowd seemed to be looking for a leader to speak for them. Nodding heads turned into a murmur of assent. A swarthy ram with a bulging neck and thickset horns just below Ben finally called up, "You have our word, Senator. We came to protect the princess. We never meant to kill anyone. If any of your guards are critically wounded, bring them out. I, Portius Boldrustle, guarantee their safety."

Warbuckle tugged on Ben's pant leg. "Do you realize how dangerous this is?"

"I think we should show that we trust them. Think of your men, Captain."

The captain wiped his brow against his knee. He looked over at the wounded guard lying a ways from him on the verandah. Finally, he stood up next to Ben and addressed the crowd, "Will you promise not to take advantage of the open doors and rush into the Capitol?"

Again, murmurs of assent led to the answer from the swarthy ram. "We promise." Then to Ben's amazement, the ram turned around and called out to the crowd. "Bow your heads now as I call out to the Lord of Grace." Hats came off and heads bowed. Boldrustle's voice rumbled into his prayer: "Lord of Grace, we call on you to rescue our princess. . . ."

Ben turned from the wall and rushed to Erlichson's side. The medic and another guard were already placing him on a stretcher that someone had brought from inside. Ben looked up toward the roof of the building.

The medic took his arm and shook his head. "Neither of the men up there has survived. Erlichson here is the only one we need to take out."

"Then I was too late to save their lives," Ben said.

"He'll thank you for his," the medic said, nodding at Erlichson, "and maybe you can get me to your friend Benedict in time. Your page told me about him."

Ben nodded. "Let's go."

The medic and another guard lifted the stretcher, and Ben followed them to the ramp that led to the first floor. As he closed the door, he could still hear the faint voice of the burly ram praying down below. Inside, he faced a very different atmosphere. Shouting voices collided with them as they descended the ramp. When Ben pushed open the panel in the wall, he found Captain Warbuckle staring down another soldier, a weathered looking man with a large moustache.

"Are you out of your mind, Captain? It's a ruse. We've finally got the door secured."

"I've spoken to you calmly until now, but you are challenging my authority, Sergeant."

"Your authority? I'm challenging your sanity."

"We'll deal with your insubordination later. Follow the order."

The other guards backed away from the sergeant—they had no desire to question the captain's authority—but at the same time, moving the furniture and opening the door was putting the Senate in great jeopardy.

Ben hurried ahead of the men with the stretcher. "Gentlemen," he said, "I have authorized your captain to open the doors. Your comrade is hurt and needs a doctor. The crowd has agreed to put their weapons down and let us through. Two men have died already. Do you want another to lose his life?"

"Follow the order," the captain repeated calmly.

Two guards stepped forward cautiously, averting their eyes from their sergeant's, and pried a carpet from the line of furniture. Two more followed, dragging the tall cabinet that blocked the door to the side of the entrance.

The sergeant stood by, his arms folded.

When the space in front of the door was clear, Warbuckle put his horns to the beam that held it shut. He hesitated and looked at Ben.

"I can do it if you don't want the responsibility," Ben said.

The captain shook his head calmly. "We have our orders." He turned to the other guards. "Have your weapons ready, but hold your fire unless the senator or I change the order. Creating a combat situation when the door is open would put the Senate in the greatest jeopardy imaginable. The risk we are taking depends on a peaceful transaction." He nodded to several of the guards. "Cliveson, I want you to unbar the door. Pullmanson and Wainwright, you open it. When Erlichson's gurney is through, the doors shut. I want no wasted time."

Pullmanson and Wainwright took their positions beside the door. Cliveson stood ready, his large hands on the bar. Warbuckle drew his rapier. Arrows were fixed on bows.

The captain nodded. Cliveson hefted the bar aside, and the two guards opened the doors. Ben stared into the faces of the crowd. Those in the front were trying to back away to give room for the emerging men, but bodies had pressed in thickly.

Boldrustle, the swarthy ram who had spoken before, took control. "Back away. Make room."

The crowd backed away in waves. Ben turned around and motioned the medics to follow him out of the building. Behind them the guards' eyes swept the crowd, arrows ready. Ben backed into the crowd hesitantly. An avenue of space slowly formed behind him. The guardsmen grunted with the weight of the gurney, and Erlichson groaned as they descended the short ramp from the door.

Pullmanson and Wainwright started to shut the doors. Ben nodded a goodbye to Captain Warbuckle. The captain had already started to turn from the closing doors when suddenly a shaft pierced the air near Ben's ear. Ben's eyes locked with the sergeant's a split second before the doors slammed shut. He felt the crowd behind him freeze in stunned surprise. The eyes of the medic who stood directly in front of him widened in fear. Ben slowly turned.

A burly man standing in a spot where the space had just widened still teetered, an arrow through his neck and terror in his face. His arms held a bow, an arrow set loosely on the string. A ewe near him suddenly bleated the cry that had choked every throat. The man fell on his face. The crowd erupted into frenzied yells, and rushed forward at the doors. Ben panicked, but there was nowhere to run. The world became a mass of flailing fists and hooves. He told himself to stay on his feet, whatever happened. If he went down, he would be trampled to death. They attacked him. Battered from every direction, he covered his head with his arms and tried to press through the crowd away from the doors. Fists slammed into his arms, his sides, his back. Hands tore at his hair, ripped his clothes. In a few moments, he had been separated from Erlichson and the men bearing him. The roar of the crowd was deafening. Only hope drove his feet forward. He held onto a vague idea that if he could get to where the crowd was thinner, he would be past the frenzy, and they might settle for taking him prisoner.

Angry voices shouted in his ear:

"Traitor!"

"Villain!"

"Double-crosser!"

A sheep bit his shin to the bone. He tried to shake his leg free, but couldn't get it loose. Looking down through his folded arms, he saw an enormously fat ewe. She let go and sneered up at him, a strip of his pant leg hanging out of her mouth.

"I'm on your side!" he shouted.

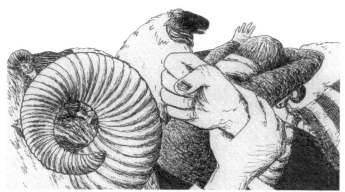

She probably didn't even hear him. The crowd buffeted him away before she could answer. He staggered and nearly fell. He had been hit in so many places that all of his wounds swelled in one big throbbing pain.

Then two men grabbed his arms and held on, dragged him forcibly through the crowd. His captors pushed others aside, yelling something about the king's prisoner. With great difficulty, they steered him through the unrelenting crowd. Several times he was wrenched from them and beaten over the back, but he kept his arms around his head and felt their grasp again. They dragged him along with a sense of authority, their grasps bony and claw-like, harsh, but the crowd was thinning. The blows abated, turned into taunts and shoves. His captors were warding others off with weapons. He caught the flash of a sword to his right.

"He's a valued prisoner, you fools!" the other cried, releasing his arm and flailing at a group of angry sheep to his left.

Ben tried to get his bearings, but it was impossible with all the pushing and shoving.

"In there," one of his captors shouted, yanking him to his left. They stumbled clear of the crowd into the shade of an awning, and shoved him against a wall. One of them hissed in his ear, "Keep your head covered if you value what's left of your life."

The other was fumbling with a door. "I don't have the right key!" he shouted. "He ought to have it. Get it from him."

The first one felt along the outside of Ben's pockets. "Here," he said, producing the key to the Senate Suites that Ben had received the day before.

"There weren't two keys?" the other asked, a note of alarm in his voice.

"Just the one," the first shouted. "Come on, get us inside!"

After another hesitation, Ben saw the bottom of the door open, and the two men shoved him through it. The door slammed behind him, reducing the din of the crowd to a distant roar. The two men released his arms and stood gasping for breath.

"I can't do this kind of thing anymore," one of them said.

Something in his voice sounded familiar. Ben slowly lowered his arms and raised his head. He found himself staring into Roderick's eyes.

The old man smiled widely. "You were in a rough spot there."

Ben stood speechless. He looked from Roderick to the man standing by his side. He was a tall, gaunt gentleman, not as old as Roderick, but more weather-warn. His dark eyes shone with a keen brilliance.

Roderick lifted his hand to his comrade's elbow. "Ben, we have no time for formal introductions. Say hello to your king."

Chapter 18
Authority

"King!" Ben stared for a moment, came to his senses, and fell on one knee—which would have seemed very noble except that he landed on the spot where the angry sow had bit him during the pandemonium. He yelped and toppled onto his side, yelping again when he hit the floor.

Roderick chuckled. "You were banged up enough the first time I saw you."

King Reinard reached down and lifted Ben by his shoulders. "Thank you," he said. "I appreciate what you've done—taking care of my girl."

Ben shook his head. "I left her. I didn't—"

"I'm sorry we're in such a hurry," the king interrupted. "The mob might have already burst through that door. Now that you're safe, we need to move quickly."

"Where to?" Ben asked.

Reinard hesitated. "To be honest with you, we don't have much of a plan. I should have revealed myself when all was quiet. I really thought that your words had quelled the villainy within them, and then suddenly all was chaos again."

Roderick cleared his throat. "We also had this wild hope that maybe Miriam had—well, we think she may have a key."

Steadying himself against the wall, Ben slowly rose to his feet. The last few days was swinging into clarity before his eyes, as though Ben had been walking blindly up a mountain path and had emerged on a vista. He could see that all the turns he had made, sometimes in faith, sometimes in what seemed to be blind luck, were the right ones. At the very bottom, he saw Clovenhoof's fire, a fork where the Lord of Grace had yanked him off the beaten road and into the woods. He had fought the murderer, befriended the orphan, fooled the spy, comforted the dying, rescued the kidnapped, argued for the life of the princess, and calmed the mob—what else he couldn't say. And all along he had felt only like a blind wanderer. Now he would act. Now perhaps he would crown a king.

Ben sprang into action. "Come with me, your Majesty," he said, starting down the hall. "She did have a key."

Reinard ran after Ben. "The little thief! I might have known it!"

"If I were a betting man, you'd owe me a few coins," Roderick said. "Which room is it?"

Ben stopped in front of Jacobson's door and tried the knob. It was unlocked. He opened it with a sense of foreboding. As he had expected, Commander Stanch's body lay sprawled across the floor, face down. Though it seemed a hopeless gesture, Ben turned him over and felt along his neck for a pulse. What would he find when they opened the trap door? Roderick and the king froze in the doorway.

Ben looked up at them. "He's dead. I wasn't expecting anything different. There's another below though—" He rose to his feet. "Help me with this cabinet."

The three men tipped the cabinet and walked it off the trap door. Ben tried lifting the door, but his body was too exhausted to get it more than a few inches above the floor. The king and Roderick heaved it open together. Ben stared down into the darkness. "Anyone down there? Colonel?"

At first, only silence greeted his call. Then a quiet shuffling rose from the depths, as though someone were rolling over or sitting up. "Ben? Is that you?" Colonel's voice rose hesitantly.

"Am I in time?"

"Thank the Lord of Grace! Yes, you are. Have you brought a doctor?"

"No, just two—uh, well—but they're strong enough to help him up the ramp."

"Roderick here is as good as a doctor," Reinard said. "He can stay with your patient."

"I'm here to protect you," Roderick answered. "You've been looking for a way to leave me behind since we left my cottage."

"You'll simply have to do as I order. It involves a young man's life." The king headed down the ramp without waiting for an answer.

278

Roderick looked at Ben for help, but Ben was too happy to find someone who could care for Benedict to give him any satisfaction. "Come on," he said. "We'll need your help bringing him up."

They muddled in the dark at the bottom of the ramp, but managed to bring Benedict up. They laid him on Jacobson's couch and put a pillow under his head. Seeing his wound, Roderick set to work without further argument. He sent Colonel to the kitchen for soap and water, while he gently unwound the dirty bandage.

Reinard grabbed Ben's sleeve. "It's time for us to move on."

Ben nodded. "Colonel, the key."

Colonel returned with a bucket of water in his mouth. He set it down and rooted in a pocket for the key.

When the king saw it, his face lit up like a torch. "That's it," he cried, grabbing it from the startled Colonel. He all but sprinted down the ramp and into the darkness.

Ben smiled a goodbye to Colonel and followed his king. He felt a new vigor come over him that laughed at his bruises. At the bottom of the ramp, Reinard stopped, thought for a moment, then plowed ahead in the right direction. When he came to the turn, he hurried around it without losing stride. Ben found himself breathing hard to keep up. They were at the door and the king was fumbling with the lock before Ben could ask what he was planning.

"I don't know," Reinard said. "Save my daughter. Save the Republic. Punish the villains. We can't really plan if we don't know what's going on up there. This a blind charge, Senator. Are you up for it?"

It took Ben a second to reply. The king had called him "Senator." He was every bit the republican that Miriam had described. "I'll follow your lead, your Majesty."

Reinard shoved the door open and without hesitating, started climbing the ladder. "Let me know if you have any ideas of your own," he huffed. "I'm not proud."

Ben took hold of the ladder and climbed after him. Halfway up, Reinard had to rest, and Ben found himself grateful for it. His bruised shoulders and chest ached miserably. The two were gathering their strength in the dark when a small voice descended from above them.

"Senator Edmundson, Sir?"

"Thistle?"

"I thought you might come back through the tunnel if you managed to find a way to help Benedict. Is he all right?"

"He's in good hands. Wait right there. We're coming up."

"Is someone with you, Sir?"

"The king of Redland is with me."

Ben heard Thistle's quick intake, a tiny gasp. The king was ascending again. Ben followed him rung by rung, his confidence rising with each step. At the top, he rolled into the closet after the king. In the dim light, he found Thistle staring out a crack in the closet door and the king looking over her shoulder.

"Hello, Miss Thistle," Reinard said. "It looks as though the mob hasn't made it beyond the hallways. Tell us what's happened in quick and easy terms."

She looked up at him, still dumbfounded—he had spoken her name—but gathered herself. "They had already started taking the votes after Senator Severnson's speech."

Reinard broke in, "Severnson? An elderly gentleman?"

"He spoke on your behalf, Your Majesty. It might be he's saved Miriam's life." She turned to Ben. "He said you had spoken to him this morning, had convinced him. There were as many votes for her as against her before we were interrupted. We suddenly heard loud shouting from one of the doorways. A page at the back yelled out that the Royalists had broken through one of the outside doors. We could hear the fighting. Everyone panicked. The Chairman tried to call us to order, but pages were running this way and that, checking doors for a way of escape. Some senators were brandishing swords. Others were just shouting at each other. No one paid any attention to the Chairman."

"And Miriam?" Reinard asked.

"I ran up to her and told her about the tunnel. I tried to get her to come with me, but she wouldn't leave the chair."

"Stubborn child!" Reinard exclaimed.

"So what's the situation now?" Ben asked.

"The Royalists have taken the hallway around the Senate Chamber. I slipped out as the guards were backing through the doorways, but it was all confusion. The guards were keeping the mob in the hallway, but they won't be able to do it for long."

The king unsheathed his sword. "Thistle, I have a special job for you. If you slip into the next room over from here—" he pointed to his left— "you'll find the royal regalia." He paused and thought for a moment. "You will, that is, if they haven't moved things in the last forty years." He looked around the closet for a moment and found a bucket. "Find my crown and robe. You'll probably have to break the glass case. Roll up the crown inside the robe. Cram it in this bucket and bring it to me." He cocked his head at the bucket. "It probably won't completely fit in there, but you can manage it."

Thistle's eyes flashed. "Miriam already broke the glass this morning, Your Majesty. Where will I find you?"

Reinard turned to Ben. "Take this sword. You're a lot younger than I am. That mob is bound to break through. When they do, you get me to the platform. Are you willing to fight?"

Ben nodded.

"Let's go then."

Reinard pulled the door open and shoved Ben out into the hallway, hanging onto the back of his shirt. The hall was a mass of bodies, surging forward and falling backward in irregular waves. Ben wondered if anyone would recognize him, but no one even turned to look at his face. Rage burned in every eye. The crowd started to chant again, "Death to the Senate, release our Princess," this time in a low, savage fury. The words seemed to form deep within them, in the lowest cave of their lungs.

Ben shouldered his way forward, frightened at their passion. How much blood would they shed before the king stopped them? Could the king stop them at all? He clawed his way through with more brutal force.

An angry ram refused to budge in front of him. He stood on his hind legs and spat at Ben, "Wait your turn! You'll have your blood soon enough!" His words thudded against the chant of the crowd and were drowned in its wake. Ben waited behind the ram, his skin tingling with anticipation.

And then without warning, the crowd fell forward, people stumbling over sheep, cries confused with bleats. The ranks of the guards had been breached. Ben dropped to his knees, but scrabbled forward on his hands and found his feet. He felt the king's tug on his shirt and shoved his way ahead, following the angry ram who had made him wait. Inside the doors, Ben stumbled over the dead and injured. The angry mob fanned out into the chamber. Guards fought them fiercely backing slowly down the aisles. Most of the senators were huddled in a ring in the far corner. Warbuckle was gathering his men to form a circle around them, shouting, "Fall back! Form ranks!" A fierce joy gleamed in his eyes even as he raced from one aisle to the other, his rapier flashing in his mouth. Ben's heart soared at the sight of it. But where was Miriam? His gaze swept across the platform to the Traitor's Chair. There she sat in stoical silence, her legs drawn up beneath her in an elegant repose. Only her eyes moved, darting back and forth with each clash of arms.

"Come alive, Ben! My people are killing each other!" Reinard dragged Ben into one of the cubicles. "We'll go over the top. I can do this. Just lead the way."

Ben broke away from the crowd and climbed over the first barrier, helping the king over it behind him. Guards were backing toward them, fighting fiercely as the crowd pressed in. Ben jumped into the next cubicle and pulled Reinard over the barrier just as the guards converged back to back behind them. One of the guards pierced his man through the side and kicked him over onto two sheep who were rushing toward him. Ben turned and vaulted over the barrier into the next aisle. A guard leaped in front of him, his sword raised to strike.

"I'm a senator!" Ben cried. "Senator Edmundson!"

The guard hesitated, a look of recognition in his eye. Behind the guard, a bulky ram lowered his forehead, his horns poised to strike.

"Behind you!" Ben cried. He shoved the guard to the side and planted his boot on the ram's forehead, between the horns. The guard whirled and sent his sword through the ram's back. Ben cringed.

Reinard was already in the next cubicle and pulling on his arm. "Almost there," he cried. "Speed is everything!" Without waiting for Ben, he hurled himself into the next aisle. Ben followed him, his heart pounding. A guard grabbed the king by the collar as he tried to climb over the next barrier. Ben knocked him over the head with the hilt of his sword, and the guard fell to the floor, pulling Reinard down with him. Ben wrenched the king from his clutch and laid his sword against the guard's neck.

"Yield!" he cried.

The guard stared at him, stunned from the blow to his head.

"Never mind him!" Reinard cried, rising to his feet and pointing. "Look!"

The crowd was now pressing close to the front, closing the ring around the frightened senators. The guards were fighting valiantly, but with each man or sheep that fell, another pressed forward. Each sword stroke seemed to jar the king, as though he felt it against his own skin. His people were killing each other. He hurled himself over the next barrier with renewed energy. Ben kicked the guard's sword away from his hand and followed the king. They stumbled over the last two barriers without resistance and reached the aisle in front of the platform.

"Climb up," Ben said, cradling his hands to give the king a foothold.

Reinard stepped up and lifted himself onto the platform. He was reaching down to give Ben a hand when he suddenly cried out. Ben turned in time to see a huge ram charging him. It was Boldrustle, the same bulk of a ram who had spoken for the crowd in the courtyard. He had recognized Ben and broken past the guards. Ben clutched Reinard's arm and threw his legs in the air. Boldrustle smashed into the platform beneath him. Ben hooked his heel on the platform and hung precariously on the edge. Reinard tried to draw him up with his arm, but the sheep caught his shirt in his mouth. Ben's rib ground against the corner of the platform. His legs searched desperately for a hold. He had seen the king safely to the platform, and he was out of energy. Even as his will gave in, the sheep's mouth was wrenched from his shirt, and he rolled over onto the stage, out of breath.

Below him in the front aisle, Boldrustle stood to face the aggressor who had bowled him over. Captain Warbuckle stared him down, shaking his horns. A flicker of understanding passed between the two sheep. Calmly, Warbuckle backed a few steps back, stamping a hoof menacingly.

Boldrustle waited for him, snorting and stamping. He eyed the stripes on Warbuckle's uniform. "A captain, is it?" Boldrustle snarled. "A captain of the treacherous! A captain of the cowardly!"

"I could have killed you just now," Warbuckle snarled back. "I will if I have to. Stand down."

"We trusted you to deliver your wounded without incident!" Boldrustle bleated.

"How dare you speak of treachery on the heels of laying siege to your own capitol!"

And now a strange thing happened. Whether it was because the initial surge through the doors had waned with the fierce fighting of the Guard, or because battles carry a certain momentum and this one was simply ebbing, or because the two champions at the front held so much of their comrades' respect, Ben couldn't tell. The sound of clashing weapons ceased for the moment. Everyone seemed to catch his breath and turn his attention to the two rams in the front aisle.

Captain Warbuckle was clearly the smaller of the two, but the calm with which he circled his opponent was awe-inspiring. The larger ram eyed him with a surly malevolence. Suddenly they flung themselves at each other, horns lowered to hammer the other off his feet.

286

Their foreheads met with a thundering crash. Warbuckle tottered, but found his hooves under him. Boldrustle toppled onto his left shoulder and rolled over, dazed. He shook his head violently and rose with a snorting vehemence. For a moment he lost his bearings and couldn't find Warbuckle. This seemed to infuriate him even more. Stamping his hooves in rage, he turned and faced his rival again.

Warbuckle grunted as if to tell Boldrustle he was ready. He shifted his weight to his powerful hind legs, poised to spring. All this time, his eyes had been riveted to his enemy, but now at the moment of action, they suddenly lost their focus and veered off in confusion. At first Ben wondered if the clash between the two sheep had finally taken its toll on him. Warbuckle's legs folded, and he fell forward onto his knees, his eyes fixed on a position behind Ben in an expression that Ben could only describe as reverence.

Boldrustle stared at Warbuckle. He stepped back cautiously and turned his head in the direction at which Warbuckle was gazing. Boldrustle's mouth fell open. He slowly turned his back on Warbuckle, a look of shock spread across his face. Up the aisles, others fell on their knees, both rebel and guardsman. Ben lifted himself onto a knee and looked behind him.

There stood the king, his crown sparkling on his head. He was sticking his arm through the sleeve of a glimmering, cobalt royal robe. Thistle stood beside him with his belt in her mouth, exultation flashing in her eyes. A few yards away, Miriam sat in the Traitor's Chair staring intently at her father. Ben couldn't read her face. There might have been as much concern as there was joy. The whole Senate Chamber was falling into a hush. Shouts had dwindled to whispers. Every guardsman had followed his captain's example and had fallen to his knees. One by one, members of the Royalist mob were sinking to their knees. Every head in the aisles or amidst the partitions was raised in wonder or bowed in reverence.

The senators in their cornered clump eyed each other in confusion. A moment before, they had feared for their lives. The king's presence had quelled the mob. They had only to bow the knee and they would leave the chamber alive. Gratitude is an oil that will not dissolve. Though beautiful in all of its rich color, it cannot mix with the water of hardened ideals. The senators were Republicans and Socialists. How could they bend the knee to a king? And yet Thistle had said that some had already voted to allow the king to return. Where were these senators? Why wouldn't they kneel?

The Chairman took a step forward. He blinked at Ben for a moment as though he had made up his mind how to act but couldn't bring his body to follow through. Slowly, he clopped forward and ascended the ramp to the platform. By the time he reached Ben, Barkloin had recovered his usual swagger. It sickened Ben. He saw himself in it. It stood for everything he had turned his back on in the past few days. It stood for the reasoned measuring of checks and balances. It proclaimed, "I cannot give myself to something lest it take advantage of my weakness." Ben turned from the Chairman and bowed his own head before the king.

He heard Barkloin's steps approach. With his head to his knee, Ben could see nothing of what was happening. This was what it meant to serve a king, to let the matter rest in another's hands, to acknowledge periphery. It did not demean. In fact, he felt a fellowship with those around him—Miriam, Thistle, Warbuckle, even the crowd that had recently beat him—in offering himself to something larger than himself.

Barkloin addressed the king, "The Senate and all of Redland welcomes you back, Sir, with all honor due a former king. Come and let me embrace you."

"I passed the army on my way here," the king replied. "My friend inquired where they were headed, and an officer told him that they were on their way to greet me. The battle gear of our army is a glorious thing to behold, Chairman. Truly impressive."

The Chairman hesitated. "Sir, I apologize. Our intelligence hinted of an invasion of the Fortimai."

Reinard seemed to consider this for a moment. "A small troop of the Fortimai were kind enough to escort me to the border. It's funny how things can become blown out of proportion. And to think that the real threat to the nation's security was right here in the city. These loyal—"

"Sir," Barkloin interrupted, "your own republican beliefs are well known to us. If you could clarify to these people that—"

"Well known?" the king suddenly stormed. "If they were so well known, why was an army sent out to face me? Chairman, you have begun to believe in the convenient lies you've put into your history books to safeguard the Republic."

"Then you haven't come to reclaim your throne? If that is the case, tell your followers here—"

"I will not be ordered," the king broke in. His voice trembled and broke. When he had recovered himself, he spoke in a steady voice. "Ingratitude is the fountainhead of chaos. When gifts become rights, the soul of a society dies. Ribald Barkloin, son of Redland, will you not bow before your king?"

An interminable silence followed. Ben's knee had started to hurt. His ankle felt cramped, and his head, low to the floor, throbbed with each beat of his heart. Others had been on their knees longer than he had, yet no one had moved. Then he heard a collective gasp from the senators. Ben rolled his head to look behind him.

The Chairman had knelt.

One by one, starting with Severnson, the old senator with whom Ben had spoken at the Crane's Neck, the senators lowered themselves to their knees.

When the last senator had knelt, the king spoke. "Rise, all of you, and sheathe your weapons. Look to your fallen countrymen around you and weep with me. Help the injured."

Ben rose to his feet slowly, stretching his tired joints. He slid the king's sword into the sheath at his side. His eyes met Miriam's, and a hesitant smile flickered across her face. He stretched his arm out to beckon her to him, but she seemed reluctant to leave the chair. In the aisles, Royalists and Guardsmen helped each other to their feet and began tending to the wounded. The senators took tentative steps away from their knot of security.

Jacobson pushed past some of the others and ascended the ramp to the platform. "Your Majesty," he said.

The king had turned to take his belt from Thistle and did not hear him at first.

"Your Majesty," Jacobson repeated. His voice wheezed with added volume, and the chamber grew hushed again. "Your Majesty, the bloodshed here on both sides has been a great tragedy. I am sure that my fellow senators will stand with me on this. I propose in the spirit of reconciliation that a general amnesty be extended to anyone involved with the perpetuation of today's riot." He waved his arm in the direction of the crowd of Royalists with a generous sweep. "We must put aside our differences of opinion and remember that the bonds that tie us together as countrymen are greater than—"

"Rubbish and lies!" Thistle's tiny voice suddenly bleated, its pitch uncannily similar to the senators.

Jacobson stopped in his tracks near the Traitor's Chair, surprised by the interruption. His towering form teetered like a ship with too much rigging.

Thistle stomped her hoof. "You killed my parents over those differences! You started this riot. I don't know how you did, but I know you did."

Jacobson's face broke into a patronizing smile. He looked from the lamb to the king. "Your majesty, how could I—"

"I know how you did," Ben said. "You leaked the news that the princess was here, that her life was in danger on the Traitor's Chair. I even know which guardsman took the news to the Royalists. He told me himself as he was dying for this cause that you now think isn't worth dying for."

Jacobson suddenly reached down and yanked Miriam up from the Traitor's Chair. Holding her in front of him, he flashed his chisel to her throat. "Someone may die yet!" he said. "I think you've all seen my handiwork with this instrument. I know how to use it. I'm not giving up on the Republic simply because everyone in this chamber has lost his head in the presence of an old man with a crown. Think about what this conflict has been about. If she dies, your monarchy dies." He began to back her toward a door at the rear of the platform.

Ben reached slowly for the sword at his side.

"No, Senator," Jacobson hissed, and he pressed the chisel against Miriam's throat so that a fine line of blood appeared on the edge of the blade.

Miriam's eyes widened. Her hands clutched at the air, but Jacobson's other arm, long and beefy, held her arms in check. "Go ahead and struggle, traitor," he said.

"If you kill me, they'll kill you," she said.

"Try me," he said. "I'm willing to die for my cause. Are you willing to die for yours?"

Miriam's eyes searched her father's. Ben could see her trying to read him. If he wanted her to resist, she would. Yet the Chisel's eyes were still fixed on Ben. There was nothing he could do.

"Sergeant!" Jacobson suddenly called. "Take the king. What are you waiting for?"

All was silent for a moment. Then Ben heard footsteps behind him ascending the side ramp to the platform. He slowly turned around. The sergeant who had shot the arrow through the doorway was approaching the king, a hesitant smile on his face. He drew his sword and waved it at Thistle as if to tell her to step out of the way. Thistle snorted at him and held her position. The look on her face was at once funny and inspiring. She was such a tiny thing that she held her bravery like a giant door swinging on a small hinge, yet something in her face—what was it—he couldn't put his finger on it until the sergeant spoke again and she frowned. . . .

"Out of the way, lamb," the sergeant said.

And there it was, the look the old professor had given him just before the knife plunged. In the face of death, Clovenhoof had been a tiny thing too. Who couldn't be? And yet he too had swung his faith around like a dog with some sort of ancient monster's bone in his mouth.

It came more as an impulse than a thought—and maybe this was what grace meant, that it was given to one to do what others would think foolish—Ben leaped forward, unsheathing his sword. It clanged against the sergeant's sword a foot above Thistle's head. The sergeant swung his blade back around in an arc, this time slicing at Ben's neck, but Ben leaned back just below the deadly swipe. Recovering, he thrust his own sword up at the sergeant's chest, only to find it repelled by a dagger in the sergeant's other hand. The sergeant's speed was staggering. Fear gripped Ben as he stared into the man's eager, smiling face. The sergeant's arms swung in serpentine motions. Ben parried with his sword, but the dagger caught him on the wrist. His sword flew from his hand and clattered close to the back wall.

For a split second, Ben knew that his life hung on the brink, but in that same moment his mind registered two things almost as though they were distractions from eternity. A little lamb flew between his legs with heroic ferocity, and an arrow whizzed past him at the edge of his vision. Just as Thistle sank her teeth into the leg of the sergeant and altered the angle of his sword stroke, an arrow struck the Chisel below his left collarbone, an inch above Miriam's shoulder. Ben's eyes took in the sword as it sliced past him and followed the same trajectory in the wake of the arrow to see Jacobson pierced through. Every muscle in the senator's body contracted like the plucked string of a musical instrument. The chisel fell from his hand. His arms sprung wide. Miriam fell forward onto her hands and knees, gasping. A second arrow pierced

Jacobson's heart, and he fell over backwards. Thistle's snarl brought Ben back to his own enemy. The sergeant had kicked her loose, and she was approaching again, ears back in a seething rage. But the sergeant had seen his comrade fall. Checking Thistle with his sword in case she lunged again, he scanned the back of the chamber.

Ben's eyes found the archer first. He smiled and shook his head. Warwick, the cowardly tracker, stood in the back row with an arrow fixed on the sergeant's heart.

"One move and you're a dead man, Sergeant," Ben said.

The sergeant's eyes landed on Warwick. He lowered his sword and knife. He fell to one knee, placed his weapons in front of him, and bowed his head.

Thistle, who had not seen either of the arrows shoot past her, looked at the sergeant in confusion. "Why? Me?"

Ben burst out laughing. "You're a fierce warrior," he said. "Historians will praise your exploits."

The king reached his arm out and took Barkloin's hoof. "Mr. Chairman, I'd like the Senate to reconvene tomorrow morning so that I may address them and clarify our roles in the new government."

Barkloin nodded slowly. "The Senate is yours to command, Your Majesty."

A few whispers passed among the senators.

"I understand your worries," the king said, walking over to the edge of the platform near the senators. "Have faith in the king who gave you your republic. Why would he undo his greatest achievement? The Senate will continue as the law making body of this republic. As king, among other things I will mention tomorrow, I retain the right to pardon whom I see fit to pardon." He faced Miriam. "Princess, you deliberately disobeyed your king in secretly coming back to this country. You bear some blame in today's happenings."

Miriam shrank from her father. She took a step back, tripping over Jacobson's boot, and nearly fell on him.

"I recognize that you acted out of love," the king continued. "I pardon you with a strict warning never to test me again. As for the claim you have made on the Traitor's Chair, as this institution was created during the kingdom, I retain the right to rule on it." He eyed the senators to see if anyone would object, but by this time, none would dare oppose him. The king smiled. "I acknowledge your claim that I have a right to return in peace. I hold your claim noble and just. I release you from the binding power of the chair."

Strength returned visibly to Miriam's limbs. Could it be that all this time she had been more afraid of her father than the senators, the mob, or even the Chisel's blade? She managed a deferential smile.

King Reinard then swiveled and stretched his arms out as if to embrace all of his people. "It is finished then. Now rise and see to the wounded. Help your enemies. Be reconciled with each other. If there are more perpetrators in league with these two traitors to the state and people, we will seek them out in due course. Their sentence will be banishment. I've seen too much death today."

Relief brushed through the room like a cool breeze. Guardsmen and Royalists alike helped each other to their feet. The senators slowly fanned out from their corner. Captain Warbuckle came onto the stage and addressed the kneeling sergeant. "Can I trust you to turn yourself in for trial?"

The sergeant rose to his feet, clicked his heels together, and saluted his captain. "Sir." His face was grim, but determined, as he strode off the platform. Two other guardsmen joined him on the floor and escorted him out of the chamber.

Ben's mind came back to Warwick. He had brought the Chisel down and forced the sergeant to surrender, but he was a murderer none the less. The mountain woman's face as she lay in her cave close to death hovered in his mind. He had also played a role in the death of Thistle's parents. Ben searched the back row of the chamber, but the man seemed to have vanished.

A finger tapped on Ben's shoulder. Something prevented him from turning around. Perhaps he wanted to savor the anticipation. Miriam would be standing there smiling at him, and he would soak up her radiance, but not yet.

She put her hands on his arms just below his shoulders and turned him around. She was not smiling. She was looking seriously into his face. "You turned your back on me and walked away."

"I'm sorry," he said. "It was the hardest thing I've ever done."

"Harder than the Sacrifice?"

"Yes. No." He thought for a moment. "They're one and the same really. The one called me to the other. You

297

are the treasure that I had to throw away."

"I'm honored." She smiled up at him. "You kissed me last night. When I slipped in here this morning, before I sat down on the chair, it's the thing that made me pause."

"I don't know what came over me," he said, reddening.

"After you walked out—not right away, but later—when they were voting on whether to kill me or not, it's what I thought about. I decided I was glad you kissed me. It was nice to have something like that to leave behind."

"I've felt more in the past few days than in my whole life put together," he said. "It's made me a bit more daring."

"And sacrificial," she said.

Ben reflected for a moment. "It comes to the same thing doesn't it? The cup overflows. You want to empty it because you know so much more will flow in. And you think, if it doesn't, well, it was already full, so—"

"Will you kiss me again?"

He kissed her, and when their lips parted, he saw the smile he had imagined—not something close to it, but the very same thing, another gift from the Lord of Grace.

Chapter 19
Repentance

"Justice dies in mercy's mouth
Ravaged by relentless teeth.
Kings forgive with every breath
That murderers may hide from truth,
Pack their bags, and wander south . . ."

Thistle's bitter song rose in the mountain air like a poisoned arrow with nothing to strike. The words seemed to drift out, lose force, and sink helplessly into the trees. She had been walking ahead of Ben and Miriam since dawn in spite of a layer of snow that she had to plow through. As they climbed, they passed in and out of the shadows of small cotton-like clouds that drifted eastward overhead. Ben felt hot one moment and cool the next. He unbuttoned his jacket.

Miriam was showing signs of irritation, thrusting her hands in and out of her pockets, alternately glaring up at Thistle and frowning at herself. Ben found himself glancing at her frowns, enjoying each piece of the emotion that composed her face—the narrowed dark brown eyes that flashed each time the sun hit them, the arch of her cheekbone, the puckered lip.

"Don't be too hard on Thistle," he said. "She loves your father, but she'd like to fly at him right now. Warwick helped kill her parents. At the very least, he led the murderer to them. Thistle expected justice, and banishment seems like a pardon."

"And yet he saved my life," Miriam said. "It's hard to know what to think. In the end, maybe he found the courage to be the person he had always wanted to be."

"I don't know. You can't let cowardice be an excuse for heinous evil. As for finding courage, shooting the Chisel was just a gamble he was willing to take. If he saved your life, the king might pardon him."

"My father doesn't make trades like that. It wasn't because he saved my life—there were others who were pardoned."

"Warwick didn't know your father, and really, if you think about it, neither does Thistle."

"Neither do all the gossipers in Redland." Miriam stooped over and packed a snowball in her mittens. Taking aim with a malicious frown, she threw it at a nearby tree.

Ben patted her on the back. The touch felt awkward. Since kissing her on the platform of the Senate Chamber, he had had little opportunity to be alone with her. The Republic seemed to have stolen her from him in a frenzy of love for their new princess. He himself had been loaded down with Senate proceedings, and when he had a moment to breathe, Thistle was tending to him in her naïve officious way.

He had at first worried that others would hound them about their romance, but in the general relief of the moment, few had noticed the kiss. A senator had alluded to it the next day, but only as a symbol of the union between the Senate and the King. People were so eager to avoid a civil war that they were ready to read a truce into every gesture between the two factions. Still, he had overheard arguments in The Crane's Neck suggesting that the king had been too lenient with the conspirators within the Senate Guard. Thistle had been there, and though Colonel had tried to make light of it, interrupting the conversation to ask if a tune on his belloret would calm everyone's spirits, the injustice had taken root in her mind.

All of Redland had embraced Colonel's heroics with as much vigor as they had Ben's. The story had developed legendary qualities overnight. Colonel and his page Benedict, who was now slowly recovering from serious wounds, had defended a secret tunnel into the Capitol. They had secured the key that would allow the king to sneak in, had led him personally to the secret entrance. Trapped underground for hours, Colonel had nursed his page, dressed his wounds in blind darkness, kept him alive in the worst of conditions. . . .

The mountain trail had reached a steep spot. Ben stopped for a moment to stretch his limbs and look around. In the week since the mob had attacked him, the bite on his leg had scabbed over, his bruises had faded slowly, his rib was even losing its tenderness, yet his body still felt stiff when he got up in the morning. He had been hesitant to take this trip back up over the mountains, not because of the physical strain, but for another reason that he hadn't wanted to admit.

The king had come to him a few nights after his return. "Is there anything you can do for Miriam? There's something weighing on her conscience, but she won't tell me what it is."

"It's hard to tell a father things," Ben had said.

"She's never kept anything from me."

"There was that matter of the tunnel key."

"You know what I mean. Something is crushing her heart, but she won't talk about it. I'm her father. Does she think anything she has done can keep me from loving her?"

Ben had turned away, unable to look Reinard in the face. It was as though the king had reached out and yanked his tender rib. Ben had been pretending that it was all over, that everything had been done, but he had yet to tell his own father about the Sacrifice. Though he hadn't consciously kept it a secret, Ben had not made a public statement about it, yet sooner or later folks were bound to miss Clovenhoof and wonder what had happened to him. It would be much better if his father heard it from him than someone else. The thought had made him cringe. His father's face unfurled before him, red and angry, like an enemy flag. Could he believe that this was a false image, that his father could forgive him? He owed him the opportunity.

The king had waited.

"Will you let me take her back up into the mountains?" Ben had asked. "There's something she needs to see." He had paused. "I need to go back over the mountains myself. We can both face our shame."

Ben had forced Thistle to come along as well. She had been performing her duties in a quiet rage, squinting her eyes and grunting in the back of her throat every time someone mentioned the king's name. Ben had felt that a long hike would help her work out some of the frustration of her grief.

Now they were nearing the summit where Ben had seen Miriam's parka. Thistle disappeared over the crest in front of them. Miriam was slowing her pace, looking from tree to tree with a mix of recognition and dread. Ben caught up to her and took her hand. She held it limply as though it held little reassurance. She couldn't seem to look him in the eye.

Then Thistle reappeared, backing up, her body tense in a stunned knot. He could see the wool on her neck sticking straight up.

"What's the matter?" Ben called, but she did not answer. The leopard cub flashed into Ben's mind. Would it still be around, looking for its master? Would it attack a small lamb like Thistle? No, that was ridiculous. It was a tiny, helpless thing.

"Something's wrong," Miriam said, shaking her hand free and breaking into a run.

"Wait!" he cried, "We don't know what's up there," but she barreled ahead of him.

Something kept Thistle's fear in a kind of trance, but did not cause her to run. Ben angled his climb off the path to a thick pine a few yards from her, drawing his knife from beneath his jacket. Before Miriam could reach her, Thistle disappeared over the crest again. At the top, Ben saw what had so troubled her. Before the marker that Ben had placed on the ground a few yards from the cave knelt Warwick, his head bowed to the ground. He remained where he was even as Thistle approached him. She could have driven a dagger into his back, and she might have if she had been carrying one. Much of the snow on the Western slope had melted off in the afternoon sun. Warwick knelt in a muddy patch of grass, his knees and pant legs above his boots soaked. Ben had never seen him look so calm before. Had he fallen asleep?

Thistle stopped a few yards from him. "What are you doing here?" she shouted, her voice a trembling rage.

Warwick shook his head slowly and said something Ben couldn't catch.

"You were banished!" Thistle shouted. "Go on and get out of here! You don't belong here!"

Warwick raised himself to one knee and looked at her. "I'm sorry," he said. He fixed his gaze on her, his eyes imploring, but steady.

"Coward!" Thistle cried. "Spineless coward!"

Warwick nodded his head. "I have been a coward. I'm sorry."

"Why did it have to be you?"

Warwick seemed confused by the question. His eyes wandered up to Ben and over to Miriam. The princess stood weakly on the crest of the mountain, staring down past Warwick at the marker. It seemed to Ben that her knees might buckle at any moment and she would wilt to the ground. Thistle's shouts had blown right past her.

"Why did it have to be you?" It came out the second time in a tortured cry. Thistle's rage was wearing down. Tears dripped from her eyes. "You don't even—" She looked up at him imploringly as though he might supply the words she couldn't say.

Warwick shook his head. "I suppose you wish you had a real villain to hate," he said. "That's the trouble with evil when you really get to know it. Even the Chisel—I can't tell you how much he scared me, and yet in the end he hid behind a woman, didn't he? We're not worth your hatred."

He wiped his nose with the back of his hand and sat back in the muddy grass. As he shifted his position, Ben could see that he had placed wildflowers in front of the marker.

"I'm sorry about your parents," Warwick said.

A long silence ensued, Thistle staring at the ground, Warwick waiting patiently for her reply.

It was Miriam who broke the silence. Strength had returned to her limbs as she listened to Warwick. She walked resolutely down the slope and knelt down beside him. Placing her hand on his cheek, she said, "We—we killed this girl."

Warwick took her hand, enclosed it in both of his hands, and lowered his head onto it. One heavy sob passed through his body, and then he lifted his face to her. His eyes were glassy with tears, his face curved in a sad smile. Miriam placed her other hand over his hands and smiled back at him.

And now Thistle's tears streamed from her face. She wailed without restraint. All the pent up grief she had held in since her parents' death burst from her. Miriam beckoned her to come close, but she stood where she was, bellowing her sad cries, more pitiful than all of her sad songs put together. Ben wanted to run down to her, but his better judgment held him back. His eyes wandered to the mouth of the cave.

To his surprise, he saw the leopard cub emerging, sleepy eyed as though it had been woken from hibernation. The cub picked its way around rocks and patches of snow to Thistle. Heedless of her cries—or was it because of them—the cub drew up next to the little lamb and placed its head soothingly over her neck.

Ben suddenly felt foolish standing on the ridge, staring at them. He walked down to the mouth of the cave and looked in. Warwick had left his pack on the ledge where the mountain woman had lain. He picked up one of the woman's cups and examined it, not for any particular reason, just to be doing something. He was ready to set it down again when it inexplicably fell from his hands with a clatter. The cave warped and narrowed, closing in on him as though someone were squeezing a sack.

He yelped, his yelp became a laugh, and his laugh became a call, and his call became a song—a loud, raucous, stamping chorus—and he was Clovenhoof. He was not the old professor with sagging jowls and weak eyes, but a young, brawny ram with a quick step and carefree laugh. People and sheep surrounded him, clapping to his song, in a great hall with wide, open windows. Light streamed through the hall, not in straight lines from the windows, but in wandering rivers that illuminated this and that with something capricious more like wind than light.

"Arise, my lads, lift high your muzzle;
The final piece is in the puzzle!
The royal flag commands the roof,
So sing your song and stomp your hoof!

Hey ditty ho ditty hey ditty hey
The Lord of Grace will dance today!

Rejoice my lads and stomp your feet
Let voices court the merry beat
The priest has said his final mass
So feast and drink and swing your lass!

Hey ditty ho ditty hey ditty hey
The Lord of Grace will dance today!"

As he sang and danced, his eyes came to rest on a magnificent sheep with flashing eyes and a smile as gentle and wild as all nature. Ben knew who it was. His hooves teetered.

"I am coming soon," said the glorious ram.

When the cave relinquished its squeeze and resumed its old hollow shape, Ben found himself on the floor with the broken cup, smiling up at Miriam.

She was kneeling over him, half worried, half bemused, her dark hair streaming softly around her face. "I heard the cup shatter. Are you all right?"

Ben sat up. The back of his head hurt, and when he touched it, he felt a lump forming. "I was dancing," he said stupidly.

"Dancing?" She looked up at the ceiling where several stalactites hung menacingly low.

"I was Clovenhoof."

"Did he tell you to turn your back on me again?"

"He said we should dance. The Lord of Grace, he—" but Ben couldn't put it into words.

Miriam waited expectantly, but the words wouldn't come.

Ben glanced toward the mouth of the cave. "Where's Thistle?"

Miriam smiled. "She's saying goodbye to her arch-enemy. He doesn't have a clue where to go once he leaves the country. 'Anywhere but Uulantep,' I said. So he's headed for Svegeby, and he's going to try fishing. It did my father a world of good—" Her voice suddenly dropped off. "Why are you looking at me like that?"

He blinked at her. In the dim light of the cave, her face wore a rich, deep beauty. He looked into her dark eyes. "Will you dance with me?"

She swiveled her head around. "Not in here. You already knocked yourself out once."

"Never mind that then," he said, rising to one knee before her and feeling as silly as he was serious. "Will you marry me?"

She stared at him.

"Miriam, I love you," he said. "I want to dance with you in caves, kiss you in your baggy marauder clothes, chase you around the streets at night, find you in  mountain shacks where you'll bash me over the head, and I don't know what else, but I want to do it for the rest of my life, however short or long it is. Will you marry me?"

She bit her lower lip and looked at him as though he were a cliff she was about to plunge over. He wanted to hang onto that look, bottle it, hoard it in a hole somewhere, his own hidden treasure, but he knew better. Everything of value is given and received. If you understood that, you wouldn't clutch the kernel of life, but toss it freely into the wind and chase after it with joy.

"Yes," she said and nodded vigorously. "I will be your wife." She grabbed hold of his head in both her hands and kissed him.

And the Lord of Grace did dance that day. Of course Roderick would say that he has been dancing since the king returned to Redland, for all is prepared and his

309

coming is imminent. If you listen very closely in the feathery quiet of dusk, or in the din of a loud laughing crowd, you might hear his hoof beats.

23476014R00184

Made in the USA
Charleston, SC
24 October 2013